MORE PRAISE FOR *MIN[...]*
THE FIRST BO[...]
F.R.E.A.K.S. SQUAD INVE[...]

"Chills and laughter share equal time in Harlow's fresh and funny debut … Sure to amass an army of fans, all of whom will be gnashing their teeth in anticipation of the next installment."

—*Library Journal*

"If Donald Westlake had gotten around to paranormal mystery, it would have sounded like this. Harlow's debut is funny, creepy, and refreshingly brash."

—*Kirkus Reviews*

"Readers can look forward to plenty of high-energy chases after odd supernatural baddies in future installments."

—*Publishers Weekly*

"Monstrously fun! Monstrously suspenseful! Monstrously good! Jennifer Harlow's debut had me laughing and gasping from start to finish!"

—Victoria Laurie, *New York Times* bestselling author

"Funny, scary, and creepy—and ridiculous amounts of fun!"

—Kat Richardson, author of the Greywalker novels

"A non-stop rollercoaster ride that fans of urban fantasy will love! Fast-paced, fun, and wildly entertaining, Jennifer Harlow has given the paranormal police procedural a fresh spin with her loveable machete-wielding heroine. A quirky cast of characters and sharp writing make *Mind Over Monsters* a wholly wonderful debut. I can't wait to read more!"

—Jeannie Holmes, author of *Blood Law* and *Blood Secrets*

"With its breezy style and exuberant sense of fun, this monstery mystery is a total delight!"

—Carolyn Crane, author of *Mind Games* and *Double Cross*

"Wildly fun and funny, Harlow offers treats for every paranormal lover to relish, with plenty of action, thrills, and laughter."

—Leanna Renee Hieber, award-winning and bestselling author of the Strangely Beautiful series

"In her funny, fast-paced debut, Jennifer Harlow gives us an urban fantasy that sharply blends murder-mystery and horror, and introduces us to a world where the monster in your closet really does exist. Using both humor and logic to help solve a grisly double-murder, reluctant heroine Beatrice Alexander is a woman you can (and do) root for as she struggles to control her powerful telekinetic gift and to find her place in this brave (and sometimes scary) new world."

—Kelly Meding, author of *Three Days to Dead*

TO CATCH A
VAMPIRE

OTHER BOOKS BY JENNIFER HARLOW

Mind Over Monsters: A F.R.E.A.K.S. Squad Investigation
(Midnight Ink, 2011)
What's a Witch to Do?: A Midnight Magic Mystery
(Midnight Ink, spring 2013)
A F.R.E.A.K.S. Squad Investigation, Number 3
(Midnight Ink, fall 2013)

JENNIFER HARLOW

TO CATCH A
VAMPIRE

MIDNIGHT INK
WOODBURY, MINNESOTA

First Edition
First Printing, 2012

Book design and format by Donna Burch
Cover design by Kevin R. Brown
Cover illustration © Carlos Lara Lopez
Editing by Nicole Edman

Midnight Ink, an imprint of Llewellyn Worldwide Ltd.

Library of Congress Cataloging-in-Publication Data
Harlow, Jennifer, 1983-
  To catch a vampire : a F.R.E.A.K.S. squad investigation / Jennifer Harlow. — 1st ed.
    p. cm.
  ISBN 978-0-7387-2711-0
1. Occult crime investigation—Fiction. 2. Vampires—Fiction. I. Title.
  PS3608.A7443T6 2012
  813'.6—dc23
                          2012009428

Midnight Ink
Llewellyn Worldwide Ltd.
2143 Wooddale Drive
Woodbury, MN 55125-2989
www.midnightinkbooks.com

Printed in the United States of America

There's a stake in your
fat black heart
And the villagers never
liked you.
They are dancing and
stamping on you.
They always knew it was you.
—"Daddy" by Sylvia Plath

You just make friends everywhere, don't you?
—Beatrice Alexander to Oliver Montrose

ONE

BROTHERLY LOVE

I THINK I JUST officially realized I am a true-blue freak. Drat.

For the past two months—God, has it only been that long?—I've been fighting the good fight against creatures of the night, and you know what? Sitting in this Starbucks, drinking an overpriced coffee, surrounded by people chatting with friends or working on their novel, it dawns on me: There isn't one normal thing about my life. I am not a part of this world anymore. I live in a mansion in the middle of Kansas with psychics and monsters, jetting to places like Butte, Montana, and Trenton, New Jersey, in order to stop homicidal, preternatural nasties. Now I drink my coffee in the middle of the night in diners, sitting across from either a werewolf eating more meat than a pack of lions, or a vampire grinning at me with bloody teeth. Meeting my brother, who I almost accidently killed a few months ago, is the first ordinary thing I've done in awhile. How freaking sad.

To say Brian hates me is an understatement. He blames me for killing our mother eighteen years ago. On a bad day, I blame me too, but I didn't force her head into our gas oven, though trying telling Brian that. As if the "you ruined my life" thing wasn't bad enough, he's also deathly afraid people will judge him for being related to me. To a man who models everything he does, down to what brand of socks he buys, on other people's reactions, having a sister who can pick up a Buick without lifting a finger doesn't exactly scream normal.

When he was living just a couple of hours from me, he never spoke to me or bothered to call except when absolutely necessary. Yet when I'm a plane ride away, I get a call to meet for coffee. He can't stand to be in the same room as me, and now he's volunteered to do it? This is not going to be fun.

I've been waiting ten minutes, growing more apprehensive with each passing second. I don't know what to expect. The last time I saw Brian, I almost killed him. Accidently. Really. I had no control over my curs—sorry, *gift*. He was calling me nasty names and I blew my top; came close to literally blowing his off too. No excuse, I know, for almost giving someone a brain aneurysm, but it was bad. *Really bad.* Thank God there was no permanent damage, at least to his physical self.

I pull down the sleeves of my turtleneck and make sure the high neck covers the two circular scars the size of pencil erasers. The long sleeves cover the chunk of skin missing from my arm. I feel like a walking hot dog in the July heat, but it'd be just too hard to explain the marks. As far as my family knows, I'm running a daycare program for a national company and living alone in a crummy apartment. I wish the government could have come up with a more glamorous cover story. That way I could have driven Oliver's Jaguar convertible to this meeting instead of a seven-year-old Camry. At least then I could console myself with the fact my materialistic brother would turn green with envy.

I see Brian before he sees me. My defenses immediately go up. I tense as he walks up to the door, cell phone stapled to his ear as always. The person on the other end says something very amusing judging from the smile on Brian's face. Smiling, that's a good sign. He closes the phone a moment later, and walks in. Within seconds, he catches sight of me, and the smile disappears. Bad sign. Very bad sign. This is going to be heck.

Avoiding my gaze, he walks around the other tables to my booth. He's out of place here in his gray suit and red tie, surrounded by people in jeans and tank tops. They probably think he's here for a business meeting. It would never cross their minds that we're brother and sister. Well, technically we're half brother and sister. Different fathers. Brian's was some musician who dumped our mother when she was five months pregnant. All she told me about mine was that he was mysterious, handsome, and "the one night we shared together was the most magical of my life." In other words, I am the product of a one-night stand with a man whose name she never bothered to get. Both Brian and I inherited Mom's brown eyes and thin lips, but the similarities stop there. He has straight, medium-brown hair cut short and is a thin six feet tall. I am stuck with frizzy, wavy brown hair and a sturdy peasant build that no amount of time on the treadmill can make pass for "slim." I should be the one who hates him.

As he slips into the chair across from me, I give him a smile. It isn't returned. "I didn't order for you," I say.

"It's okay," he says, "I can't stay long."

"Oh. Why?"

"I'm just in town to get some contracts signed. Hugh Jackman is filming a movie here." Brian's in entertainment law. He can name drop with the best of them. "Nana wanted me to check on you."

"Oh."

"You look ... well. Lost weight?"

"Yeah, a little."

He glances at his watch. "Good. Good."

"You look good too. How's the job going?"

"Fine. Yours?"

"Fine. Interesting."

"Oh."

We sit in silence, neither looking at the other. The elephant in the room practically trumpets. It's my elephant, I'll put it down. "I was surprised to hear from you. *Glad,* but surprised. I thought—"

"Look, whatever you *thought,* you thought wrong. I am here simply because Nana asked me to see you while I was in the Midwest. Nothing else." His phone chirps. When he reaches for it, the gold ring on his left hand catches my eye. "And now I can tell her you're alive with all limbs intact." He opens the phone, scanning the message. "Damn it!"

Brian stands, flipping the phone closed. He doesn't give me so much as a glance as he walks out of the shop. I'm not even worth a goodbye.

I sit glued to my seat, my mouth slack. That's it? I drove an hour to have my brother take one look at me and leave? Now, old Bea would hang her head, slink back to her car, and cry her eyes out. She'd make excuses for him. She'd let him get away with this.

But the new and improved, monster-hunter Bea picks up her purse and follows the jerk out of the coffee shop.

I catch sight of him right away in the parking lot. "Brian!" He glances back but continues walking. I run after him, but he refuses to stop walking.

"Leave me alone," he says, still walking.

"No. We need to talk. I'll follow you to your hotel if I have to!" This stops him. I've hit his Achilles heel: introducing his oddball sister to his colleagues.

He spins around. "I have nothing to say to you."

"Well, I do!"

He folds his arms. His anger rolls into me like a tapeworm. I hate when emotions hit so unexpectedly that my stomach doesn't have time to prepare. "Then speak!"

"Please don't yell at me! God, I'm trying to apologize here!"

"Right," he scoffs. "Well, I don't want your fucking apology. You tried to kill me."

"That was an accident."

"I could give a damn! I had to miss two days of work because I was in the fucking hospital being poked and tested! I still get migraines, and will for the rest of my life. Not to mention you scared the hell out of Nana. So, your apology means *shit* to me." He starts playing with his wedding ring. "The only consolation out of the whole debacle is you moved a thousand fucking miles away from everyone I care about so you don't almost kill them too. And if you give a damn about any of us, you'll stay here and never come back. We don't want you there."

"Does that *we* include your wife?"

His righteous anger disappears, replaced with the look of a young boy caught looking at Daddy's secret magazines. "Nana told you?"

"Your wedding ring told me." He stops playing with it, and I'm chagrined to hear my voice grow quieter. "You got married and weren't even going to tell me about it?"

He clears his throat, refusing to look at me. I've learned through two months of investigating that this is a sign of a guilty man. He squares his shoulders to regain some dignity. "I didn't want you there."

"Is it Rennie?"

"Of course it's Rennie." He'd been dating Renata Goldman, daughter of Hollywood producer James Goldman, for almost two years. She's the one who got him the entertainment lawyer gig at Sunrise Studios. (That's one other thing Brian and I have in common: our love of old movies. Nana's influence.) I've only met Rennie a few times in passing. Skinny, rich, beautiful, classy, but Nana says she's sweet. It's just typical; my brother marries into the movie world, and I don't even have time to watch them anymore. Life stinks.

"And you're going to find out eventually, so I might as well tell you now. She's pregnant."

This time I'm the one with the surprised look. "Really?"

"Yeah. She wants to have it. I couldn't convince her otherwise."

I'm taken aback. "Why would you?"

He scoffs again. "Why the fuck do you think? It could be like *you*. Some … freak. Just what I need in my life, another you." He sneers. "Just stay away from my family, okay?" He glances at his watch. "Shit, I'm going to be late now. Don't follow me." He turns

6

his back and walks away. I don't move until his car, a Mustang convertible, pulls away. He doesn't look back once. Good. He doesn't see me wiping away stupid tears. Yes, even freaks cry.

———

Jab. Jab! Jab. Right hook! Jab. Kick! Jab. *Die.* Kick! *Stupid.* Uppercut! *Bag!* I stop attacking the defenseless hardbag to catch my breath and wipe the sweat off my face. My arms quiver as I raise them. Crud, I overdid it. I won't be able to pick up so much as a pencil for the next hour. So worth it though. An hour of crying in the car followed by an ice cream sundae, a Cary Grant movie, and a half hour of hitting an inanimate object just makes things better for some reason. It was probably more the sundae than the punching though. Sugar tends to quell my homicidal tendencies.

"You are a stalking, creepy pervert who needs a hobby," I say, pulling the straps off my gloves.

I look over my shoulder at the gorgeous creature filling the doorway. Oliver Montrose, vampire pain in my butt, leans against the door sipping what I'll pretend is fruit punch from a yellow mug with "Florida" written on it. At least it's not his "World's Greatest Lover" mug. Even better, he's not shirtless as he usually is around me. He looks just as good though in a sky blue dress shirt and khakis—more like an investment banker on Martha's Vineyard than a creature of the night. He must be going to town. That's the only time he retires the red silk and leather jacket.

"I am simply—"

"Admiring the view," I cut in. "Yeah, get a new line please." I yank off the gloves and hang them on the bag. "Seriously, I am close to taking a restraining order out against you. Every time I come down here, there you are!"

"How long have you known I was standing here?"

"Since you got there. I could feel your eyes on my behind." I so have to remember to wear my sweatpants instead of the spandex ones.

He glides—yes, glides—into the room. There is nothing clunky about this man or anything he does. Ballerinas could take lessons on grace from him. "And yet, you let me stay." He stops a few feet away, a small all-too-familiar grin plastered on his face. I call this one "Oliver Full of Himself, Number Three." With the other two, he resembles a fanged Cheshire cat.

"Because I don't have the energy to deal with you tonight," I say, picking up my towel and wiping my cheeks. "So, let's just sum this up. 'Oh, Trixie, you are so sexy sweating like that. Let's you and me do something in my bedroom where we can sweat together.' 'Oliver, Paris Hilton will be a member of MENSA before that happens.' The end. See, saved us ten minutes." I collect my water bottle and walk past him. Darned if I don't feel his eyes on my derriere again.

"Something has upset you," he says. I turn back around. "You attacked the bag with the ferocity of a lioness defending her cubs."

"Well, I was thinking about you," I say like a mouthy teenager. "That must explain it."

"The meeting with your brother did not go well I take it?"

My mouth drops open. "How did you know about that? I didn't tell anyone." Well, not anyone who is currently in this house, and I doubt Will said anything, especially to Oliver.

"There are no secrets in this house, my dear." He steps closer, meeting my eyes. "What did he say to distress you so?"

I don't want to tell him. I want to superglue my lips together, but those gray eyes rimmed with thick black lashes do something to me. It's not vampire magic, as numerous boring tests in the lab have proven I'm immune to for some reason. No, it's *that look*. That look of "If you share with me I will do everything in my power, I will rearrange heaven, to make it all better." It's moments like this where I almost want to … well, lips in naughty places are involved. I look away before I become the whore of Kansas.

"He said the usual. I'm a freak, he wants nothing to do with me, and I should never set foot in California again. Oh, and then he told me he got married and didn't invite me. And that my new sister-in-law is pregnant, but if the kid turns out like me, it won't be an Alexander for long. So yeah, *great* meeting. Thanks for making me relive it again. Good night, I'm going to get plastered."

I turn back around and *poof*! He's moved five feet in a millisecond. I've actually gotten used to the "poofing" by now. Maybe in two more months my knee will be ready for his groin when he does it. "Move or I move you," I say.

"No."

"Seriously, don't mess with me tonight, Oliver. I'm just itching to make something bleed, okay?"

"He should not have said those things to you. It was done solely to hurt you."

"Well, it worked, didn't it?"

"He remains in town still?"

"I suppose. He didn't exactly share his plans with me."

"Would you like me to take care of him?"

"Um …" I'm stunned into silence. I wait for him to crack a smile but wait in vain. The expression I've only seen about six times in two months remains. It's usually followed by violence. "Did—did you just offer to kill my brother?"

"You said it, I did not. Is that what you wish?"

Honestly, the thought crossed my mind, but to have it out there … "You'd do that for me?"

He doesn't move or even twitch. I meet his eyes again. I should be scared, right? That is the appropriate response. Then why do I have the strongest urge to smash my lips against his? I laugh nervously instead and look away. "Good one. I'm going to tattle to Will, you know," I chuckle. "Finally give him a reason to stake you."

"If it brought a smile to your beautiful face, it would be worth it."

"Right. Thanks for the offer, but I'll take the chocolate and vodka route instead."

"Well, if the desire for another guilty pleasure strikes you, it will be my great honor to satiate it for you."

"Remember those snowmen in hell I've mentioned a million times before? Don't think they've arrived yet."

He isn't paying attention to my banter. His head cocks to the right, listening to something I can't hear. "My dear, excuse me. I believe I am receiving the call I have been waiting for. Will you be alright?"

"I'm fine."

"I will check on you later."

"That won't be nec—"

He disappears.

He always gets the last darn word.

———

Vodka, God's greatest invention next to antibiotics and Gandhi. It's even better with … um … that orange stuff made from oranges. What's it called? Whatever it's called, it rocks. This stuff, plus *From Here to Eternity*, almost makes me forget my crappy brother and crappy ass life. Oops, I said a bad word. I owe Nana a nickel.

I love this movie. Burt Lancaster is my ultimate, super-duper fave. So strong, so virile, so funny. If he were still alive, I'd so have wild hot monkey sex with him. Is it weird having sexual fantasies about a dead man? Oh, wait, make that two dead men. *No*. Not allowed to think about him. I am so not going there tonight.

Oh, here it is! The scene! Yep, there they go. The ocean drenches their locked bodies, but they don't notice because they're so into each other. God, that'd be nice. I tried to get my ex-boyfriend Steven to act out that scene, but he refused. Didn't want to get sand in his pants. Stupid Steven. He was never that adventurous, reason number thirty-six we split up. I do miss him—well, the *idea* of him—sometimes, like tonight. I could use a semi-pleasant distraction for a few minutes. A very few minutes in his case. Heh, heh. Alas, the only person I'd even seriously consider as a distraction is somewhere in nowheresville Maryland on vacation, and I'm not even sure he wants to distract me.

God, it's so unfair! My stupid, jerk, poopy ass—damn, another nickel—brother gets a gorgeous, rich woman who probably makes him chocolate cake in the nude, *and* soon a cute little baby to hold and play with. Meanwhile, I—who has saved countless lives and am nice to old people and animals—am stuck in flipping Kansas with only Mr. Shaky in the nightstand for company. Sure, I could throw myself at the living dead man, but alcohol hasn't totally eaten away my reason. Three more drinks maybe. Oh, Will, why aren't you here? I would have already jumped your bones by now, whether you wanted me to or not.

Stupid Will. Why did he pick now to go on vacation? He's been gone for a week, with one more to go, camping and fishing and running with the wolves or whatever. One of the packs invited him for some male werewolf bonding. Got their own compound and everything. How he can still go camping, I don't know. His wife became steak tartare and he was turned into a werewolf on a camping trip years ago. He won't talk about it but still camps, go figure.

Two months, and the only things I know about him are he's brave, he's a natural leader, his butt looks perfect in jeans, and I make his skin crawl. Well, *I* don't make his skin crawl, my curse does. At least that's what he says. Like it matters, crawling is crawling.

I hate my life. Damn my brother. Maybe I should call a witch and have her put a curse on him. Yeah, all his hair could fall out. That'd be awesome! Oops, drink's empty. Time for another.

I toss off the covers, and with glass in hand, walk toward my good buddy vodka and its friend OJ. Okay, the world's a little wobbly. At least this time it's not due to a concussion. Shoot, how many have I had? Three, but all mild. That's still a lot.

This time, three parts vodka and one part juice. That's the word I couldn't remember! *Juice!* I pour and taste. Lord! My body shimmies. Strong. I am *so* paying for this in the morning. Still worth it. No more homicidal or suicidal thoughts here. I am incredibly horny, though.

Someone knocks on the door. Oh, bloody heck. Why can't people just leave me alone? Nancy literally popped into my room and did her best to cheer me up by talking nonstop about the new Johnny Depp movie. I hate living with a teleporter. No privacy. I managed to stand her babbling for fifteen minutes before kicking her out. Even Irie and Agent Wolfe stopped by to check on me after their date. They're probably off distracting each other like crazy right now, having hot pyrokinetic/special agent fun. Jerks. I hate them.

Eff it, whoever's at the door will go away soon enough. I can't stand any more cheering up. The person knocks again. "I can hear you breathing in there," Oliver says on the other side. I don't move, and even stop breathing. Maybe he'll take the hint. "Please open the door." Guess not.

"Sleeping," I shout. "Come back tomorrow. Or never. Never is better."

"If you open the door, I will give you a gift," he teases.

"Oh, I can just imagine what that 'gift' is. No, thank you."

"Please open the door. I will wait here as long as I must."

He will too. I once made the mistake of saying I'd go to a movie with him but changed my mind and decided to watch *NCIS* with Andrew. (Hey, Andrew is not very social, so I had to take the opportunity for camaraderie when it presented itself.) Oliver stood outside my door for over half an hour, humming and knocking. I finally had to push him down the hall with my mind. He shot like a missile, breaking the vase on the end table. Sometimes I don't know my own strength. So, I know I have two choices: torture us both by making him wait a few hours while he knocks every thirty seconds, or give him the satisfaction of me giving in. If Burt wasn't on …

"Open, my dear. I really do have a gift for you."

"If this gift involves any part of your anatomy, I *swear* I will send you flying through the wall again," I say as I wobble toward the door and fling it open.

He leans against the doorframe, both hands behind his back, with that cat-that-killed-the-canary grin, Number Two. Slight fang action. He's still prepped out in khakis, but now his shoulder-length brown and golden hair is slicked back, held in a ponytail. Bar sluts beware.

"What? I'm missing a shirtless Burt Lancaster for this."

"You reek of alcohol."

"Sorry, *Dad*."

"The hangover tomorrow will be intolerable."

"Problems I don't have right now. What do you want? And where is my present?"

"May I enter?"

I stretch my arm across the doorway. "No. Go away. I have more vodka to drink."

"We have an assignment," he says.

"I didn't hear the alarm." Even drunk—heck, even dead—you can't miss a Klaxon bell louder than an Ozzy Osbourne concert.

"Special assignment. Just you and I. George will brief you on the particulars tomorrow when you are more … receptive."

I raise an eyebrow. "I'm not going anywhere alone with you."

"You do not trust me?" he asks with amusement, but the grin drops.

"No comment."

Grin Number Three returns. "Perhaps it is yourself you do not trust."

I scoff. "You wish."

"I did not know you were a mind reader as well."

"An amoeba could tell what's on your mind right now. You do know that trying to get me into bed on your way to pick up other girls isn't the best tactic, right?"

"I am giving you a chance to have me all to yourself."

"No, you're not; you're here to annoy me with stupid sexual innuendo like 'special assignment' because I'm all vulnerable. I am *not* having sex with you. Deal!"

"I believe you were the party who brought up sexual relations, my dear. I am here solely on official business. And to give you this." Arms move and out comes something black and lacy. Big shocker. He holds it by the straps with crooked fingers and that grin, Number One, the one with the raised eyebrows and massive fang action. I haven't seen something like this getup outside of Frederick's of Hollywood. It's a bustier with black lace over dark purple satin, and a corset with boning complete with a lace-up back. Jenna Jameson meets Jane Austen.

"You'll look cute in it. On your way to *Rocky Horror*?"

"Clever. No, it is is for you."

"I am not wearing that, you pig."

"You will."

"And why would I do that?" He releases one of the straps and yanks at the side of the corset. The fabric rips off with the sound of Velcro.

Oh, wow. In between where the boning was are thin silver throwing daggers with crosses for handles and more engraved on the blades. "Awesome."

"I thought you would enjoy that." He reattaches the cover so it's skanky as new, handing it to me. "It should fit."

"What exactly am I supposed to do with this thing?"

"Practice." He makes a graceful little throwing motion.

"Why? What's the assignment?"

Grin Number Three surfaces again. "I cannot wait to see you in it. Till tomorrow." He turns and walks down the hall, out to hunt for a distraction. I gaze down at my sexy/deadly present. I've got a bad feeling about this.

Nothing in my closet matches it.

TWO

SPECIAL ASSIGNMENT

CONCENTRATE ON THE RED circle. No, *be* the red circle. There are no black circles around it, no white background. There is nothing but that red circle. Holding the blade by the cross hilt, I raise my arm to the level of my head and throw with all my might at the target. Crud! The handle reaches the wall first, not even close to the target. Darn it! Once, just *once*, I'd like to get near the stupid piece of paper. Rambo made it look so easy.

"I'm blaming the hangover," I say.

"Or you can blame it on your weak ass arms," Irie says, still pumping away on the exercise bike.

"Like you could do any better."

"*I* don't have to. He gave you those knives for a reason. You better learn to use them by tonight."

I walk over to the wall and pick up the six knives from the blue mat on the floor. They're so thin, probably less than a millimeter, but sharp as heck. "You ever had to use these?"

17

"Couple times. The bra was too big, but the knives did the job. Not enough to kill, unless you hit the heart several times. Hurts vamps and weres like a motherfucker, though. Makes them stop chasing you every time."

"So this assignment has something to do with vamps or weres?"

"If I had to guess, this 'special assignment' has more to do with getting you alone wearing next to nothing than any fighting."

"That thought has crossed my mind." I walk back to my position twenty feet from the target and stare down at the knives in my hands. "But just in case…" All the knives float out of my hands into the air, lined up in a row. As fast as bullets, they shoot across the room, three hitting the bull's eye and the rest surrounding the red eye.

"Nice," Irie says.

I stroll back to the target, tugging at one of the knives. Shoot, it won't come out. I pull a few more times, and out it comes. I have the same problem with the other five. "Maybe I do need to work on my upper body strength."

"Oh, I'm sure Will won't have a problem staring down your shirt while you sweat and moan on the bench press," she says in an insinuating tone a deaf man could catch.

Three times a week Will and I exercise together, if you can call it that. He basically makes me weight train for ten minutes—my complaining always gets the better of him—then he "teaches" me martial arts. Judo, Krav Maga, anything he thinks is useful. Of course, I spend most of the time on my back, and not in a good way.

"I liked you better when you weren't getting any. You're about as smutty-minded as Oliver now." I start placing the daggers back into the corset.

"I'm happy! Is it so wrong I want everyone else to be happy too?"

"No, it's just annoying."

"Come on, Bea. It's just us girls here. You can admit you miss him. Just a little."

"Yeah, I *so* miss getting my butt kicked three times a week by a werewolf. Fun times."

"You don't miss being pinned under him, your slick bodies touching, his musk filling your every sense ..."

"*Definitely* liked you better when you weren't getting any."

She chuckles, and pedals even faster. "Seriously though, has he called at all?"

I climb onto the bike next to her. Cardio time. "Just once or twice to check in." Or maybe five times, each lasting over an hour, but who's counting?

"And you don't think it's strange that he's only called you?"

I groan. "Will you please stop? We're friends, end of story."

"Well, I know he'll be pissed when he hears you and Oliver went off to destinations unknown, one of you wearing lingerie."

"It's not lingerie, it's a weapon. And hopefully, Will won't find out. I'm tired of pulling those two apart. I feel like I'm back at elementary school."

"We used to just let them go at it. It was funny."

Poof! Nancy, teenage teleporter, appears like magic dressed literally head to toe in black. Black hair cut like Bettie Page's, thick black-framed glasses, sweater, Capri pants, and Mary Janes. She's going through a black phase now, which in my opinion is a vast improvement on the polka dot phase last month. My black sweater hangs on her rail-thin body. I've been looking for that. The past two months have made me realize I'm happy I never had a sister. "Hey," she says. "What you up to?"

"What the hell are you doing teleporting? What if your tutor saw?" Irie says.

"She's gone. Chill. I'm not, like, totally brain dead. I've been sent to get Bea. George wants you. What's going on? He wouldn't tell me. What's that for?" she asks, pointing to the bustier. "And why did Oliver leave me a note asking me to let you, like, borrow my clothes?"

"He what?"

"Yeah. Like all my Goth shirts, even my chains and stuff. I left them on your bed. But they'll all, like, be too tight on you."

"That's probably the point," Irie says.

"The point of what? What does she know that I don't?" Nancy asks.

"Nance, you know about as much as I do." I climb off the bike and pick up my secret weapon. "George in the briefing room?"

"Yeah," Nancy replies.

"I'll drop off my slut clothes later," Irie says as I walk out.

"Yeah, because they're so gonna fit me," I call back.

The gym takes up half of sub-basement two, with the gun/skills training center taking up the other half. There is a small concrete cell where Will wolfs out once a month, but I hate going in there. It smells. I walk through the tiny hallway to the elevator. Up one floor to sub-basement one, home to our briefing room and Oliver's bedroom, the only room in the house I haven't been in. I won't even take a peek. I'm sure red satin lines the walls with a black silk bed taking up half the room. The briefing room is the first door on the left, which is where George awaits me.

Dr. George Black, Ph.D., the man who runs the whole F.R.E.A.K.S. show. He does the research, deals with the bureaucracy, and makes a mean Chimichanga. He's been part of the team for over forty years. First as a consultant, then as the head of the F.R.E.A.K.S., a clandestine offshoot of the FBI. Technically, we don't exist, but here we are, smack dab in the middle of the country like Area 51. (Not that I've been there; I've asked, but I'm not allowed to take a tour.)

George sits at the head of the long table, his face obscured behind the file marked "Classified," so only his gray hair shows. He looks up when I clear my throat. "Sorry," he says. "I was just familiarizing myself a bit more with the case."

"What?" I ask, sitting across from him. "You didn't prep it?"

"Afraid not. Oliver left it on my desk this morning with detailed instructions as to hotels and supplies. I have to say, he does a better job than I do."

"I doubt it. So, what's the deal? Am I acting as trashy bait or what? Let me guess, he's cast me as either a stripper or a hooker. Or possibly a stripping hooker?"

George points the remote in his hand at the projector on the back wall, and the lights dim. We use this room to watch movies sometimes with our feet up on the table—only time we can get away with that.

Up pops a picture of a thirty-something woman standing behind a bar with enough booze to supply a frat party. George flicks to the next slide of a teenage girl. Pretty, skinny, dressed in a long blue gown with a clean-cut boy standing next to her in a tux. The next picture is of an African American man in his forties sitting on a motorcycle.

"Who are they?" I ask.

He flips to a photo of a girl in her late teens in full Goth garb. Black hair, black lips, dog collar, and fake white skin. Then another of a picture of a man and woman my age holding up wine glasses in a toast. "That's the last one."

"So, who are they?"

"Missing persons from the Dallas area." He looks in the file. "The first two are Suzie Thal and Kate Bending. Suzie disappeared two and a half months ago, and Kate weeks after that. The man was Antoine Baker, police officer with Fort Worth police. He went missing a week after Kate. The Goth was Donna Zahn, missing two weeks. Finally, the couple are Don and Linda Costarello, both vanished one week ago."

"What's the connection?"

"Nothing, as far as I can tell. All different races, ages. The FBI and local police have treated them as separate cases."

"And we know better?"

"The only commonality was their enjoyment of the night life, but none frequented the same clubs, according to the reports. The Costarellos and Donna Zahn lived in Dallas, Bending in Grapevine. Suzie Thal worked and lived in Weatherford."

"But Oliver found a connection. How?"

"One of the reasons he was brought on the team was his … network of associates. He is fairly well known in the vampire community."

I scoff. "As what?"

"He told me 'a fun man.' We've found it handy in situations like this."

"So, someone called him and said all the people are connected?"

"Yes."

"Who?"

"I have no idea. He never reveals his sources," George says.

"Then how do we know this person isn't making this up to ambush us or something?"

"Oliver hasn't been wrong in the past."

"Then we all go investigate. Why the special assignment?" I ask.

"Oliver feels, and I agree, that an undercover operation is the best tactic in this situation."

"So, I *am* supposed to be a stripping hooker?"

He chuckles. "No, nothing that extreme. Your cover is lovers looking to join the Dallas vampire scene. You infiltrate and discreetly ask questions. According to the source, the disappearances can be attributed to a group of approximately seven vampires traveling together."

"A cabal? Perfect." A cabal is a group of vamps who live and play together. I've only heard bad and worse things about them. I shake my head. "I'm sorry, but shouldn't Irie be the one going? All I can do is toss things at them, she can burn them up."

"Oliver was insistent you go. For experience."

"Of course he was. There'll be kissing and touching involved?"

"There is no way Oliver would put his lustful feelings over the well being of others," George says as if I've just insulted the Pope. "I trust him, and so should you."

He's right. Lecherous though he may be, Oliver is great at this job. "I'm sorry. I just really don't want to go."

"There's no reason to be nervous. You'll be in communication with us the entire time. We'll be an hour away by plane if anything should happen. This is simply a fact-finding mission on your part. When you locate the cabal, the rest of the team will join and help take it out if necessary. It isn't the first time we've done this. You'll be fine." He stands up. "The plane leaves in an hour. All the supplies you need are loaded already. We've arranged for a service to pick you up at the airfield and take you to a hotel that caters to vampires."

"So, I'm the dutiful girlfriend making sure her man gets there safely. I think I can manage that."

"Excellent. I have no doubt you'll do just fine." He pats my hand as he passes out the door.

Well, that makes one of us.

———

He has got to be kidding. I look … like my grandmother's worst nightmare. I wouldn't wear this stuff on Halloween. Black mesh top under a bustier? Tacky. Too-tight black leather mini-skirt? I think I can see my cellulite imprinted on the fabric. I'll put the black stiletto boots on before we land and not a moment sooner. It'll be a miracle if I can take two steps in them. I haven't even decided on makeup, except red lips with lots of powder and eyeliner. If sexy was the aim, we've missed the target by about fifty feet and landed in the red light district. I feel ridiculous. Crud, it's time to go.

This is going to suck so bad—pun intended.

I zip up my suitcase with a sigh. Why is he doing this? What does he think, I'll be so wrapped up in our cover that I'll just fall into his arms? If he puts one hand on me—

The telephone rings. This is a rare occurrence, since most of the people I now know on this planet live in this house. I only get two calls a week, if that. One from Nana, the other from my best friend, April, and they both called in the past few days. I pick it up. "Hello?"

"Hello," says a voice that lets loose every variety of butterfly into my stomach.

"Oh! Hi!" I say, my voice raising an octave. "How are you? How's it going? You good?" *Stop babbling, Bea.*

"I'm fine," Will says. "I'm sorry I didn't call yesterday. How did things go with your brother?"

He remembered. He called to check on me on his vacation! I am squealing for joy inside, but not outside. Cool is my middle name. I sit on the bed as best as I can in this skirt. "About what I expected. Nasty names, hurt feelings. I should have known better, I don't know what I was thinking."

"You thought he'd act like a brother. As he should have. Nothing wrong with that."

"He seemed to think so." I sigh. "I'll know better next time. I did sort of deserve it. You know, the whole 'almost killing him' thing."

"No, you don't," he states emphatically. "You have to stop beating yourself up over that. It was an accident. And you've made sure it will never happen again. That's more than most people would do. Focus on that."

"I'll try," I say with a smile.

25

"Still, I wish there was something I could do."

Hop on the next flight and ravage me when you walk in the door? My smile widens from cheek to cheek. "That's sweet, thank you. I'm over it for the most part. You know me, I try not to dwell on things."

"I know. It's one of the things I admire most about you. You're a good person." Neither of us says anything for a few seconds. This is standard for almost all our conversations, uncomfortable silences. We're working on it. We didn't start with awkwardness, that's progress. I broke it last time, so it's his turn now. "Am I missing anything else interesting there?"

Crud, he just had to ask. Okay, I have two choices. I can tell him about Operation Lovebirds and he'll either A) dwell on the fact Oliver is leading an operation without him, but do nothing, or B) in a grand romantic gesture, order me not to go and hop on the first flight back to stop me. Either way, it'll ruin his first vacation in years, and I'll still have to go. Plus, if he goes with Option A, it could break my heart. On to my second idea. "Nothing. Same old, same old. I'm boring. What about you? Having fun getting in touch with your inner wolf?"

"I suppose. I'm learning a lot about…"

"Your gift?" He hates calling it that as much as I do. As if turning into a wolf against your will, or almost giving your brother a brain aneurysm, is something akin to a bracelet from Tiffany's. "What have you learned since we last spoke?"

"I think I have partial transformation down."

"What's that?"

"If I concentrate hard enough on one part of my body, I can change it from human to wolf and back again."

"Wow! Really? Like your hand can become a paw?"

"Yeah, but it's getting things back to normal that I have problems with. Yesterday, I spent the whole day walking around with a paw. Everyone acted like it was nothing."

"That must be refreshing."

"Not really. I'm actually still homesick. I think it's getting worse by the hour."

"You miss us?" I ask.

He pauses. "Some more than others."

My smile could light up Vegas. "Well, *Nancy* misses you horribly."

"Does she?"

"Yeah. She's moping around. Told me she's constantly thinking about you. It's downright pathetic."

Another pause. "Well, tell her the feeling is mutual. I miss her more than I thought I would."

I feel my cheeks flaring up, and I clear my throat. "So, they still treating you okay?" They being the Eastern Pack, a group of werewolves who hold domain over all the wolves from the Mississippi River east. Will met them right when he turned and got on with the Alpha, or leader, Jason Dahl. Will has an open invitation to permanently join them but probably never will. Too much kumbayaing and rules.

"I guess. It's all too upbeat for my taste, but otherwise I guess I'm having a good time."

"What do you mean, *upbeat*?"

"The whole time I've been here, they've been drumming into my head this 'proud to be a werewolf' rhetoric. I wouldn't be surprised if they asked me to be in a parade or something."

"I'd like to see that," I chuckle. "You'll all be carrying banners and howling in Baltimore."

"Well, if it happens I'll send you a plane ticket."

"We can march and chant together! I'll even dress up! We can wear matching fur coats while singing 'Who Let the Dogs Out.'"

"No singing. I've heard you sing. We wouldn't want to clear the streets."

"Shut up. I'm not that bad."

"You really are," he chuckles. "But I'd let you walk with and hold my leash, how's that?"

"I'm honored you'd trust me with that responsibility," I laugh.

Someone knocks on my door, and it opens before I can respond. Agent Wolfe, Irie's nighttime playmate and one of the actual FBI agents assigned here, pokes his head in. "The plane's waiting."

"Is someone there?" Will asks.

Covering the phone with one hand, I wave Agent Wolfe away mouthing the words, "Just a minute." Releasing the receiver I say, "Will, sorry, I have to go. Nancy's waiting for me."

"Oh, okay," he says, sounding disappointed. The feeling is mutual.

"I'm sorry. She's been waiting for half an hour. I'll see you in a few days, okay? Try to have fun. Bye." I hang up before he says another word.

"You didn't tell him, did you?" Wolfe asks.

I stand up, pulling my skirt down. "Of course not. And you better not either."

"And have him eat the messenger? I don't think so." Wolfe steps into the room, picking up both my suitcases. He glances at me and smiles. "You look ... nice."

I pick up my boots from the floor. "Shut up. I look like an Elvira reject."

"Then you'll fit in with everyone else there. And don't be nervous. Just stick close to Oliver and follow everything he says. Do that, and you'll be fine."

Right. I am so doomed.

THREE

MR. AND MRS. OLIVER SMYTHE

I know people flying in private jets with unlimited financial resources shouldn't be miserable, or at least that's what I thought when I'd watch those celebrity shows, but it does happen. I'd rather be in my old Volvo without air conditioning on my way to anywhere but Dallas, Texas, in this Cessna. I've seen Dallas. Lived there, done that. Of course at the time I was six. A lot has changed since. Instead of pink jelly shoes and overalls, now I'm barely wearing clothes, and the shoes I have on might kill me before any vampire does. Either a man or a sadomasochistic woman invented these things. Even sitting down, they're as comfortable as the Rack. The clothes and makeup—all two inches of it to make me resemble a corpse—aren't any better. "Slut" has never been a good look for me. My best friend, April, would laugh if she saw me now. She was always trying to get me to dress like this when we went out as teenagers. One look now and she'd bite her tongue clean off. My jelly-shoe-wearing self would run away crying.

This will never work, not in a billion years. Nobody will ever believe I belong in the vampire world. I mean, I've only ever met one, and if he's any indication, I'll stick out like a redhead in Asia. I'm not sophisticated, I'm sure as heck not sexy, even in costume. *Especially* in this costume. I'm cute, and on a good day pretty, but there hasn't been a single millisecond of my life on this Earth that I've been sexy. I'm a child playing dress up as a mother's worst nightmare.

Oh goody, we've begun our descent onto a private airstrip just outside Dallas. Maybe, if I ask, the pilot will fly me home to San Diego instead. I wouldn't mind this assignment as much if it was anywhere but Dallas. Bad memories. The last time I was here, I was that six-year-old in jelly shoes. Mom was working as a wait-ress/singer at a bar and shacking up with some guy named Chuck or Buck or something equally fitting for a man she met at the bar and moved us in with a week later. We were in his trailer one night and Mom didn't have dinner ready on time. He smacked her so hard she almost lost a tooth. A plate flew across the room, smash-ing into his head and knocking him unconscious. I was on the other side of the room from it, but I knew I threw it. That's the first time I can remember using my power. Not a happy memory.

The plane touches down onto the tarmac with no problems. Like most airstrips we land on, this one is small and desolate with maybe two runways and one hanger. We can't fly commercial be-cause we usually bring flamethrowers and machetes with us. Not to mention it might draw attention if we pick up a coffin at bag-gage claim. Of course, our pick-up at the strips are pre-arranged with local FBI, so I just climb into a car and go to our destination. Here, I have no idea what to expect. Having an FBI escort would compromise our cover. I just hope I don't have to sneak Oliver's coffin into the hotel myself.

The plane jerks to a complete stop, and I manage to stand up. Four inch heels, three inches more than I like. Crud, I have to concentrate just to walk, how am I going to fight? God, I hope I don't have to fight—or run, as I'm more apt to do surrounded by scary monsters. Ugh. This entire situation has disaster written all over it. The plane door unfolds from the outside, and I hobble down the steps.

"Mrs. Smythe?" a man asks the moment I step outside. Lord, it is hot! I feel the perspiration on my forehead already. There goes my makeup. At least the sun is setting, so it'll be eighty-nine degrees instead of ninety in a few hours. I shield the sun with my free hand. "You Mrs. Smythe?" the man asks again.

I gaze from the sun down to the burly man in a pit-stained wife beater waiting at the bottom of the stairs. Behind him, a white truck with "Damon's Plumbing" idles. Oliver *would* hire a plumber to greet me. "I'm sorry, who are you?"

"Look lady, I don't have all day. I'm sweating like a pig. Are you Beatrice Smythe or not? I'm here to pick up Beatrice and Oliver Smythe."

We're *married?* "I'm her." I think.

"Good. Is he in the cargo?" Clearly he knows the vampire thing. "Yes."

The man—Damon, I guess—backs up the van to the plane and jumps out again. He opens the back of the van and the cargo hold on the plane, pulling a ramp up to the plane. The gorilla tosses my bags to the ground, getting them all dirty from the dust covering this whole state. Only two of the bags are mine, so the other two must be Oliver's. Louis Vuitton: definitely his. When the final one, a black duffel, hits the ground, the unmistakable sound of metal on metal escapes it. A gun might as well have gone off. The man glances at the bag, then me. My body tenses. That has to be the weapons bag. Does he know I'm a fraud? Was our cover blown already? What—

"You gonna get those?" he asks. "I ain't a fucking valet, lady."

"Right," I mumble. "Sorry."

While my rude helper sets up the ramp, I put the suitcases in the back of the van. Effing heck, this duffel is heavy. Do we have an atom bomb in there or something? I swear, carrying something that weighs as much as you do in stilettos should be an event in the Olympics. When I manage to get the bag in the back of the van (giving Magilla Gorilla a brief view of Victoria's secret, no doubt), I wipe my brow with a sigh. I spent half my flight here on my makeup and hair, and it's ruined in three minutes. Well, he can get that coffin in all by himself, thank you very much. I climb into the passenger's side, turn the key, and crank up the AC. Aah, much better.

Five minutes later, Mr. Grumpy secures the coffin, and we're on our way out of the airstrip. The man turns on the radio, and Shania Twain belts out "Any Man of Mine," a personal favorite of mine. Up until age eight I moved up, down, and sideways across the Southwest, so tunes from Tanya Tucker and Garth Brooks became my lullabies. I've always loved country music, even when people make fun of me for it. Southern Californians *do not* listen to country music. Boy bands, yes; Johnny Cash, no. With Shania's help, I calm down a little. Well, as calm as someone who's riding with a perfect stranger going to an unknown destination with a vampire asleep in the back can be. Okay, nervous again.

"We're going to the Dauphine, right?" the man asks.

"Um, right," I say.

The man pauses then says, "Too rich for my blood. Hear they got silk sheets or some such shit."

"Wouldn't surprise me," I say, inwardly rolling my eyes. Oliver *would* pick the hotel decorated by Hugh Hefner.

"First time here?"

Crud, personal questions. I have no idea if this is Mrs. Smythe's first time in Dallas. What if Oliver or George or whomever mentioned something over the phone when arranging this? Wing it. No other choice. "Yeah. We're just here to visit some friends. *Vampire* friends, not my friends. I have no friends here, right, because I've never been here before." *Shut up!* "Is it nice?"

"No better, no worse than anyplace else."

Not a glowing endorsement. "So, you pick up a lot of vampires?"

He scoffs. "You must be new. Lady, the V word is forbidden. They'll cut your tongue out if you use it to outsiders. Literally."

Oh. Not even to the hotel, and I've made a faux pas. "I will definitely remember that, thank you." We ride in silence for a few seconds, except for Brooks & Dunn, but I'm not good with silence. "How's the party scene here? Oliver, that's my husband, says it's wild."

"How the fuck would I know? I don't associate with you people. Besides picking you up, I want nothing to do with y'all."

"I'm sorry? You people?" Okay, now I—I mean *Mrs. Smythe*—is offended. "A bit judgmental, aren't we? You don't seem to have a problem taking money from 'us people.'"

"Taking money is one thing lady, fucking 'em and getting gnawed on like a bone is another."

My mouth drops open. "Just shut up and drive, jerk-off." That was Mrs. Smythe swearing, not me.

He shuts up and drives. Good boy.

A long fifteen minutes later, we pull into a residential area of antebellum mansions behind brick and metal fences. High houses with columns holding up balconies and wraparound porches are surrounded by perfect lawns of emerald green grass with lush trees and the odd fountain. This is not the Dallas I knew. Not a trailer park in sight. We turn the corner on Dauphine Street to find more of the same. The van stops at one of the more hospitable gates. Ivy covers half the metal fence. The gorilla rolls down his window, allowing a gust of hot air into the cool interior. He reaches to the call box, pushing the red button.

"Yes?" a man says over the intercom a moment later.

"Dropping off Smythe."

"Password?"

"Daffodil."

The box buzzes, and the gate slowly opens like the parting of an ivy sea. The rest of the house comes into view. Oh my goodness, I'm staying at Tara from *Gone with the Wind*. It's beautiful. I live in a mansion now, but I'm still a sucker for a grand house. Three stories with a wraparound porch on all three levels secured with roman columns and metal fences around the perimeter. We pull up the red brick driveway past oak trees covered in Spanish moss.

There have to be close to a dozen windows on each floor, strangely some showing white lace curtains and others blacked out. Patio furniture is placed around the three porches: tables, chairs, even a swing per level. The ivy—

Oh. My. God.

No way … is that … my mouth drops open. A naked woman! There is a naked woman—naked!—lounging in a deck chair on the top floor! She's totally naked! What the heck kind of place is this with people being naked in public? *Shame*, don't these people know the word? I swear that if Oliver picked the only nudist hotel in Dallas, I'll stake him myself. If the driver notices Lady Godiva up there, he doesn't show it. Or worse, maybe he's used to it.

A man in a crisp white shirt and khakis strides out of the double doors just as the van reaches the brick steps. He's a tad younger than me with curly blonde hair and a perfect jaw line. Even the staff is beautiful in the vampire world. That red-headed stepchild feeling creeps back. No way they'll believe Oliver and I are an item.

We're so going to be killed.

The preppy hunk opens my door. "Mrs. Smythe?" he asks in an adorable Texas drawl. "Welcome to the Dauphine." He holds out his hand to help me out of the car, which I take. I need all the help I can get in these heels. The heat and humidity hit, and I'm immediately in a sauna. I think I can actually feel my hair frizzing. "Hot enough for you, ma'am?" Golden boy chuckles. He leads me up the stairs to the door.

"What about—"

"We'll take your bags and companion to the room. Don't you worry."

What, me, worry?

36

We walk through the doors, both of which have stained glass windows with a blooming rose, as the van rolls away. Strangely, my anxiety spikes as the van disappears from view. I'm alone. Oliver's totally helpless—literally dead to the world—but not having him close scares the snot out of me. Not that he could do anything, but still.

I jump when the gorgeous man touches my arm. "Is there something wrong?"

"Um, just tired, thank you."

"Right this way. I'm Cole, by the way. Anything you need, I'm your man. We'll get you to your room as quick as we can."

Cole leads me past the winding wraparound staircase and oil paintings of men dressed in animal skins or Confederate uniforms holding guns. Compared to outside, the house is as dark as a well. The walls are covered with rich purple wallpaper with black Fleur-de-lis patterns up and down. Brown mahogany furniture complete with a grandfather clock fills the small space. At the top of the stairs hangs a painting that would cover the entire ceiling of my old apartment. In it, a woman with dark brown hair pinned up with only curly ringlets free, latté Latin skin, red bee-stung lips, and a huge pink dress to rival Scarlet O'Hara's lounges in a chair. Pre–Civil War. "That's Marianna De Fuerte," Cole says. "She owns the hotel. If you ask, she'll tell you who was better in bed, General Santa Ana or Davy Crockett." Huh. I wonder if he wore the coonskin cap to bed.

Cole gently takes my arm, guiding me into the study. Two dark green leather chairs sit in the corner next to a matching fainting couch. More paintings fill the remaining two walls. The one of the

Regency foxhunt is particularly bold. Men with guns watch smiling as two hounds rip apart what was once a fox. Lovely.

"Please have a seat," Cole says as he sits behind the desk that holds the only thing from the last century. Even vampires have jumped into the computer age.

I sit in the tall chair across from him. "All my credit cards are in my bags," I lie. I doubt Beatrice Smythe has one.

"There's no need. Your companion already wired the first three night's fee into the account."

"Of course he did," I say. "I'm sorry, I'm totally tired. Long night, long flight." And my hangover headache is creeping back.

"Then I will try to make this as fast as possible," he says typing away. "I have you in 303 with an excellent view of both the garden and front lawn. Mr. Puccio and his consort are the only others on that floor."

"Will they be able to hear us?" Vampires have super-hearing, and I don't want Mr. Puccio to hear shoptalk … or us *not* having sex. "I mean …"

"All the rooms are soundproof, ma'am." The printer starts whirring and spitting out papers.

"Great."

With a smile, Cole hands me the pages and a fountain pen. "Please sign on the second page."

I scan the first page. Blah, blah, blah, responsible for all damages. Blah, blah, blah no fires or holy items allowed. Blah, blah, blah when in town must follow all laws and decrees of Lord Frederick St. Clair without question. Breaking the last rule is punishable by death. Death? That seems a bit harsh.

"I'm sorry, but what laws and orders are the death ones?"

"All. It's a standard clause. It just means we can't intervene on your behalf should something happen. You haven't seen it before? It's standard at all hotels."

"Um, my husband is usually the one who handles these things," I say, doing my ditz impression. With a smile, I sign. "Are there any strange rules the Lord has that I should know about? Am I allowed to wear white shoes after Labor Day, or will he chop off my feet?"

Vampires have their own type of government, or I guess *aristocracy* is a better word. Each territory has a Lord or Lady who oversees the others and keeps the peace, like a governor. Other vamps pay taxes and basically do whatever the Lord wants; in return, they get protection and community. How big a territory depends on how much a Lord is willing to face off against other equally powerful vamps to expand. According to my reading, it doesn't happen often. The last documented case was fifty years ago when the Lord of Phoenix fought the Lady of Tucson. The Lady now controls the entire state of Arizona. The biggest territory covers Idaho, Montana, and Wyoming, but it's not the most happening spot.

More common is the fight to become a Lord or Lady. Vamps give the phrase "hostile takeover" a whole new meaning. The only way to kill the reigning monarch is in a duel, Musketeer style, until only one stands. If you poison them or something else sneaky, it doesn't count. Regardless, these duels don't happen often. Lords act like Tony Soprano, banishing or just plain killing anyone they see as a threat. I'd rather be a rogue like Oliver, without allegiance.

The only vamp higher than a Lord is the King or Queen, depending what land mass you're on. North America has two, one supposedly in New York and the other in Vancouver. They split the continent right down the middle. Their identities are secret and they only reveal themselves when you've been naughty and they've come for your head. Literally.

"When your husband rises, he'll have to sign too."

"Not a problem."

"Good, then let me show you to your room," he says, standing.

I rise, wobbling a little. "Thank you."

I follow him out and up the stairs. "Right now we have three other couples staying, including a celebrity." He leans in and whispers, "Jim Morrison."

"The Doors' Jim Morrison?"

"Yes, but he's checking out first thing tonight."

"Oh. Too bad." Him, I'd like to meet.

We start down a dark hallway where gas candelabras hang from the ceiling. The flames flicker inside the glass bulbs. Reminds me of the gas lamp district in San Diego. Quaint, but dangerous. The paintings are even more interesting. I pass one of a tall vase with wildflowers, and in the next frame a serene meadow of tall grass wafting in the wind. The following one stops me in my four-inch heels. A pale, beautiful woman dressed in a pitch-black cloak hovers over a naked sleeping man in repose, his red hair lying like a fan on a pillow. And his throat is covered in blood.

"Mistress Marianna painted that one," Cole says. "Striking, isn't it?"

"It's … something else." I am so locking, bolting, and welding my door shut tonight. I stare at my boots the rest of the way to the staircase.

"Is this your first time in Dallas?" Cole asks.

"Yes. Oliver, *my husband*, has friends here."

"Oh." Both men just stare at me for a few moments. "Oh! Tip!" I run over to the suitcases on the other side of the bed to get my purse. Crud, all I have is five dollars in singles. "Um ..." I hand Cole three dollars and the rest to muscles. "Sorry. I didn't get a chance to get to the bank before we came."

Muscles rolls his eyes and walks out. Cole, smiling sympathetically, pockets the money. "Not a problem." He pulls out three keys and hands them to me. "Here are your room keys and the key to your automobile in the garage on the side of the house."

I take them. "Thank you."

"The remotes for the windows and television are on the dresser," he says, pointing. "The windows themselves open onto the patio." He opens the armoire to reveal a flat-screen television. "The television has three hundred channels. Room service is twenty-four hours, just dial 66. The menu is located in the desk along with the phone book. If you need to secure jewels or cash, we have a safe downstairs. The number for the front desk is 77. Any questions?"

"Nope."

"Every night at sundown room service brings two pints of complimentary warm blood. More can be ordered at an additional charge. Around seven every night Mistress Marianna hosts an informal get-together. You can meet the other guests and chat."

"We'll try to make it."

"Excellent. Pool, hot tub, sauna outside in the back. Now, most of the hotel is accessible, but if a door is locked or there is a restricted sign, please don't enter. I believe that's it. Anything else, don't hesitate to ask."

"Thank you."

With a polite nod, he walks out, shutting the door behind him. I dead bolt it. God, I thought he'd never leave. First things first. I hop on the bed and literally strip off my boots. Oh, God... that feels good. I wiggle my toes until the feeling returns. Next: off come the fishnets. I toss them next to the evil shoes. That is *so* much better. If it didn't take so long, I'd take it all off and be as naked as my next-door neighbor. At least I'd fit in.

I have about an hour and a half before sundown, and there is no way I'm leaving this room without backup. Well, that and I don't want to put the evil shoes on again. I know; I'll unpack. No, I don't want to do that. If we have to leave in a hurry, I don't want clothes to slow us down. Instead, I pull out the menu and order dinner after careful perusal. Lamb chops with asparagus and antipasto. Over thirty bucks, but I'm not paying. Thank you, taxpayers. Still have over an hour to kill now. The black duffel bag on the floor catches my interest.

Geez, it's heavy. Easily sixty pounds. I manage to get it on the bed and unzip it. Holy cow, which country are we invading? I pull out an honest-to-goodness silver sword, laying it on the bed. Next are three guns: two 9mm and one snub nosed .38 with black holsters. Five—no, six—boxes of silver bullets. We have them specially made with little crosses on the tips. Burns vamps bad, as if a bullet hole wasn't bad enough. Next, a Taser that crackles when I push the button. Under that, a stiletto with a cross on either side of the blade. Then out comes the silver and garlic pepper spray, along with a sawed-off shotgun, rounds, two pairs of handcuffs, and finally, my Bette.

I feel safer with her in my hands. Bette is my machete, souvenir from my first case. She's been improved, if that's at all possible.

The weapon maker who does our bullets dipped her in silver. She's over a foot and a half of shining, severing beauty. I added the yellow flowers and wrote her name on the blade in red nail polish. A girl should always look her best when chopping. I don't leave home without her.

I return the weapons to the bag, shoving it under the bed. Oddly, I feel a lot better now. Sure, I only know how to use a few of the weapons effectively, but at least they're there. If I'm lucky, I won't have to use a single one of them. I scoff. Raise your hand if you think that's going to happen.

Lacking anything better to do, I curl up in the puffy chair and turn on the television. There's nothing good on TCM or Comedy Central. I flip until I reach SyFy. Oh, *Serenity*. I am such a sucker for authoritative, witty men in space. Dinner arrives just as I'm getting into the movie, and I chow down. Darn, I was hungry. I puked everything out this morning and only had a candy bar on the plane. They sent wine with dinner, but I stick to water. Must keep a level head.

I'm immersed in the big spaceship dogfight and the last of the asparagus when there is a thump from inside the coffin next to me. I jump. Jeez! I almost forgot it was here. The knock on the room door a moment later warrants another jump. So much for a level head. I open the door. The same woman who brought my dinner stands in the hallway holding a coffee thermos and wine glass. "Blood," she says. "O positive."

"Human?" I ask, taking the goods.

"Of course. Have a nice night." She walks away.

I shut the door, holding human blood. I know Oliver usually drinks pig blood (I asked), and I've only seen him once after trying the human variety. It was not a pretty sight. Black eyes, torn flesh, fun scar on my neck. Don't want a repeat. I set the thermos on the desk as the coffin thumps again. Suddenly, hot space pirates aren't that interesting. I can't take my eyes off the coffin.

There are two clicks inside it. Using the remote, I lower the black window slats to snuff out the remaining light from outside. Even the slightest sliver of UV light can light up a vamp like a brush fire during the Santa Anas. "It's safe to come out now," I say, when the last of the light disappears.

The lid lifts. Huh, I was wrong. I thought for sure red satin lining, not white silk. Of course, the boxers he's sporting—and nothing else—are red. I can't help myself, I take him all in. His skin's almost the color of the lining. I've never seen him this pale before, with dozens of soft blue veins cascading and crisscrossing all over his body. It makes him look... vulnerable. It doesn't help that his skin is drawn across his face like a bad face-lift with sunken-in eyes to boot. A corpse. He looks like a corpse.

His gray eyes fly open, darting immediately to me. He blinks a few times to focus. "Blood," he croaks.

I leap up, wanting to get away from him. I grab the thermos, twist off the cap, and hand it to him. He snatches it out of my hand, gulping down the blood, Adam's apple bobbing. The red liquid drips from both sides of his mouth, landing on his muscular torso. I watch as the veins fade away and the pink returns to his skin. Even his brown hair revitalizes, gaining back its shampoo commercial volume and shine. The thermos leaves his lips, and he wipes the blood off his chin, smudging it. "Will you please get me a wet towel? I made a mess of myself."

I do as he asks, returning as he steps out of the coffin. "Thank you," he says, taking the towel. I watch with my mouth half open as he wipes his broad chest. *Hello*. The memory of the last minute fades from memory. As he moves, his muscles become taut. I don't know much about his life before becoming a vamp, but Irie told me he was a farmer somewhere in England. I believe it. He's muscle bound, but not in that scary way popular with Hollywood. He just has the outline of a six-pack and pecs, with well-toned arms, and only the beginnings of love handles. I've seen him shirtless before, but I've never taken him all in like this. Okay, I'm lying. *Every* time he has his shirt off I check him out. I can't *not*. Like all the other times, my whole body heats up from the inside. Oliver notices me and raises an eyebrow. "Do you enjoy what you see?"

I snap out of it. "You are such a jerk," is the best I can come up with. "And you're a messy eater."

"Dying does that to me, my dear."

"Whatever. Put some clothes on, please. You're not at home alone, okay?"

"We are a couple, *darling*. We should at least act as if we have seen each other in a state of undress."

"We're alone. Put. Some. Clothes. On." I glare, but he smiles. He doesn't move. "Look, I'm tired, hung over, weirded out, and royally peeved at you right now. If I have to, I will push you out the window and watch you fry! Now, get dressed!"

Grin Number Three disappears. "As you wish."

I plop back into my chair, pretending to watch the movie while Oliver selects his clothes. Without a word, he retreats to the bathroom, shutting the door. Well, he wanted to be a married couple.

Water runs, I think teeth are brushed, and mouth wash is gargled. I didn't know vamps brushed their teeth. He's in there long enough for me to finish dinner and the movie. He steps out just as I push the room service tray outside.

My, my. We are a pair. He's dressed in black leather pants that hug each centimeter. Pretty sure the boxers are gone now. His top is crushed velvet in cerulean, which brings out the blue in his eyes. Me, I look ridiculous in Goth getup, but Oliver could wear a muumuu and still look gorgeous. I don't know if he looked better before in nothing or like this. Tough call.

"You look nice," I say, closing the door.

"You look like a child playing dress up," he says.

I scoff. "You're the one who told me to dress like this."

"Your outfit is too flamboyant. Keep the skirt and bustier. The shirt underneath must go. Did you pack sheer black pantyhose? Fishnets are so garish."

Okay, that's it. I have had it. I so don't need this. I pick up one of my boots from the floor, and fling it at his head. "Jerk!"

He dodges it. I get the other and toss. It misses again.

"Please calm down, Trixie," he says in a condescending tone.

"The heck I will! I did not put up with a killer headache, a rude driver, or a nymphomaniac just to be insulted. Is this even a real assignment? Because I don't think so! I think this is just some elaborate setup to get me alone and uncomfortable because you enjoy torturing me. That's what I think! Some people are missing? No real connection? Give me a break!"

"I would not waste either of our times on such a scheme when I know you will eventually come to me willingly," he says with absolute certainty.

Rolling eyes time. "Then why am I here? Why not Irie? I'm sure she's gone undercover before. And *she* doesn't mind putting up with you."

"You possess an ability she does not have. A natural immunity to my kind. You cannot be swayed by our mind tricks. It is an invaluable asset in this circumstance."

"That's it?"

"That and I thought it would be better for you to keep busy instead of dwelling on the unfortunate occurrence yesterday. That was my only ulterior motive."

I meet his eyes. Crud. He's telling the truth. "Then…oh."

"I forgive you."

I sigh, letting some of the tension out. Not much, but some. Just because this trip is legit doesn't mean he won't use it to his advantage. I'm still not completely at ease. I need a guarantee he won't overstep his bounds. "Just know one thing: If anything happens, if there is *any* unprofessional behavior on your part during this case, it ends. I call Will."

"You would tattle to William about me?" he asks with a genuine smile.

"Yes. And we both know what would happen after that."

World War III complete with claws and fangs.

"I promise you my dear, I will be the height of professionalism."

"Good. Then let's get to work."

FOUR

KEEPING UP WITH THE JONESES

I HATE IT WHEN he's right. I *so* hate it. Luckily, he's only been right about three times since we've met. I look so much better without the fishnets, mesh top, and five inches of makeup. Sitting on the toilet, I roll on the black pantyhose—control top, if you must know—and pull down my skirt. I re-apply my neutral base, red lipstick, and mascara before adjusting the girls in the bustier. Darn. Cleavage up to my nose. It'll be a miracle if I don't pop out at least once. I'm wearing a coat even if it's two hundred degrees.

I do one final check through. Okay … wow. I look good. Real good. Bordering on sexy even, a look I have never been able to pull off before. My medium-brown hair cascades down my back frizz free. The clothes may be uncomfortable, but they pull the right things in, giving me a perfect hourglass silhouette. Not the ideal in the land of the impossibly gorgeous, but I'll pass. No stomach too. Still need to lose about fifteen pounds and grow five inches, but overall not bad. I cover my hair with more hairspray and step out.

My "husband" stands by the bed, rooting around in the duffel bag. He looks up as I step out. He doesn't move, doesn't even blink for a few seconds. His eyes rove my body from toes to top, where they rest on my breasts. My entire body heats up in embarrassment.

"This is better, I take it?" I ask with a nervous chuckle.

"Yes," he says in a husky voice. He finally blinks and looks away. An embarrassed vamp, there's something you don't see every day.

"I need you to do up the laces," I say, turning my back to him.

He hesitates for a moment, then says, "Very well."

I brush my hair off to the side as he joins me by the bathroom door. If he had breath, I'd feel it on my back now. I tense a little as I sense his eyes on my bare neck. This is where trust comes in. He's tempted; I'd be a fool not to know this. This is like shoving a Big Mac in the face of someone on a diet. I mean, bare neck just inches from his mouth? But I know he won't succumb. I just do. Weird, right? I don't understand it myself. I trust my instincts. That and I have no choice; I can't do the laces myself.

We stand completely still for a moment. The butterflies that have taken up permanent residence in my stomach since I took this job spread their wings and soar for the second time today. They have no loyalty. As his hand moves toward me, I visibly tense this time. He doesn't touch me; his hand moves to the laces. He yanks the bottom one.

"This must bring back memories, huh?" I ask.

"I beg your pardon?"

"I'll bet you've done up a hundred corsets through the years, what with all those Victorian women you no doubt seduced."

"I have done my fair share, yes. I was usually undoing them, though." He pulls the final one and ties the back. "Done."

Thank God.

"Thanks." I flip my hair back and step away. Darn. The girls rose another inch. "Just like a married couple, huh? Me serving you dinner, you doing up my dress. We might actually pass."

His left eyebrow lifts. "Married?"

"Yeah. You didn't fill me in on our cover story, so I had to improvise. We were married a year ago in Vegas. I thought it might explain why we're not so moony-eyed over each other. The thrill is gone, *pookie*."

Grin Number Three surfaces. "And is there anything else I should know? Do we have children or pets?"

I sit on the desk chair facing him. The butterflies return to their perches. "I did my best."

"And you did beautifully. I do apologize for your ill preparedness. I did not have time while making all the other arrangements to provide a complete cover. If it is any consolation, I knew you would succeed without one."

"I'm sure you did. So, care to share now? You do have a plan, right?"

"Of course," he says, sitting on the bed right across from me. "The last three victims were last seen in Dallas at two clubs often frequented by human and vampire alike."

"So we go there and ask questions?"

"Discreetly."

"Didn't the police already do that?"

"Yes, but the clientele were less than forthcoming. You and I will claim to be friends of the suspects. A cabal of seven vamps will be noticeable."

"Right, but whoever these vamps are, they've probably moved on by now."

"Possibly, but there still might be witnesses who can lead us in the appropriate direction," Oliver says.

I scoff. "I'm sorry, but that's your plan? Hit a couple bars, ask questions, and pray we luck out on the off chance these vamps even exist?"

"They exist. My source is convinced."

"And you trust this person?"

"To a point. He has never led me astray, but I do question his motives."

"Who is he?"

"It is not important. An accusation of a crime has been made, and as officers of the law, we are duty bound to investigate. And so we shall."

"Do we even have a description of these vamps? Something to go on?"

"Yes, we have the description of one. Six-foot even, thin, blue eyes, midnight black hair. Answers to the name JR."

"That's it? I'll bet half the men in this town are named JR."

"If it helps, the source will continue to aide us when he is able."

"Yeah, and until then we have to play lovey dovey."

With an honest-to-God smile, Oliver reaches over and places his hand over mine. A feeling like warm honey trickles down my spine. His eyes meet mine, gray and clear. If I could, I'd turn to goo right now. "My darling, will that really be such a hardship?"

Someone takes control of my body, not me I don't think, and pulls my hand away. Thank you unconscious mind. "Inappropriate touching," I hiss. I stand above him. "I warned you."

"My dear, if this farce is going to work, there must be some touching and, as you say, lovey dovey involved."

"Yes, out there," I say, pointing to the door. "Inside this room there will be no touching, flirting, nothing. Think you can handle that?"

"Do you?" he asks, serious as pneumonia.

My heart skips. "I can't do this. Call Irie. I can't do this."

He stands up, now towering above me. "I do not want her here. I want you."

My mouth flops open. "Did you not hear a word I said?"

"I will admit that the, how do you say it, 'icing on the cake' is a few days alone with you. We both know that. I do not deny it. But you are immune to vampire mind tricks. And we are about to enter a precarious world where we need every weapon in our arsenal. You cannot be forced to turn against me or yourself. We both experienced how horrible that can be." He gazes at my neck, at the two ragged scars he put there. It wasn't his fault, he wasn't in control of his body, but I know he still feels responsible. Instinctively, I cover my neck with my hand as if I'm rubbing it. Oliver steps toward the television with his back to me. "You should not let them know about this immunity, of course. Do what they say, within reason. And try not to use your gift. We need to blend in, draw no undue attention to ourselves."

"Got it." It was my specialty in high school.

"Well, then. I think it is time to face the world."

"You do know that clubs don't get busy until at least ten?"

"I have been to a few in my day, yes," he says, checking his hair in the mirror. He's leaving it loose and wavy tonight. I like it better this way, but I'd never tell him that. It would mean I've actually thought about him. Don't need to give him any more ammunition. "But it is customary for guests to pay homage to his or her host on the first night. Marianna is a stickler for tradition."

"You know her?"

"Our paths have crossed," he says with a private smile. Oh, great. She's an ex. Just what I need.

"When?"

"About two hundred and fifty years ago in Barcelona."

"And you two were … friends?"

Grin Number One with full fangs surfaces. "Do I detect a hint of jealousy?"

Yes, but only an itty-bitty spark. It barely registers, I swear. "No," I scoff, "but I'm supposed to be your wife. I need to know how to act around her."

"It will come to you, I am sure." He kneels down on the other side of the bed, pulling out his suitcase. Out comes a pair of black cowboy boots with white embroidery. I get my boots off the floor and sit in the chair, pulling them on as well.

"Nice boots," I say. "Going native already?"

"One must adapt," he says, putting them on. "If you are a good girl, perhaps I will buy you a matching pair."

"Oh, we are not one of those couples. I hate those couples."

He twists his body around to face me. "And what type of couple are we?"

"The kind that avoids each other as much as possible. A normal married couple. Think you can handle that?"

"Why did I ever marry you?" he asks, mock serious.

"I'm asking myself the same question," I say, matching his tone. "Now, are you ready? Don't want to keep your ex-girlfriend waiting." I stand, smoothing my skirt.

"Yes, my darling."

We walk out of the room, locking everything we can and putting the "Do Not Disturb" sign on the door. My stomach starts doing somersaults when the door closes but tumbles faster as we reach the steps. I hold onto the guardrail for dear life taking each step slowly.

"Here, let me help you," Oliver says, taking my left arm. "Lean against me." Reluctantly, I do. My left arm wraps around his right and I clutch onto his hard bicep. "Tomorrow you will buy more sensible shoes. You are no good to me with broken ankles."

"Yes, pookie."

We reach the bottom of the stairs and I pull away, but he holds onto my arm. "Oliver..."

"You are my wife," he says seriously. "I *help* you."

He's right, darn it. We walk arm in arm down to the lower level, past the portrait of Marianna. Someone cackles in the other room, and I near jump out of my skin. I'm a terrible, horrible liar. What if they find out? What if I become dinner? What if they laugh at me? Oliver must sense my fear. He stops us at the bottom, doing something unexpected. He kisses my cheek, slightly cold lips on my hot face. I look at him, not sure what to do. Do I pull away? Do I slap him? I just stare. "Do not worry, my beloved," he whispers. "I will not let the wolves feast tonight."

"There you are," a woman says in the other room. Gloria, the nudist next door, steps into the entranceway—fully dressed, thank

58

the Lord. She's in a skintight silver satin dress, her boobs barely contained. We match in that respect. Martini in her hand, she looks Oliver up and down as he often does to me. He allows her to do it, expressionless. "My, my, I can see why you don't want to share. I certainly hope you change your mind."

Another woman, almost identical to the nudist, except with bright red hair and even bigger boobs encased in white lace steps out. She moves behind Gloria, placing her hand lightly on Gloria's shoulder. I'm Raggedy Ann at a Barbie convention. The woman eye schtups Oliver too, bee-stung lips pursed in approval. Again, he does nothing. A tsunami of anger washes the anxiety away. Beatrice Smythe doesn't let sluts mentally undress her husband right in front of her.

"Excuse us," I say through clenched teeth. I tug on Oliver's arm to get him moving. We walk past the vultures, my head back and high. Oliver grins like a fool, either from the attention or my reaction. Most likely both.

We're the last to arrive at the party. The others sit in black and red silk chairs or on the matching couch. The walls and floors are the same dark wood as the rest of the house. Cole, the concierge, stands behind the bar with martini, scotch, and brandy glasses all lined up with bottles of alcohol and blood. The walls, except for the one with the stone fireplace, are filled with photographs and paintings from various eras. The Wild West, the Thirties—it's a historical society's dream room. Above the fireplace is another portrait of Marianna, this time lying nude on a bearskin rug with her black hair styled like Veronica Lake's.

The woman herself lounges on another fainting couch near a huge globe, sipping blood out of a martini glass. Unlike the rest, she's dressed rather conservatively in black velvet capris and white button-down shirt with charm bracelet dangling from her small wrist. Her black hair rests on one shoulder, not a frizz anywhere. Her light brown skin, the same tone as my friend April's, darn near glows. Her huge lips are painted red, or it could be from the blood. When we enter, her black eyes drink us in. "So good of you to show up," she says. "I was beginning to worry."

The others wait for Oliver's response. A boy and girl, seventeen if they're a day, sit next to each other on the couch, the girl's long red fingernail caressing the boy's thigh. They could be twins, with the same sandy blonde hair, dark blue eyes, long limbs, and even the same nose. Heck, they even wear the same style clothes, both in black leather suits. Red Barbie slinks in behind us and sits next to the girl, putting her slender arm around the girl's shoulders and resting her head on her shoulder.

The other stranger sits in a chair, cigar in his mouth and ash-tray on his ample thigh. He's a large man, and even the expensive pinstripe suit can't hide that fact. His belly rivals a pregnant woman's. The rest of him is about as appealing as the potbelly. A bald head with a crown of dark brown hair from ear to ear with a matching mustache covering his top lip. I hate to admit it, but I'm relieved to not be the ugliest person in the room.

"I apologize, Marianna," Oliver says. "My wife and I were ... distracted." He wraps his right arm around my waist.

"Glo, while you're up, get me a drink," the cigar man says.

Passing us, Gloria flips her hair back on the way to the bar. Cole pours some blood into a brandy sifter. *He's* a vampire? Wonder how that happened. Normally, from what Oliver told me, a vamp gets lonely or bored and the first person they come across or are doing the horizontal mambo with is turned. Of course, usually they look like someone who struts on a catwalk. Who wants to spend fifty or so years making love to someone they have to pretend is Ryan Gosling every night? Cigar man has a story.

Marianna raises her hand, palm side up, presenting her cappuccino wrist. Without a word, Oliver releases me, strolling over to Marianna. Taking her hand, he raises it to his lips, kissing the thin skin where the veins meet. "You are as beautiful as I remember," he says, mouth still hovering centimeters from her skin.

"As are you," she says with a smile. "Still enjoy making love with your shoes on?"

He releases her hand. "Now, you know the only reason I did that was Gustave was returning any moment. It was a good thing I had them on, if you remember."

"As if I could ever forget you."

Gag me.

"And who is this … lovely creature you've brought with you," Marianna asks, eyeing me.

"I'm his wife," I say harshly.

Marianna looks at Oliver, mouth agape. "You married?"

"Yes. A year ago."

"Now, I know you are lying," she says, smiling. My body locks up again, all joints buckling. I've blown our cover. They're going to eat us.

Oliver stays as cool as the Fonz. "Why do you say that?"

"The very thought of you in any form of relationship longer than a weekend is incredulous," she chuckles.

I have to agree with her.

"I am a changed man. Love transformed me."

"You must be some form of magician, kitten," she says to me. "You have performed the impossible."

"I'm good like that," I reply.

"You look it," the boy on the couch says in a thick German accent. He reaches across to touch my leg, but I move away, flinching. He wouldn't have gotten me anyway. Oliver moves faster than I can see. One moment he's next to Marianna, and the next he's got the boy's wrist in his hand, teeth snarled.

"Attempt to touch my wife again and I will break every bone in your hand. Twice."

The German snarls back, making his gaunt face close to skeletal. His companion matches his look, but hisses like a snake too. The German yanks his arm away.

"Everyone," Marianna says in a calm tone, "we are all friends here. Let us not fight."

I touch Oliver's shoulder, leaning in and whispering, "Let it go."

He glances at me and drops the vampire face. The Gruesome Twosome remains poised to strike.

"Klaus. Ingrid," Marianna says like a scolding mother.

It takes a moment, but their faces return to normal. Snooty, but normal. They still shoot daggers at us with their eyes. Oliver crosses his arms across his chest, I'm sure mentally willing them to try again. Gloria, who lounges on the armrest of Mr. Cigar's chair, winks at me. I suddenly feel like a hick in Beverly Hills, out of place and pitied. Marianna sits up, stretching her long legs in front of her, staring at me. "Kitten, you must have been Helen of Troy in a past life. We almost had a war on our hands." She pats the now empty seat next to her. "Come. Sit. Oliver, prepare some drinks for me and your lovely wife."

Like a good boy, he does as she says, as do I. All eyes follow me to the couch. I slowly sit, delaying the inevitable a second longer. My body remains at a state of readiness just in case she does strike, but I do cross my ankles to keep Gloria and Klaus from getting a cheap look. (Their eyes do glance there.) Oliver starts mixing, but doesn't take his eyes off me. My protector.

"So, tell me about yourself Beatrice. It is Beatrice, correct?"

"Yeah, Um, not much to tell. I was born, now I'm here," I chuckle nervously.

"Well, how did you meet *our* Oliver?" she asks.

"*I* met *my* husband … um … at the library." Not a total lie, we did meet in a library. "He was checking out books on … knitting." Oh yeah, I'm a jerk. Oliver stops pouring vodka, raising an eyebrow.

"Knitting?" Cigar asks.

"I have been alive almost five hundred years. I am running short on things to learn," Oliver says, not missing a beat.

"Whatever," Cigar says, sniffing said item. He hasn't taken a single puff. Gloria takes it out of his hand. She inhales, and blows smoke in his face. O … kay.

"Was it love at first sight?" Marianna asks.

"Actually, no. I couldn't stand him," I don't lie. "He was rude, crude, obnoxious, he scared me, and hit on me at the most inappropriate times." I meet his eyes. Grin Number Three greets me. I smile back, then look away. "But then he showed his real self. He helped me when I really needed a friend, and my opinion changed. We were married a year later in Vegas. It was one of those places with Elvis. I know it's not official, but it means something to us both."

"You don't have rings," Cole, the concierge says.

"I don't like jewelry," I say. "I'm allergic to gold and he's allergic to silver."

"The sign of our commitment is in a location we intend only each other to ever view," Oliver says, staring at me.

That was for the knitting remark, I know it. Okay, enough about me. "And how did the three of you meet?" I ask the scary Germans.

"We are brother and sister," Ingrid answers with her hand still on his thigh. Oh. My. God. Mondo grossness. Eww.

"Oh," I say for lack of something better. "And you?" I ask the redhead.

"Gigi is our consort," Klaus says harshly.

"And what about you two?" I ask Gloria.

Oliver, balancing three glasses, two filled with blood and another with a screwdriver, walks toward us. He hands us our drinks and walks behind me, putting his hand on the back of my neck. Kudos to me, I don't flinch.

"I was a dancer at one of Sal's clubs," Gloria says.

"I was big time in Detroit in, you know, waste management. I got the head honcho out there out of some trouble, and he turned me in return. I hooked up with Glo about a year later."

So there's incest, lying, stripping, and the mafia all crammed into one house. I gulp my screwdriver.

"What about you, kitten? Thinking of joining us, or has this naughty boy never offered?"

"He offered and I declined. Like Queen said, Who wants to live forever?" Everyone in the room stares at me blankly. Wrong question to pose to this group. I clear my throat. "I may change my mind."

"There is no rush," Oliver says. "We are quite content with how things are."

"I just cannot picture it. How do you live?" Marianna asks.

"Blissfully," Oliver answers with grin Number One, full fang.

"Well, you won't catch me settling down," Sal says. "Glo here knows the score," he says, patting her hand. If this bothers her, it doesn't show. She sips her martini. "I did that whole married, kids crap for over twenty years. I got my balls back from that woman; I ain't giving them up again."

"Trixie does not 'have my balls' as you so eloquently put it," Oliver says.

"Bet she has you gardening or some such shit," Sal laughs.

"Hardly. We travel."

"Yeah? Where you been since Gidget got her hooks into you? She doesn't strike me as the adventurous type, if you catch my drift."

Um, hello? I'm in the room.

Oliver's grip in my neck tightens. "I believe you are mistaking adventurous for whorish. Not surprising considering the company you keep."

"Hey!" Sal says.

"And for your information, I have shown my wife the best of the world. Paris, London, Cairo, Rio to name but a few."

"Paris, huh? Been there three times," Sal says.

"We have been there four."

Okay, they're about to whip out their johnsons and compare size. Macho men drive me nuts. I stand, tugging down my skirt. "Well, I think I've had enough socializing for one night. Nice to meet you all. Oliver?"

With my chin up, I walk past the Gruesome Twosome out the door. I'm halfway up the staircase when Oliver catches up, taking my elbow. We don't speak until the door to our room shuts.

"We don't have to do that every night, do we?" I ask, finishing my screwdriver.

"Thankfully, no. I am sorry for how they treated you. It was inexcusable."

"They're predators, it's their nature to toy with food. And you didn't help matters. Can you please not get into a fight while we're here? The guy touched me, he wasn't going any further. Low profile, remember?"

"I was a husband defending his wife."

"No, you overreacted. I don't know about you, but I don't want to get dragged into vampire court if I can help it."

For a fleeting moment, something passes over his face. His mouth tenses and eyes double in size, but it's gone so fast maybe I imagined it. Was he scared? I've only seen him frightened three other times, and they were *bad* situations. Like, we-almost-died situations. "Oh, crud. What's wrong?"

"Nothing. You are right, I will control my temper."

"You didn't have a *nothing* face. Is there something you're not telling me? Because if—"

"Trixie, dear, you are looking for trouble where there is none, I assure you. Now, we should leave. I had George arrange for us to review copies of the case files on the missing. They are expecting us."

"You're kidding, right? I can't walk into an FBI building dressed like this. Can't we do it tomorrow?"

"Would you rather stay in this house, alone with me?"

Good point. "Don't want to keep the Feds waiting," I say, picking up my purse from the floor. I also pull out my suitcase feeling in the side flap for my credentials. There it is. I love this thing. It's like a black card case, but when opened, there's a gold shield with "Federal Bureau of Investigation" written on it. This thing can get me into anywhere: people's homes, work, you name it. It's also great if you've been caught speeding. (I was doing eighty in a fifty-five, and the guy let me off with a smile.)

I also take out my fitted black leather jacket that flares out at the waist. My best friend in the universe, April, made me buy it, convincing me I looked rock-and-roll in it. It was a bargain at half my paycheck. With the matching leather skirt I definitely feel rock-and-roll, but more on the groupie side. If Nana could see me now, she'd throw me in reform school.

"That is a fetching look on you," Oliver says throwing on his own leather jacket. He loves that thing. It reaches down to his hips and hangs loose. What a pair we are.

"Did they give you keys to a vehicle?" Oliver asks.

"Desk," I answer, putting the suitcase back under the bed.

He grabs them. "Are we ready?"

"I was born ready."

FIVE

THE FBI AGENT RODE A BLACK MOTORCYCLE

WE MAKE IT DOWNSTAIRS and past the still-chatting group without incident. The Germans glare as we walk out the front door, and Marianna shouts "Have fun you two," but that's it. The breath I hold escapes when the door shuts. At least it's a nice, clear night. The temperature has gone down about twenty degrees, but considering it was a hundred before, that isn't saying much. The still-hundred-percent humidity doesn't help either. I don't like eating soup, let alone having to walk around in it. Leather in the middle of summer is never a good idea. Get me in air conditioning fast.

The door to the garage is unlocked. Even though Oliver walks in first, I'm the one who flicks the light switch by the wood door. Holy mackerel. It's like James Bond's garage in here. A black Porsche, a vintage green Aston Martin, a red BMW, and a silver Mercedes. How the other half live.

"I am so driving. Give me the keys."

Oh, no. Grin Number Two surfaces. "You do not know how to operate our motor vehicle."

"What?"

Oliver steps away from the Porsche he was leaning against. Instead, he walks over to the other side of the garage where the black BMW motorcycle with matching helmets rests. "Our chariot."

"You have got to be kidding me," I say, hands instinctively moving to my hips. "I am not riding on that thing with you."

"It is a perfectly safe mode of transportation, I assure you."

"No way. Uh uh. I draw the line here."

"You do not trust me?"

"No, I just see right through you. You chose this so I'd have to hold onto you on something that … vibrates."

Grin Number Two becomes grin Number One, the widest with fangs. "Would I do something as underhanded as that?"

"Oliver, you are such a creep."

"It is too late now, unless you wish to go back inside and speak to Marianna." He raises an eyebrow. "Alone."

It would take a nuclear explosion to get me back in that room. With a scowl, I push the button to open the garage. The motor above grinds to life. "Tomorrow we take the Aston. And I drive."

"I can live with that."

"You're not alive," I mutter.

He climbs on first, kicking out the stand and leveling the bike. I put the helmet on. There goes my hair. Oliver puts his on too, flipping the tinted visor down over his eyes. I do the same. Now comes the tricky part. In the tight skirt, I can't lift my leg up high. I try but almost topple in the stupid boots.

I have no choice. I hike up the skirt so the world can practically see the control top of my pantyhose. I'll be flashing my nether regions to all of Dallas tonight. Oh, joy. If people could die of embarrassment, I'd be a corpse right now. To his microscopic credit, Oliver doesn't turn to get a look at the view. I manage to get my leg over this time and sit on the bike feet up on the metal rests. I swing my purse around to my back, and scoot up so my front touches Oliver's back. I know he's grinning even though I can't see his face as I loop my arms around his torso, clutching onto my own wrists for dear life. Motorcycles have always made me nervous ever since April's brother fell off one and was in a coma for two days.

Oliver turns the key and kicks the starter. Like a bear, the bike growls to life then hums. The entire body shakes lightly to the hums. Hello. My unmentionable place jumps to life as well, drawing much more attention than I like to give it outside the privacy of my own room. Think unsexy thoughts. Baseball, doing the dishes, old Jack Palance. He so planned this. If I have an orgasm on the interstate, Bette will get a workout tonight.

"Are you comfortable back there?" Oliver asks.

You have no idea. "Let's just go!"

And we're off. The bike jerks forward out of the garage and down the driveway. I hug Oliver tighter. If he could breathe, he'd be gasping right now. The gate opens as we approach. We pass through and he guns the engine, which roars louder than a chainsaw. I scream and darn near break Oliver's ribs as we zoom down the quiet street. The possibility of becoming a road pancake sure does take my mind off the other problem. He slows a bit as we turn the corner but ignores the stop sign.

"Are you trying to kill us?" I scream hysterically over the engine.

"Calm yourself, my darling," he shouts back. "I have never had an accident."

We round another corner, tilting so close to the asphalt my ankle glides an inch from it. "Slow down now!" I scream again.

To my surprise, our speed drops by ten miles per hour. "My darling, you are about to crush in my chest."

With hesitation, I loosen my grip a little. "Then drive like a sane person!"

"But I so enjoy you holding me close."

"And I so enjoy not being the star of *Blood on the Highway*."

He maintains speed until we hit traffic a moment later, the dreaded stop-and-go of worker bees on their way home from work. The drivers can't see our faces behind the helmets, but I can see theirs. They are all the same with their SUVs, thinning or graying hair, and white shirts done up with hideous ties. They're old enough to be my father, but they can't take their eyes off my exposed thigh. Green with envy, no doubt. We look like a freedom fantasy come to life. Open road, leather, semi-hot chick on the back of the hog. The man to my left, even though no doubt talking to his wife on the phone, stares at my hiked up skirt at the area only my gynecologist should see. I wish he could see my glaring face. The light changes and we move to the next red one. The sweat drips down my back and cleavage.

It continues like this for ten minutes: stop, stare, move a foot. The helmet might as well be a plastic bag wrapped around my face for all the breathing I can do. I flip the visor, taking in lung fulls of exhaust from the cars.

"Are you alright, my dear?" Oliver asks, flipping his visor.

"No," I say in a huff. "It is a thousand degrees, I'm in leather, I can't breathe, and the whole town is looking up my skirt. How much longer?"

"If we continue like this, forty-five minutes. It is possible to arrive sooner ..."

"Then do it!"

"As you wish."

The engine revs and we rocket off, narrowly missing the truck in front of us. The bike glides between the stalled cars, so close on either side I don't know where they stop and my legs start. I asked for this, I know, so I can't complain. I clutch onto Oliver as tight as I can, but bite my lower lip. *Please don't let us crash, please don't let us—*

The red pickup a few feet ahead of us changes lanes. The motorcycle skips to a stop. I yelp and close my eyes. Oliver, unfazed, guns it again. I open my eyes as the truck clears. He is about five seconds from losing his driving privileges forever.

We make it to Justice Way fifteen minutes later, pulling into a lot down the street for ten bucks an hour. First thing I do is pull down my skirt, then peel off my jacket. That's better, but not by much. I can see the waves of heat rising from my skin. Carrying our helmets, we walk toward the Dallas field office of the FBI. From the outside, you would never think this place was FBI. It looks like a regular office building. The few people who filter out in their business suits and pantyhose unabashedly stare at us as we reach the door. Oliver ignores them, but I blush. I've never turned heads before. Don't know if I like it.

I pull my badge out of the hidden pocket of my purse, and Oliver takes his out of his coat. The tall, African American security guard touches his gun as we walk in. The hand moves back when he notices our credentials.

"We have an appointment with Special Agent Michael Tully," Oliver says.

"Are you armed?" the guard asks.

"Yes."

Thank goodness we don't have to go through the metal detectors, or they'd have a field day as I take out all the knives from my bra. The guard waves us through to the man in the reception area sitting behind the bullet-resistant glass. He examines our badges and with a moment of hesitation calls Tully. "He'll be down in a few minutes," the receptionist says. "You can have a seat."

Don't have to tell me twice. I flop down in a chair with a sigh. I had better spend the whole night sitting or I'll never be able to walk again. The cold air from above chills the sweat on my torso, face, and legs. Oliver takes the chair next to me, staring at the display of the far wall of all the agents who lost their lives in the line of duty. The last one is a familiar face. Special Agent Spencer Konrad. He died on my first case, eaten alive by zombies. The official story was that a crazy cult member shot him. I barely knew him, didn't even know his first name, but seeing him looking so serious with dark brown hair slicked back, a pang of sadness grips me. He died serving his country. The only consolation is the man who was responsible died by my hand—or my mind, to be more accurate. I look away from Konrad's picture. I don't want to think about that again. Ever.

More people in suits walk through the turnstiles past us, staring. What they must think. Pimp and prostitute? Biker gang informant and girlfriend? That's what I'd assume. I hug my helmet

73

close, and look down at the floor. Oliver watches them go by, meeting a few eyes. The people look away.

"People can be so rude," Oliver says.

"Well, we do look like S&M Ken and Barbie," I point out. "I don't think I've ever been so embarrassed in all my life."

"You are young."

"Not helpful."

"Perhaps it is that they have never seen as beautiful a woman here before."

"Can it. Time to be professional."

A man in his early forties with receding hairline, ice blue eyes, and white dress shirt pushes through the turnstile and zones in on us. He smiles, holding out his hand. "Agents Montrose and Alexander?" he asks.

We stand, and a sharp pain shoots up my right leg. "Nice to meet you," I say, shaking his hand.

He can't help it. His eyes zoom in on my boobs for a moment. Men. "You as well."

He takes Oliver's hand, but Oliver grips it so tight, bones and tendons crack. Tully winces, pulling his arm away. "Nice grip."

"Thank you for meeting with us," I say.

"No problem. Follow me."

I swipe my visitor badge and walk through the turnstile after Tully with Oliver behind us. More sideways glances greet us as we walk down the hall to the elevator. Tully pushes the button, and in we go.

"Where are you two staying?" Tully asks.

"The Radisson," Oliver replies as we step out of the elevator.

"Nice place," Tully says.

"I suppose," Oliver says.

Tully leads us down a beige hallway with a gaggle of closed doors with keypads on them. The movies have it so wrong. You'd think that places like an FBI facility would be a bit more exciting. A gun range, wall of televisions, or people running around like crazy talking about serial killers or bombings. It's nothing but cubicles with the odd office. Total letdown. We end up in a conference room where a stack of files awaits us. Oh, joy. Homework.

"I was surprised to hear from you guys," Tully says. "I don't know what these can tell you. I went through them; I didn't find a single commonality."

"Appearances can be deceiving," Oliver says. He takes off his jacket, sitting in one of the swivel chairs. "Are these all of them?"

"All the ones you requested."

"You looked through all of these?" I ask, glancing at the stack, which has to be six inches thick.

"Yeah. When I got the call you'd be coming, I went through them. If you want my opinion, whoever told you the same perps did these was jerking your chain. I didn't see anything warranting an undercover op."

"We shall see," Oliver says, meeting the agent's eyes. "Thank you. That will be all. If we have any questions, we will be sure to call for you."

"Um," he says, running his hand through his hair, "I think I should stay. The Costarellos are still my case, and ..."

Oliver meets Tully's eyes again, but this time the agent's expression changes. A familiar vacant face with dull eyes and slack jaw surfaces. "Leave now," Oliver says in a soft voice. Like a good mind slave, Tully walks out, shutting the door behind himself.

"Was that really necessary?" I ask.

"I did not like him."

"You just met him."

"He was … crude."

"Says the man who dressed me in bondage gear," I say, taking the first file.

Victimology time.

Let's begin at the beginning with Suzie Harriet Thal, age thirty-one. Occupation: bartender at Club Pain which caters to the S&M crowd. I can just imagine what her uniform looked like; we could probably be twins. She'd only been working there two weeks, hadn't made any friends, nobody knew much about her. According to the file, she was originally from New York. A child of the foster system who left when she was seventeen and got married. Divorced a year later. She alternated between waitress, stripper, and bartender all over the country. Married and divorced a second time and had a child. No contact with either for over a year. Ex is remarried and has an alibi as well as full custody.

Suzie often went home with a man from the bar, and the night she disappeared was no different. One waitress saw a twenty-something man, tall with brown hair, helping Suzie into her car. It was dark, so the waitress didn't get a good look at the man. No sign of life since. She was skinny, tall, with long dark-brown hair. She reminds me a lot of my mom.

Next, Kathryn "Kate" Michelle Bending, age eighteen, student at Grapevine High School in Grapevine, victim number two. Good student, long-distance runner on the varsity track team, well liked. Both parents are doctors, no signs of abuse, and no priors on either. Kate didn't have a boyfriend, ex or otherwise, so no viable suspects. Kate and her friends Amanda and Petra used their fake IDs to get into the Glass Cactus, a local nightspot. They danced and drank, but that's all the girls remembered. Amanda and Petra woke up the next day covered in bruises with no idea what happened or how they got home. Kate wasn't as lucky.

The working theory is the girls were drugged, and then horrible, despicable things were done to them, but they managed to get away. The girls were interviewed three times by the police, who got nowhere. The only evidence of foul play were the multiple bruises on their thighs and necks. No sign of Kate since. A waitress and bartender saw the girls bumping and grinding with a couple they had never seen before. They couldn't give a description except for good-looking and the girl had bright blonde hair. Why they let the other two go, I don't know. We'll have to ask the creeps before we take them in.

Victim number three is Officer Antoine Baker, age forty-one. He lived and worked in Forth Worth as a police officer. Fifteen years on the force, a few commendations, one citation for excessive force two years ago. Married ten years, two children, avid motorcycle enthusiast. Also avid horn dog. Per his partner, Shane Nashaw, Antoine had a new girlfriend every month. The wife, Lashandra, should be the prime suspect, but she had an airtight alibi. She was away in Houston singing with her church choir. Doesn't get much better than that.

The night he disappeared, Antoine and flavor-of-the-month Rochelle went to the Red Goose Saloon for drinks. Rochelle left when Antoine started flirting with a woman Rochelle can't remember a thing about. The police think she's lying, but the bartender remembers Rochelle leaving with her roommate. They were together for the rest of the night. Two bar patrons remember Antoine making out with a "Naomi Campbell lookalike," and leaving with her and some friends. The sketch is close to the one provided by a witness of the couple's later disappearance. No sign of the victim since. The entire force was out looking for "Naomi" and her posse to no avail. The cabal had already moved onto Donna or some other place and victim we may not even know about.

Donna Bennet Zahn, number four, age sixteen at time of disappearance. Junior at Summit High School in Mansfield, Texas. Poor student with Cs and Ds, except in art. Suspended twice for smoking and once for fighting. Parents Claude and Cindy, older sibling Jeffrey. Father owns a garage, mother a nurse. Parents ruled out due to lack of priors, and though neighbor and friend interviews said their relationship was strained, they loved her. Ex-boyfriend lead suspect. Wayne Ronertson, age seventeen. Donna broke up with him two weeks before, and friends stated he was sending her notes and hanging outside her house. He was also at the same club, the Lizard Lounge, the night she disappeared. He claims he left before her. Last person to see her was her friend Cherie Martindale, who saw her dancing with a tall man with spiky brown hair named Rick.

I pull out a sketch of Rick. Late twenties, thin mouth, high forehead, brown hair, handsome even with the spiked dog collar. Apparently, he was with a group of friends, but Cherie never met any of them. The bartender from that night didn't recognize him, so the case is at a dead end. I flip past a list of items taken from Donna's bedroom to the last page. The photos of her. The first is a recent one taken for the yearbook. She's pretty, or would be if she removed the heavy white makeup, eyeliner, and black lipstick. The badly dyed jet-black hair with blonde streaks doesn't help; but the dark blue eyes, small nose, and lips with high cheekbones do. Too bad she doesn't smile. The other photo is from years ago. Absent are the horrendous makeup and hair. Instead, she had a healthy tan and strawberry blonde hair. Why she changed is anyone's guess.

Lastly, Linda and Don Costarello, the most recent missing persons. Donald Lee Costarello, age thirty-seven, originally from Chicago. Criminal lawyer at Waltham, Spektor, and Ludo with a specialty in fraud. Married previously to Tori Schneider, but divorced five years ago. She lives in Chicago with their son, Cody. Current wife was Linda Harris, age thirty, part-time personal trainer, married a year before. Happy marriage by all accounts. Don had a prior for possession of cocaine four years ago, but no other criminal history. Interesting list of items taken from the house. Dildos, chains, you get the picture. Friends said they had an open marriage. Apparently, Don enjoyed watching and occasionally joining in while his wife got it on with strange men and women. Whatever floats your boat.

Don's secretary reported him missing when he didn't show up for court on Monday. Credit card bills placed them at the club Purgatory the night they disappeared. They were regulars there and one of the waitresses, a Jodi Gibbs, remembered the couple hanging out with a group of people in their late twenties to early thirties. All she remembered about them was they only ordered one drink each, which seemed to stay full all night. She also remembered three names: JR, Serena, and Rick. The sketch of "Rick" is very close to the previous one, minus the spiked hair. JR fits the description the source gave: black hair, blue eyes, the sunken-in cheeks popular with males now, and a pointed nose. The woman, Serena, is African American with full lips, straight black hair with bangs, and wide brown eyes. Since that night there has been no credit card activity or other signs of life.

I close the Costarello file with a sigh and rub my eyes. I waded through stacks of paper to cull the relevant details out of the police jargon. I haven't read this much in one sitting since I was studying for my Biology final in college. I barely got a D.

Oliver finished reading way before I did. Right around Antoine he got up and left and hasn't been back since. He's not one for the investigative side. Our little group is split in two: investigative and retrieval. Investigative is Nancy, Carl, Andrew, and the real FBI agents all led by former Washington, D.C., detective Will. I was brought on for retrieval along with Irie, Oliver, and Will. Fueled by too many *Law and Orders* and Nancy Drew books, I wormed my way onto the investigative side. Otherwise I'd spend most of my time in hotel rooms watching soaps until it was time to kill something. The good news is I'm pretty great at it. Oliver, I've found, lacks the necessary patience. An immortal with a patience issue, go figure. Since the rest of the team's not here, I guess it's up to me.

Game plan time. It's so much easier when I'm just given an assignment and off I go. I wish Will was here. He'd know where to start, who to talk to, what evidence was important. By myself, I could just waste days while they kill another person. Okay, I need to make a pact with myself now: If I feel like I'm getting nowhere in two days, I'll call him—sooner if Oliver lays one inappropriate hand on me.

Okay, Bea. You've done this enough times by now to know where to start. No physical evidence, no DNA, no fingerprints, nothing. The nightclub in question didn't have cameras. The only witnesses had their memories wiped. Okay, why did they wipe the memories? They had to know something the vamps didn't want them to. So, how do I get that information out of them? Oliver? No help, he doesn't have the power to restore memories, only the vamp who put the whammy on them has that. Wait … if I remember Witchcraft 101, there are certain spells and potions that can open consciousness. That might work. Now I just need to find a witch in a strange city where I don't even know where the nearest grocery store is. It's not as if they advertise "Witches" in the yellow pages. I'll find one somehow. At least I'll have something to do tomorrow besides nude sunbathing.

After jotting down the addresses and telephone numbers of Amanda, Petra, and Rochelle, I gather the files and totter out of the conference room in search of a copy machine. I want copies of the composites in case we get a bite (har har) tonight. The outer cubicles are near empty, with no annoying ringing phones or banal conversation, just a high-pitch giggle in the back. Oliver leans into a cubicle, whispering to a barely-out-of-college blonde. She either finds everything he says hysterical or is having a seizure as she vibrates like a spring that's just been flicked. The blonde looks up at me, giggling even harder. Oliver rises and turns around. Grin Number Four appears, the awkward one when he's been caught doing something naughty. What the heck are they talking about? Me, probably. Lord knows what he told her.

"There you are," he says with the same grin. "I was beginning to wonder if you were slumbering in there."

"Unlike *some*, I actually read the whole files." My eyes dart to the blonde. "Where's the copier?"

"I can show you," she says, standing up. Ugh. A skirt halfway up her stick thighs, I should have guessed. So not professional. Okay, I know, glass house much right now? But I'm undercover, not a representative for the U.S. government. If her skirt was any shorter, my three-year-old goddaughter Flora couldn't even wear it. As she walks over, Oliver folds his arms across his chest and doesn't take his eyes off her butt. His eyes jump to mine for a moment, and grin Number One appears. I roll my eyes and follow the Lindsay Lohan of the FBI to the copy room.

"Here you go," the blonde says, gesturing to the machine.

"Thanks," I mutter. I pull out the sketches and start the machine.

"So, do you like undercover work?" the blonde asks.

"I've never done it before," I say, pressing the button.

"Oh." She walks over to the machine, stopping at the files. "So, how long have you two worked together?"

Subtle. "About three months. Longest three months of my life." I put the next sketch into the machine and press the button. "If I have to hear one more word about his wife and four kids, I'm going to stick a red-hot Q-tip into my ear. I'm almost as sick of hearing about them as I am about his impotence problem. I've told him time and time again 'if you put Tabasco on it, eventually it will lose all sensation.' I mean, TMI, right? But you know men." I put the final picture in, and the machine spits it out. "All done," I say cheerfully. I hand her the originals and the files.

"Um, thank you," she says.

When we walk out, me first, Oliver still waits by her desk, smiling. "I got everything I need here," I say, matching his smile. "You ready to go?"

"If you are." He takes the hand of the blonde and raises it to his lips. "Thank you for the stimulating conversation, Hayley. I hope to see you again."

Darned if she doesn't look at his crotch. "Same here."

"Thanks for all your help," I say as I start toward the elevator with Oliver behind me.

The elevator door opens right as I press the button. Love when that happens. We step in, both pressing the button. The doors close and bye-bye Hayley.

"She was a delightful girl," Oliver says.

"Yeah, she really seemed to like you. Maybe you should ask her out, see what she says."

"Perhaps I will."

"You do that."

The doors open onto the lobby and we walk out, handing back our visitor badges as we pass. I try to gain some ground away from him, but in these frigging shoes he doesn't need super-speed to reach me. He takes my arm, but I yank it away without even realizing it, shocking even myself.

"I have upset you," he says, stopping.

"Nope," I say, still walking toward the parking lot. For once he doesn't follow. "Come on! We have a club to get to," I shout back at him.

"We have at least an hour before we should arrive," he shouts back, still not moving.

Crud. Having no real choice, I stop walking and face him. "Jesus Christ,"—he winces— "can we please get moving? My feet are killing me!"

He bridges the gap between us until he's two feet away. "I apologize if I upset you. It was not my intention."

"I'm not upset, I'm uncomfortable. I honestly don't care if you and the chick were going at it Animal Planet style in front of me. Flirt with whoever you want. Not my business."

"You do care," he states as cold hard fact.

I roll my eyes. "Okay, I probably would care if you were having sex in front of me, I mean, gross, but ..." I shake my head. He always does this! I want the talking to stop, but he utters a few words and it's soliloquy time. I stop myself. "I'm not having this conversation with you again. Not when I'm dressed like a hooker in front of the FBI building. We have work to do. That is what we're here for, right? Work? So let's go. We can check out the Costarello condo."

This time we both start walking toward the parking lot, though he walks behind me. "I am sorry. I will try not to let it happen again."

And darned if I don't feel a little better.

———

The Costarellos lived in the trendy—read: ritzy—part of Dallas where the Dolce & Gabbana boutique is down the road from the Prada store, along with a Starbucks on every other block. Their high rise, a triangular building that's mainly glass, is wedged between a Dean & DeLuca and Armani Exchange. Since it's a work night and everyone but us night owls is tucked away in their beds, we manage to find a metered spot across the street. Oliver holds the helmets as I pull out my badge while we cross the street. A skeptical door man stares at the badge for a few seconds but opens the door.

The lobby is exactly as I imagined it would be: white marble, with a fake waterfall off to the side. There's even a little pond with koi. I keep my credentials out as I approach the middle-aged man in the burgundy vest behind the reception desk. His nametag reads "Rob." His expression changes from confused to absolutely puzzled as we reach him.

"Can I … help you?" Rob asks with a Texas drawl.

"I'm Special Agent Beatrice Alexander and this is Agent Oliver Montrose with the FBI. We're looking into the disappearance of Don and Linda Costarello in 602."

"Oh," Rob says, relaxing a little.

"Do you mind if we ask you a few questions?"

"The police already did. I mean, I barely knew them."

"You work the night shift?" I ask.

"Afternoon. I usually leave around midnight."

"I understand the Costarellos had many visitors at night," Oliver says.

Rob chuckles. "Yeah. And they usually looked like you two. Not my place to judge, though."

I pull out the sketches of the bad guys and lay them on the tabletop. "Do any of these people look familiar to you?"

He studies them carefully. "I don't think so."

"Okay, thank you," I say, collecting the pictures. "Can we have the spare key to 602?"

"Um … I'm afraid I can't do that. We have a strict policy about warrants."

Oliver steps forward, meeting Rob's eyes. Rob's body tenses again, and his eyes turn vacant. "Hand her the key," Oliver says.

Without a word or blink, Rob bends down and opens a drawer. He pulls out a key, putting it in my hand. Oliver plucks it out, and starts toward the elevators. Rob just stares at nothing as I follow Oliver.

"I hate it when you do that," I say as the elevator doors close. "It can't be good for them."

"You were complaining of foot pain. We would have spent the next five minutes arguing without achieving the desired result."

"Still. Taking away someone's free will like that is wrong."

"I can do nothing to please you tonight." The elevator doors open and we step into a beige hallway. "Perhaps when we retire to our room tonight, I can attempt to change that. Pleasing you, that is."

"Yeah, you can get your own room. That would please me to no end."

We reach 602 and Oliver unlocks the door but doesn't open it. Instead he keeps his hand on the handle, looking at me. "You know, my dear, one of these days I may take one of your expressions to heart and cease all my attention on you."

"I live for the day. Now open the darn door."

Changing grins to Number One, full teeth, he opens the door. I step into the dark alcove, feeling the wall for a switch. After five steps, I find it, flicking it on. Nice place. The gray tile alcove opens onto a large living room with black and white leather furniture and silver lamps all on off-white carpeting. Simplistic. On the glass coffee table in the middle of the room rests a book of Frida Kahlo's art, providing the only splash of color in the whole place besides the now brown flowers on the mantelpiece. I think they were lilies.

It's stale in here and still, almost as if the place knows its owners will never return. Homes have a feel. They pick up the energy of their owners and hold onto it. That's why there are some rooms that you can walk into and get a little pick-me-up. There are others that, even though the room is bare, make you feel unwelcome. This one is near null. They must not have spent a lot of time here.

Oliver clears his throat. "Um, Trixie, dear?"

I spin around. He's still in the hallway. "What?"

"I cannot come in until I am invited."

"It's not my house, can I do that?"

"Anyone who crosses the threshold can. Your energy is melded with theirs."

"So, I can make you stay out there if I want?" I ask with a sly smile.

"Only if you want to explore the dark apartment yourself."

"Good point. Come in."

Oliver crosses, closing the door behind himself. "Thank you."

I shrug. "It's not very homey, is it?" I ask, looking at the wedding photo on the mantle. I recognize the wedding dress Linda wore from a wedding magazine. Yes, I flip through wedding magazines sometimes. I'm a girl. It's not as if I have a subscription. Anymore. Anyway, it's a Vera Wang and costs as much as a small car.

"Some prefer a clutter-free life," Oliver says.

"Do you?"

"Not recently."

His gaze makes my cheeks flare up. "We better go to the bedroom." His eyebrow raises and grin Number One returns. "To look for clues, creep."

"Of course."

After a histrionic eye roll, we walk down the bare hall, past the exercise room, and into the master bedroom. The bed takes up the majority of the room. Oh, bad taste alert. There's a mirror above the bed. Besides those two features, the room's like the rest of the place: white and dull. My first stop is the dresser, Oliver's is the bed. He flops onto it, resting his head on his hand.

"I wouldn't touch that thing," I say, opening the drawer. "Who knows how many hundreds of people have been in that exact same spot." Nothing but expensive underwear in there. I open the next one. Designer clothes. "You could help me, you know."

"I try not to rifle through other people's treasures. It is such an invasion of privacy."

"This coming from the man who just last week asked me my bra size."

There's nothing in the dresser but at least ten thousand dollars worth of designer clothes. Next, I go over to the bed, kneeling down to get a peek underneath, which is not easy in this skirt. Nothing. After two tries I stand up, walking back to the nightstand. Nothing again but lotion, magazines, and a sleep mask. I'm about to close it when I notice a gap between the front and bottom of the bottom drawer. A hidden panel. I all but rip the drawer out, dump the contents, and watch as the false bottom gives way. As do dozens of Polaroids. Oliver sits up, suddenly interested.

"Nancy Drew would be put to shame," Oliver says.

Nancy Drew would have a heart attack or join a nunnery if she found this stuff. Linda, Don, and various men and women engage in countless lewd acts with all sorts of paraphernalia. I will never look at a stapler the same way again. Eww. I pick up another one. Okay, how does that thing even fit? He must have been sore the next day.

"Huh, um, huh," I say.

Oliver picks up a few photos, examining them. "Intriguing."

"Gross. This is just … ick. How can people, *married* people, do these with other people, let alone photograph it?"

"Many couples have open relationships."

"Well, I couldn't."

"That is because when you love, you love for eternity. You would never share that love. It is a beautiful thing."

I smile despite myself. He smiles back, not a grin, but a genuine smile. "What about you? How do you love?"

"It has been so long, I do not remember," he says with a hint of melancholy, but the smile stays in place.

I look back down at the pictures. "How sad for you."

"Yes."

For the first time, I feel him beside me. He's been there for seconds, but now I feel it. Bodies in close proximity and all. It makes me uncomfortable, but I won't let him know it. "Do you think our perps are in one of these photos?"

"I doubt it. I do not smell blood, and even if I did, they would have taken the photos with them."

"Thank God—" He winces. "Sorry. I so do not want to look through all of these. What do you think we should do with them?"

"Put them back."

"Right."

Oliver and I gather up every picture, tucking them back into the drawer. Whoever ends up with this thing is in for a big surprise.

I do a quick search of the rest of the condo but find nothing of interest. I should have known the vamps didn't come here. Not with neighbors and thin walls. They probably have a house somewhere. Another dead end.

"So, now what?" I ask Oliver as I close the door.

"Now, we go to the Church."

SIX

THE CHURCH

No, we don't actually go to church. For one, we're not dressed for it; and two, Oliver would burst into flames if he set foot in one. We pull up to the lot across the street from the Lizard Lounge, which according to Oliver becomes "the Church" every Thursday and Sunday night. This was Donna Zahn's last known location. There's a line halfway around the building consisting of the biggest group of Goths this side of a Marilyn Manson concert. For people who shun conformity, they sure do all look alike. Black, white, or rainbow hair. Mesh shirts, black trench coats, and dog collars as far as the eye can see. This is the first place tonight where I'm the conservative one.

Judging from the length of the line and my limited experience at clubs, it'll be two hours before we reach the door. By then my feet will turn gangrenous and have to be amputated. Oliver crosses the street with me close behind, but instead of joining the line, we walk right up to the linebacker at the door. The teenagers in line scoff and roll their eyes as I would too. I always hated the genetic lottery winners who get special privileges, but my feet hurt and I'll be a hypocrite if it gets me off them sooner. Sure enough, the bouncer takes one look at Oliver and parts the velvet rope.

"Go right in," the bouncer says.

"Thank you," Oliver says, passing through. As I walk behind, the bouncer gives me the once over. He's not impressed. I'm an impostor, and I can't even fool a bouncer.

The entranceway is packed with black-clad people who match the walls. Some wear capes, others miniskirts and tube tops. A girl with a purple halter top adorned with white, bats eyes at Oliver, licking her lips. This is so commonplace he doesn't even notice. As we maneuver through the crowd, other women and even men watch him. Me they don't even notice, except when I step on their feet. We make it to the coat check, turning over jackets and helmets. The music booms so loud I can feel each beat down to my marrow. A beautiful, tall blonde wearing a red tube dress breezes past. She winks. Oliver apprizes her, winking back and licking his lips. Then just as slut one vanishes, her evil twin does the same thing, garnering the same response from my fake husband. I see the same color red as that woman's lips. That's it.

Now, I am not the possessive type. I'm really not. When women flirted with my ex Steven, I shrugged it off. I didn't even care when he flirted back. But this time ... He wants a whore, I'll damn well give him one. I grab his arm, dragging him to the wall next to the dance floor entrance.

"What?" he shouts over the music.

I move in right next to him, putting his arm around my waist. He looks surprised. Not as surprised as when I put my hand in his back pocket. "If we're doing this, we're doing it right. Now, let's have some fun, *pookie*."

A gothic mix of the Gorillaz "Dare" begins as we walk in. The club is perfect for the Goth set with black walls, chandeliers, stained glass windows, and heavy red velvet curtains on the walls. A disco ball twirls above, and off to the side nubile young things gyrate on stripper poles. On the far wall near the DJ, *The Hunger* plays. Catherine Deneuve and Susan Sarandon kiss and caress on the screen. The room smells of stale sweat and a butt load of pheromones that I'm sure I'll blame for what I do next.

I lead my man to the dance floor, giving his gorgeous butt a pinch before pulling my hand out. Oliver looks at me as if I'm a stranger. With a grin, I start dancing—well, as best I can in these freaking heels. Everything but my feet move in time to the music. Hips pivot side to side in time to the music. I raise my arms above my head, hands swinging with my hips. Oliver doesn't move for a few moments with that "she's possessed by the devil" look. I swing everything: arms, hands, hair, hips. My hands find my hair, and I fan my fingers out in it. The hair falls on my exposed shoulders, tickling me. Using my knees, I bend down, still grooving side to side, and then slowly gyrate back up trailing my finger up Oliver's leather pants, chest, and slightly parted lips. Meeting his eyes, I wink. Grin Number One.

He bridges the small gap between us so our chests and legs touch, putting his leg between mine and placing his hands on my hips. The song changes to techno Korn. I rest my arms on his shoulders, bringing our faces closer too. Our skin is millimeters from contact. His eyes meet mine and a shiver cascades down my spine. *It's an act, it's an act.* I just haven't had anyone touch me for awhile. I'm a method actor. Jesus, just go with it. I do look away, though.

Our bodies sway as one, moving side to side in time. With each sway I become more and more aware of his body and mine. Hands, chest, legs, all melded. His finger making circles on my hip. My nethers separated from him only by leather and cotton panties. His neck is so close, I can kiss it.

Think of something else. Bunnies, baseball, anything. His left hand moves south to my tush, and I damn near jump out of my skin. Grin Number Two surfaces. The jerk's teasing me! He knew which buttons to push, and darned if he didn't push them like a videogame controller. Anger clouds the sexy feelings. My first impulse is to step on his foot, but instead I pull away by twirling around. He just lost touching privileges. He tries inching in closer, but I dance away. We continue dancing a few inches apart for the rest of the song. That's enough of that. I need a drink.

I maneuver through the now moshing crowd, past the go-go dancers, to the bar. An arm wraps around my waist. "I did not know you could dance," Oliver says.

"I was a teenager once. I've been to my fair share of clubs."

I order a fifteen dollar rum and Coke, Oliver a vodka rocks. Not that he can drink it, but he'd stick out without a drink. When the bartender brings back the drinks Oliver shouts, "Excuse me. We are looking for our old friends, a tall black woman named Serena and a man named JR. Thin, with black hair?"

"Sorry."

Long shot anyway. This time Oliver takes the lead, walking past the dance floor, up the stairs with a gothic metal fence along it. Luck smiles upon us as a boy with green spiked hair and girl in red corset stop making out and rise from a velvet couch. We snag it before anyone else can. Oliver sits close, draping his arm on the back of the couch. I lean back so my head rests on him. Just another happy couple. "Rest your head on my shoulder," Oliver says. I do, cuddling against his chest. We can talk without screaming now.

"Do you think they'll actually show up tonight?" I ask, taking a sip of my drink.

"It is possible," Oliver says. "This type of nightspot always attracts my kind. Especially the younglings."

"And why is that?"

"They are able to live out the fantasy, the stereotype. The elders enjoy it as there are so many willing donors. I think you will find that the majority of the clubs frequented by this set are owned by vampires as well."

"I'm just learning so much, pookie." I take another sip. Strong. "How many vamps do you think are here?"

"Just upstairs? Five. Two in the far left corner."

I look. Two thin-to-the-point-of-starvation girls in low-cut corsets with short, short skirts sit at a table playing with their neon colored drinks, watching the drones below. They have all the hallmarks of vamps: pale, full drinks, holier-than-thou attitudes.

"They look bored," I say.

"That they do. The man in the corner does not." Oliver points to a man with bright orange hair and stocky build, trailing his finger across the collarbone of a nowhere-near legal girl with brown hair. She giggles, pushing his hand away.

"If she's eighteen, I'm Elizabeth Taylor."

"My darling, you will have to fight your urge to arrest everyone here. We do not have enough handcuffs, at least not since we left the Costarellos' condo."

"Ha ha." I sip my drink. "So, do we have a plan? Ask every vamp here if they've seen our bad guys?"

"No. We let them come to us. We must not arouse even a hint of suspicion."

"I'm not good at patience, you know that. I can't just sit here."

"I could stand it a bit longer," he says, taking a wisp of my hair between his fingers.

"You are enjoying this way too much."

"And you are not?"

No comment.

The twig and stick vamps glance our way, then again. I raise my glass to them, smiling. The girls turn away again, chatting. They then pick up their drinks and walk toward us. That didn't take long. They *must* be bored. Up close they're even skinnier, like on the cusp of organ failure if their organs still worked. Their cheeks sink in so the dark circles under their eyes look almost like makeup. And they're young, about sixteen when they turned. Forever sixteen, what a living hell.

"Hello," says Stick, the taller one with blonde hair.

"Good evening," Oliver replies.

"Can we join you?" Twig asks, pinning a tendril of her curly chocolate brown hair back.

"Of course," Oliver says. He and I scoot over as the girls sit beside him. He replaces his arm around my shoulders, fingers hovering centimeters from my boob.

"I'm Denise," Twig says. "This is Pam."

96

"I am Oliver, and this is my wife, Beatrice."

"She's human," Pam says in disgust. "Is she your consort?"

I stop myself from asking what a consort is. "No," I respond. "I'm just his favorite walking lunchbox."

"I totally didn't mean to be rude," Pam says.

"I will just assume it is the hunger. Have you two fed tonight?" Oliver asks like a father to his child.

"No," Denise says. "We're trying to cut back."

"Younglings like you need to feed at least three pints a night, otherwise you might accidently kill."

"We know," Pam says.

"How long ago were you turned?" I ask.

"Like two years?" Denise asks Pam.

"Yeah. We were in New York for fashion week and went to this party. They turned a couple of us."

"That's horrible. I'm so sorry."

"It's cool. At least we were at our goal weights," Pam says. "Can you imagine being over a hundred pounds for, like, all eternity? Gross."

I'm about to open my mouth to rip the beanpole a new one, when Oliver pipes up. "Do you reside in Dallas?"

"Yeah," Denise says. "My brother lives here. We were crashing in his basement until Lord Freddy got us our own place."

"That was nice of him," I say.

"I know, right?" Denise asks. "Like, all we have to do is sleep with some of his clients or whatever sometimes."

Or not no nice.

"Have you met Lord Freddy?' Pam asks.

"No," Oliver answers quickly. "This is our first night in town."

"You should meet him, he's totally super," Denise says. "He has *the* best parties. Blood fountains, the yummiest donors. We could introduce you!"

"No," Oliver says. "That is alright. We are only in town for a short time."

"Actually, we're looking for some old friends of Oliver's. You might know him. JR. Tall, thin, black hair. Hangs out with Rick and Serena?"

"Sounds kind of familiar," Pam says. "Didn't we see them at Purgatory a few times?"

"I think so. We didn't, like, talk or anything," Denise says.

"Any idea where they might be?" I ask.

"Sorry," Pam says.

"Oh my G, I love this song!" Denise says. I tuned the music out, as a person screaming at the top of their lungs to a beat isn't my cup of tea. Leaving her drink on the floor, Denise stands up holding her hands out to me and Pam. "Let's dance."

I glance at a grinning Oliver. I hate him. With a fake smile plastered on my face I stand up, taking her freezing hand. Pam follows as we descend the stairs onto the dance floor. I'm sure I look like the Stay Puft Marshmallow woman next to these two, but we do get approving looks from the men as we pass. I can barely move on the dance floor; it's packed like the bathroom of a modeling agency after lunch. The music, if it can be called that, changes to something I recognize, "More Human than Human" by White Zombie. At least this has something of a beat. I move my hips side to side without moving my feet. I wish I lived in the days of disco with dance moves instead of pretend sex on a dance floor.

Someone grabs me from behind, and immediately a strange pelvis grinds into my butt. It is not a pleasant situation to say the least. My head spins around and at the same time the offender, some skinny kid in a leather jacket, stumbles back as if pushed by invisible hands. And he has been—mine. Confused, the kid looks around for the answer, but of course doesn't find the cause. I'm mysterious like that. He just moves onto the next victim.

"What a total loser," Pam shouts over the music.

I look at her, smiling. "Clumsy too."

The girls chuckle and continue dancing together, bumping and grinding like something out of a porn film. All the surrounding men glance or downright stare as they nuzzle and lightly touch each other's bare skin. With her fingertips, Pam runs her hand down Denise's arm. I pretend not to notice.

"How long have you two known each other?" I shout.

"Like, all our lives," Denise shouts back. "We grew up together."

Pam smiles seductively at her friend, then plants a kiss on her lips. It is soft at first, then grows deeper and rougher. I can actually see their tongues massaging each other. Holy macaroni. They keep making out as I stand and watch with my mouth agape. It's not the fact two women are kissing that gets me—I mean I'm from Southern California, for goodness sake—but it's the fact they're friends. I love my best friend April to bits, but the thought of doing anything like this with her is just plain creepy. Like getting to second with your sister. And I'm not the only one watching a live version of *Girls Gone Wild*. All males within sight stop dancing and watch, some laughing and smacking their buddies on the chest. The women roll their eyes and continue dancing alone. Pam and Denise separate, smiling at each other. I pretend to find the disco ball above fascinating. Very ... spinney.

Pam grabs her next victim, a twenty-something with blue hair and enough piercings to set off every metal detector within a mile. Simulated sex to a beat follows. Denise eyes a few boys but takes my hand instead. She's not getting as much as a peck from me. The song changes to Depeche Mode's "Halo," a song my brother loved for all of five minutes.

"You're a great dancer," Denise says.

"Thanks," I say, swinging my arms in the air.

"Your boyfriend's, like, really cute," she says. "You can tell he totally loves you."

Really? "Thank you." I don't even correct her by pointing out that Oliver is supposed to be my husband.

"He's old, like really old, right? He's kind of scary."

"Oliver's a pussycat."

"I bet Freddy'd like to meet him. He so likes hanging out with the old ones. Always gives them, like, the freshest blood and great parties. I could totally introduce you!"

"Maybe. We'll see."

A semi-normal looking boy in khakis and black shirt smiles at Denise, who smiles back. She spins away from me to start grinding on the boy. I take this opportunity to slip off the dance floor and back up the stairs, where Oliver sits talking to a handsome African American man sporting long cornrows, sunglasses, and tight leather. Both look up from their full drinks as I approach.

"Did you enjoy yourself, my darling?" Oliver asks. "We certainly enjoyed watching you, did we not Phineus?"

Phineus smiles, showing off his fangs, white as snow. We're just making friends left and right tonight. I sit beside Oliver, who immediately drapes his arm over my shoulders, pulling me to him.

"I hope I didn't interrupt you two," I say.

"We were just comparing the nightlife now as opposed to back in the eighties."

"The 1880s," Phineus says with a thick Southern accent.

I grab my drink and sip. "Right."

"A simpler time," Oliver says.

Just what I need. Two old farts talking about the good ole' days. We'll be here all night. "Fewer people too, I bet. It's so hard to find people nowadays. It seems that even the vamp population has boomed. We've been trying to find some old friends of Oliver's, and it's been near impossible. Maybe you've seen him. JR, thin, black hair, hangs out in a group?"

Phineus isn't paying attention. He waves to a Nubian beauty in a gold dress on the other side of the room, and then stands up. "Sorry. Excuse me." Our new friend walks toward the woman.

I scoff. "Are all vamps rude? I mean, did all their manners get sucked out with the blood?"

"It would appear so," Oliver replies with a thoughtful smile. "I am sorry you are not enjoying yourself tonight."

"We're working. It's not supposed to be fun." I sip my drink. "So, now what?"

"You dance more. I do enjoy watching you."

"My feet are killing me."

"Then we sit here, taking in the ambiance, and wait for others to come."

"How do you know they will?"

"I intrigue them. They can feel my power."

"'Your power?' Conceited much?"

"I am an elder. With age comes power. That is why there is no Lord or Lady under three hundred years old ruling a territory."

"Then why aren't you off ruling Hawaii or North Carolina or something?"

"I abhor politics."

"Speaking of politics, why don't we just go talk to this Freddy guy and see if he knows our people? I mean, he's the ruler, he *should* know what's going on, right?"

"It is not an option."

"But he—"

"It. Is. Not. An. Option," he says, drawing out every word.

"Okay! I won't suggest it again."

My female intuition is tingling. There's a story here, and I'll get it out of him yet. Until then, I need another drink.

———

Three hours, two rum and Cokes, and a glass of water later, we pull into the garage of the Dauphine. And I am tired. I haven't been up until two clubbing since I was nineteen. I remember why now. My feet throb. My legs ache. I smell like a locker room. Who knew I'd feel so old at twenty-six?

And it was boring. *So* boring. We sat there for the most part waiting for vamps to approach and make polite conversation. About once every half hour one or two join us, talk for about ten minutes, and then go back to hunting. One after the other these impossibly beautiful creatures paid homage to us. And with over a thousand years between them, what did they talk about? The Black Death? The Sixties? Nope: fashion and celebrities. Maybe they've spent too much time playing human, I don't know, but I was surprised Oliver knows so much about *The Real Housewives.*

Some knew our vamps, though. Either seen them around or shared a meal with them. We got the name and description of two more: Liang and Ken, both skinny Asians with matching pixie haircuts. All were at the club Purgatory on multiple occasions, where Linda and Don were last seen. Guess where we're spending tomorrow night? Maybe there will be a staking to break the monotony.

I climb off the bike and pull down my skirt before Oliver turns around. I can breathe again when I pull the helmet off. My hair's plastered to my face by a thin layer of sweat covering my whole head. It is eighty degrees at two a.m. I hate Texas.

We walk—well, I hobble—up to the house without a word. I open the door and a blast of cold air escapes. The house is quiet. If I'm lucky everyone is out doing their bloodsucking thing. It looks as if I did luck out until we reach the stairs; Marianna steps out of the library, blood-filled glass in her hand.

"Hello, you two," she says with a sly grin. "Enjoy your night?"

"We did, thank you," Oliver says.

"Not turning in for the night, I hope? We have so much to catch up on," she says, licking her lower lip. I have the strongest urge to take off my heel and stab her with it.

"Later perhaps. Come on, my darling." He lightly presses on the small of my back. I start up the stairs with him close behind. I don't open my mouth until the second lock clicks on our door.

"What a b-word," I say, peeling off my boots. Dear Lord, does that feel good. Tomorrow I'm burning these darn things.

He drapes his jacket on the chair. "Only to some," he says.

I sit on the bed with a sigh, and start massaging my poor feet. I'll have to do this for hours to make them even ten percent better. "Oww."

"Would you like me to—"

"Absolutely not," I snap. "I think you've touched me enough for one day, thank you." Three times he lightly ran his thumb across the mound of my breast. I'll admit, the first time I got the tingles, but by the third I wanted to bite the finger off.

"I have had centuries to perfect my technique."

"So you keep reminding me." I start pressing on the other foot. "I'm sure Marianna would love to let you practice your technique." This isn't working. I'm too tense. I know what I need, something I've been dying to do since I set foot in this crappy state. "Why don't you make our report to Kansas?"

"Very well."

I pull out my suitcase and root around until I find my pjs and swimsuit. I've never been one to pass up a pool, and luckily most of the hotels we stay at have one. I'll swim, shower, and then crash. I purposely packed my ugliest pajamas: a Wango Tango oversized shirt and white cotton pants. The swimsuit is a black one-piece that hides my tummy. While I do this, Oliver retrieves his cell phone and dials Kansas. I shut the door on the bathroom.

Yikes. I haven't seen a mirror since we left. Wish I'd continued that streak. My makeup is blotchy, the eyeliner and mascara cover half my face, and my hair either sticks up or remains plastered to my head in random places. I'm scarier than any vamp. I have to literally peel off my clothes. The boning on the corset has created some funky indentations on my flesh, almost like welts. I can't look anymore. I avert my eyes as I pull on the suit. After wrapping a towel around me as tight as a mummy, I step out.

Oliver sits on the bed talking into the phone. "They were very helpful. We had no problems getting access to the files." His eyes follow me to the door. "Hold on a moment, Wolfe. Trixie, where are you going?"

I open the door. "Swimming."

"Wait!" But I close the door. As quiet as I can, I creep down the hall to the stairs. Nobody accosts me as I walk down the stairs, through the house, to the backyard.

It's as beautiful out here as the rest of the house. The same lawn furniture from the upstairs porches sits around the nearly Olympic-sized pool and hot tub. Trees and grass surround the pool, providing extra privacy. Like any body-conscious woman, I step into the blissfully cool pool before tossing off the towel while simultaneously plunging in. I instantly feel better. There is nothing like cool water on a hot night. I sigh as I just float on my back. We're far enough outside of the main city that some stars shine through. A distant half moon accompanies them. I wonder if Will's staring up at the same moon this very minute. Probably not. He hates looking at the moon. It must be like gazing at the seconds ticking by before a bomb goes off. Or maybe he is. Maybe he couldn't sleep and instinctively knows what I'm doing right now, so even though we're a thousand miles apart, we're together. I wasn't lying before. I miss him something fierce. He—

The sound of a closing door pulls me out of the night sky. Oh, wonderful. A shirtless Oliver, sporting only his red boxers, glides toward me. I scoff and roll my eyes. He places his towel on the chair nearest to me.

"I thought I would join you," he says, slipping into the pool.

"Oh, you did, did you?" I say with another scoff.

"Yes, *wife*," he says. "I did."

Oh, crud. We're in public. I should be happy to see my half-naked husband. I muster a smile. "Great."

He swims toward me, pale arms gliding in the illuminated water, then past me with grin Number Two until he reaches the edge, where he stands. "We really must purchase you a bikini."

"When pigs fly, pookie."

"Come to me." He beckons with his finger.

I swim to the edge. Immediately he grabs my hand, pulling me into him. I fall into his chest, and at the same time he slams my back into the edge. He presses his entire body onto mine so I'm wedged between concrete and a hot vamp. "What are you doing?"

He answers by lowering his head to my neck. My whole body tenses. The last time his mouth was that close to my neck, I was literally scarred for life. But my skin is met by lips, not fangs. I try to jump away, but can't. He kisses my neck, twice, then a third time. The tension becomes tingles from toes to eyes. I can't feel the cold water as my skin warms. My body, hussy it is, betrays me by pressing closer to his. His hard chest pushes into my breasts. My eyes close so there's nothing but those warm lips, and his body on mine. I think my brain shuts off, especially the reason part. I feel nothing but … yum. My toes curl. A rush of warmth cascades down my body despite the cold water. I've imagined this, those lips on me. I run my fingers through his soft hair, tugging on it to bring his lips in tighter. His mouth moves to the other side with more soft kisses. It's been a long, *long* time since someone's kissed any part of me. Pol Pot could be kissing me this way, and I'd react. Right? That's what I thought.

Oliver whispers something, but I'm in fairyland, so all I can muster is "Huh?"

The kisses stop. "I said we are being watched," he whispers after another kiss.

I wrap my arms around his neck. "Oh."

He pulls his mouth away. "It is not safe for you to wander around the house alone at night," he whispers.

With his mouth nowhere near me, I can think again. Crud, there's someone watching us. "Is that why you followed me?" I whisper.

"Yes."

The door opens behind us. He leans in, kissing my nose. I giggle like a little girl. "You're so silly."

"I do hope I am not interrupting anything," Marianna says.

I release Oliver, spinning around. Marianna saunters toward us, fake smile on her face. Her eyes give her away. They're zeroed in on me. Oliver backs away. "We were just … swimming."

"Is that what they are calling it nowadays?" she asks, raising an eyebrow.

"Um, I think I've had enough swimming for one night," I say. I walk toward the steps and grab my towel. As quick as I can, I wrap it around my wet body—but not fast enough, judging from the amused smile. I'm going to owe Nana a nickel: what a bitch. "Baby, are you coming?"

Oliver glances at me, then Marianna, then back to me. "Of course, my darling."

Ha. Take that. I hand him his towel as he climbs out, unabashedly drinking his form in with my eyes. After he wraps the towel around his waist, I take his hand, entwining my fingers in his. I pull him toward the house, giving the unmistakably evil eye to Marianna as I pass. She scoffs.

"I will be up for the rest of the night Oliver, if you get bored," she calls as we step inside. Lord, give me the strength not to stake her.

When we get back to our room I slam the door, hopefully waking up the termites so they can eat this house down around her. "I'm taking a shower," I mutter.

"It is not wise to anger Marianna," Oliver says picking up his clothes from the floor. "She has killed people for less than a cruel look." He puts back on his pants, and when I walk back out from the bathroom, he's buttoning his shirt.

"What are you doing?" I ask.

"I have delivered you safely to the room, and now I shall give you privacy. I know you are exhausted."

"You're going to talk to *her*, aren't you?"

"We are on precarious enough footing as it is. Any further trouble, and I fear we will not be able to keep our heads above water. I will attempt to smooth things over with her."

"I don't believe this! After how she treated me?"

"It must be done. This has nothing to do with—"

"You are such an unbelievable jerk! If you gave a damn about me you wouldn't even *think* about her, let alone do what we both know you're going to do! You kiss me, then you go and kiss her? You don't care about me at all, do you? You pretend you do, and make me believe you do, and then you … and then you don't … ugh! What kind of husband are you?"

Oh, crud did I just say that? We look at each other, unsure what the other is thinking. Heck, I don't even know what *I'm* thinking. It was the kissing; it scrambled my brain. To his credit, a grin doesn't form. "I'm sorry," I finally say, looking away. "I'm tired. And this whole thing is just … I'm sorry. You can do whoever you want, I don't care. No judgments. Um, have fun." I shut the bathroom door before more stupid words burble out from either of us.

What the heck is wrong with me? It's not as if *Will* was the one about to spend the night with that prozzie. I mean, he and I have future children to raise together, but Oliver is just … Oliver. So why the hell are there tears in my eyes?

SEVEN

THE WITCHES OF WINCHESTER PLACE

When I got out of the shower, he was gone. No note, nothing. So I climbed into bed, shut off the lights, and fell asleep ten minutes later. Who knew anger and embarrassment were such good narcoleptics? I didn't wake whenever he came in, but he must have, because when I woke up at ten this morning, his casket was locked. He probably stayed up until dawn "reminiscing" with that slut. Well, we're supposed to be a typical married couple. Going to bed peeved at each other is a common characteristic.

Whatever. Not going to give it a second, okay *fifth*, thought. I've got murders to solve. No time for mixed emotions or flashbacks to those kisses. Those toe-curling kisses. I make appointments with Amanda and Petra, friends of victim number two, and Rochelle, girlfriend of victim number three. All of whom have conspicuous memory loss. Those dang vamps think they're so slick, but I'm black ice.

Soon after I am driving up I-30 in my poly-blend gray suit and sensible black shoes—which had to be forced on due to last night's escapades and still kill my poor footsies—on my way to Garland, Texas, to meet a witch. At least I'm traveling in style. I wanted the Aston Martin but thought it too conspicuous for a humble FBI agent. I settled on the black BMW, which I know isn't much better, but it was the cheapest one in the garage. Rosanne Cash's "Seven Year Ache" pounds on the stereo. I feel you, girl. Why is it when you're dying to forget something, the world, especially the radio gods, seem to be against you? Before this song was "I Can't Make You Love Me" by Bonnie Raitt. Just my luck. I pull off the freeway just as the Ache ends.

The GPS guides me though the suburb, which is close in ambiance to my own hometown. Strip malls, fast food restaurants, and movie theaters. It's strange that you'd find a witch in such a normal place. A woman who not only can spot demons, produce love spells, but can also control earth/air/fire/water lives here. Not all witches can control the elements, only a "high priestess" or as I like to think of them, "uber-witches."

The woman I'm meeting, Anna West, is an uber-witch according to George. He set up the meeting this morning and gave me the CliffsNotes on the woman. Not only is she a powerful witch, but she was a member of our motley crew about thirty years ago. George was in a tizzy about something, not his normal demeanor, so he wouldn't tell me more than that. I wonder if she knew Oliver. I'd love to find out if he was as pompous a jackass then as he is now.

With a few quick turns, I leave behind the strip malls and enter a much nicer residential area. Sprinklers run on the lawns of ranch-style houses. I turn another corner. As in most neighborhoods now, all the houses look the same: boxy, too close together, two stories, beige. McMansions, I think they're called. I call them boring. A few more GPS ordered turns put me in a more interesting neighborhood. Ranches here are mixed with two-stories made of stone, adobe, or wood. Some have trees, others just patches of lush grass. A woman in khakis and white tank walks her golden retriever down the sidewalk, ponytail swishing side to side. She eyes me as I pass. As do the sweating gardeners at their posts. I actually get a massive wave of déjà vu as I drive past a park where kids play on equipment. I suppose it's possible I played here as a child, but there were so many different parks in my childhood that they all blend together. Whatever. I turn on Winchester Place past more houses.

"You have reached your destination," the GPS says. She is so polite.

I stop the car in front of the white two-story, the only one with an honest-to-god white picket fence. Lining the fence on either side are holly bushes with those little red berries. The sprinklers douse the golf course–green grass and blooming oak tree. I feel as if I'm on the set of *Leave it to Beaver*, it's so wholesome. This is the place I dreamed of as a child. A trailer was a poor substitute.

After putting on my jacket over the white shell top, I step out of the car into once-again soupy air. I walk through the gate and up the gray stone path to the front door. I push the doorbell, and a few seconds later a distorted figure appears on the other side of the hazy glass in the door. It swings open.

Okay, when someone says "witch" what immediately comes to mind is scraggly gray hair, warts, and hook nose. An old hag, basically. Boy, did I get it wrong. Anna West, uber-witch, is hands down one of the most beautiful women I have ever seen. She's about five-seven, with a dancer's figure. Thin, but muscular with curves right where they should be shown off in her black and white striped shirt and blue jeans. If she was in the F.R.E.A.K.S. thirty years ago, then she's at least in her late forties, early fifties, but she looks better than any twenty year old. Her natural blonde hair is pulled back in a ponytail. Her Caribbean blue eyes are large and perfectly spaced above her small nose. Her thin lips must be naturally pink because I don't think she's wearing a stitch of makeup. It's like she's Grace Kelly redux.

"You must be Beatrice," she says with a gracious smile.

"Yeah."

"Well, come in. It's an inferno out there."

She steps aside to let me enter. Ha! She's not perfect. I knew there had to be some flaw somewhere. Her house reeks of burnt sugar, skunk, and rotten eggs.

"Pardon the smell," she says, closing the door. "Potions always have the most repugnant smell. That's why I rarely do them." The telephone rings. No doubt Revlon calling to offer her a multi-million dollar contract. "Will you please excuse me? I have to get that."

"No problem."

With another gracious smile, she walks into the room to my left, disappearing from sight. I'm never quite sure what to do in strange people's homes. I don't want to stand at the door staring at the steps. Snooping is always a good option.

I stroll into the room Anna walked into, which turns out to be the living room. The entire house must have hardwood floors. The large space is off-white with a grand piano taking up a corner. A fluffy gray couch sits across from the huge plasma TV with book-cases on either side. Magazines lie on the window seat against the bay windows with white gauzy curtains. The black leather recliner with cup holders seems out of place here. Her husband's, no doubt. My attention is drawn to the mantelpiece above the stone fireplace. It's the usual fare of old school photos of two boys, vacation shots, a wedding photo, and one of a handsome man with piercing blue eyes, pale skin, and thick dark red hair. It's not the same man in the wedding photo or of the boys grown up. His face is vaguely familiar, but I can't place it.

The wedding photo intrigues me too. A young Anna, beauty queen beautiful in her white dress, stands next to a tall, gangly man with muddy brown hair parted on the side, wearing silver glasses and a tux. The same man, but with more in the middle and thinning hair, appears in several other pictures. It's the background of the wedding photo that stops me. I pick it up. I know that globe off to the side and those books behind them. That's the library at the mansion in Kansas where I live. Huh.

The door in the corner flips open as Anna walks in, carrying two glasses of lemonade. It swings closed behind her. I put the picture back.

"I thought you might like something to drink," she says as she approaches. "The potion won't be ready for another few minutes."

I step from the fireplace, not looking at her. I always get caught. I should know better. I take the glass. "Thank you, I was just..."

"Snooping?" she asks with a smile.

"Yeah."

"It's okay. I do the same thing myself. Just can't help it." She picks up the wedding photo. "That's my husband, Nathan."

"You two were married at the mansion?" I ask, taking a sip of the drink. Sweet, just the way I like it.

"Yes. George gave me away."

"Really? Your husband was in the F.R.E.A.K.S. too?"

"Uh huh. He was there when I was recruited." She places the photo back in its place. "There is something about those life and death situations that breeds love. I wouldn't be surprised if the team lost more members to inter-marriage than death. At least I hope so." She walks over to the couch and sits, twisting her body so she's still facing me.

"Is that why you left?"

"I got pregnant with my oldest almost right away, and Nathan was homesick. Seemed like a good time to retire."

"How long were you two in?"

"I was only there about two years. Nathan, four. He was recruited after being struck by lightning four times in one week."

I join her on the couch. "What can he do?"

"Control electricity. He's made seven of our televisions explode."

"Wow."

"What about you? What's your 'gift'?" she asks doing the quotes with her fingers.

Always the show-off, I look at the coffee table in front of us and lift it with my mind. It hovers six inches off the ground before I lower it.

Anna seems impressed. "A psychokinetic. Don't run into many of you. George must have been thrilled to find you."

"I guess," I say, feeling my cheeks go warm. I don't take compliments well.

"How long have you been a F.R.E.A.K.?"

"Almost three months."

"What did you do before?"

"I taught fourth grade."

"You taught elementary school?" she asks, face slack in shock. "That's a new one. Have you gotten used to it yet?"

"Not really. My first impulse is always to run the other way."

"Sweetie, that's just you being smart."

I so want this woman to adopt me.

Anna folds her slim legs under her body and adjusts herself on the couch, inching closer to me. "It's worthwhile work, no question. I was reluctant to join at first. Saving people … wasn't really my bag. It got better, though."

"How old were you when you joined?"

"Nineteen."

"Wow. How did they find you?"

"Through a case," she says, eyes leaving my face for the first time. Sadness hits me—her sadness. Not only am I able to move things with my mind, but I can feel strong emotions from others. If someone's really nervous, angry, you name it, I know. I *feel* it. It sucks sometimes. Like now. This nice, beautiful woman should never feel this way.

"Which one?" I ask.

"Um …" she looks at me again, face neutral, "D.C./Richmond area. Early eighties. Vampires murdered some witches."

I spent two months reviewing cases when I was in training. That one sounds vaguely familiar. It takes a moment, but I remember. The Lord of D.C. was close to war with the same werewolves Will is with now. It was resolved before too many died, but while the team was there, three vamps slaughtered an entire family of witches in neighboring Goodnight, Virginia. One baddie got away, one's fate was unknown (parts of the file were blacked out), and the last was presumed dead in a fire set by his companion, a nineteen-year-old … witch. And now I know why the red-headed man from the photo looks familiar.

"I sort of remember the case. It must have been awful."

"It was."

"The man in the picture … he was a vampire?"

Another wave of sadness washes over me, so intense I almost gasp. "You ask a lot of questions," she says, voice hard.

"Sorry," I say quickly. "It's just … I'm living around vamps for the foreseeable future. Any tips you can give me …" *Nice save, Bea.*

Her face and body slack. "I'm sorry. It's … a sensitive subject."

"No, I'm sorry. I mean, you just met me, and here I am prying. It's none of my business."

All of a sudden I want to leave. Just get in my car and go back to Kansas. I'm so embarrassed. I can't do anything right. For the last two months the longest I've spoken to anyone outside the team was when I was interrogating them. I need some real, social human interaction and fast before I forget all the rules of polite society. I can't meet Anna's eyes, so I look down at my drink and sip. She's looking at me though, studying me.

"I was raised by a vampire," Anna says finally. I look up at her expressionless face. "Asher. The man in the photo. My father, my *real* father, was an abusive son-of-a-bitch. Asher killed him and took me away when I was nine."

"Oh, my God."

"Don't misunderstand me, I had a fantastic childhood. Traveled the world. Wanted for nothing. He loved me like a daughter … and then later as something else." Oh. Her blue eyes meet mine. "Then, as vampires do, he got bored. Brought someone else into our lives, and I stood it as long as I could. He was less than happy when I tried to break away. He didn't like it one bit," she says, voice hard. "Wonderful people died. And he hurt me in a way I never thought he could. If you read the case file you know what happened next."

I nod.

"Vamps are ruled by their emotions," Anna continues. "They're spoiled. Most believe the world is their playground and humans are nothing more than toys. They are capable of great atrocities … and the deepest love and kindness. Never forget they gave up a piece of their soul in becoming what they are. Never. So, my advice to you: keep your guard up. Show no weakness. Play to their vanity. And always keep your hand at the level."

I get a chill. "Thank you."

"You're welcome."

We each take a sip of our lemonade.

The sound of a buzzer floats in from the next room, startling me a bit. Anna sets down her drink on the coffee table and stands up. "Time to add the last ingredient. Pardon me." With a perfect hostess smile, she leaves the room.

Wow. As if I wasn't petrified by vamps before. Now I'm going to pack a bazooka when we go clubbing tonight. A vamp for a father, now that's a scary thought. I'm amazed she's as normal as she is. I can't even imagine what her childhood was like. How do you explain your dad's coffin to friends? There's a reason vamps are sterile. Although there are more than a few case files on vamps stealing children and keeping them as their own. They were human once and the need to procreate and nurture must survive death. It usually did not end well. What—

The front door opens in the other room. "Mom?" a man calls with that now familiar Texas accent.

I turn my head just as the man walks into the room. I recognize him from the photos on the mantle, though he's aged about ten years from the last one. He's about my age and cute. *Really* cute. Brown hair spiked up in front, strong jaw, straight nose, blue eyes with long lashes framing them, nice long lips, medium build. The all-American quarterback. And he was one; the pictures on the mantle show it. Today he's dressed in blue jeans and white dress shirt with the sleeves rolled up.

The man steps into the house but stops when he sees me. His left eyebrow cocks with the left side of his mouth. "Um, hello."

"Hi," I say back. "Your mom's in the other room finishing up my potion."

"Oh." The man eyes me up and down with curiosity. I wish I wasn't sitting, my thighs double in size. "It must be important. She doesn't make potions for just anyone."

"I'll be out in a minute, Joe," Anna calls from the kitchen.

"Okay," he shouts back.

"It's for a federal investigation," I say.

"Wait, *you're* a F.R.E.A.K.? A genuine F.R.E.A.K.?" he asks as if I've just told him Hulk Hogan was really a woman.

It's the team's name. The Federal Response to Extra-Sensory and Kindred Supernaturals, or F.R.E.A.K.S. I really hate the name, but what can you do? It's been around practically since the Declaration of Independence was signed.

"I'm a F.R.E.A.K.," I say.

"I don't believe it," Joe says, astonished.

119

"Gee, thanks." Why is it so hard to believe a five-foot-three woman can't take on bad guys? I'm getting a little sick of that misconception.

"No, it's not that," he backpedals. "I'm sure you can kick my ass. No, I just haven't met one of you in years."

"We are an elusive bunch."

"How long you been a member?"

"Couple months. I'm the rookie."

Joe walks around to the couch, sitting next to me. He drapes his arm around the back of the sofa. "You live at the mansion?"

"Yeah."

"I went there once. It's beautiful. Isolated, but beautiful."

"Helps with camaraderie, I guess."

"I'm living proof of that." He chuckles. "Man, I'm jealous. I've wanted to join since I was a kid, but they won't take me."

"Why not?"

"I think my parents said something."

I wonder what *my* mom would have said if I told her what I was doing for a living. Nana would chain me to the bed, which is why she thinks I'm working at a daycare center. Mom would probably want to join too. She'd be the first to grab a stake and flamethrower. That woman was as impulsive as they come.

"Your parents are very smart people," I say.

"I think *overprotective* is a better word."

"Nothing wrong with that. And they're justified in this case."

"Your parents aren't the same way? Your boyfriend, maybe?" Joe asks.

"Um," I laugh, "I have none of the above."

He clears his throat. "So, what are you working on?" Joe asks.

"Missing people. Vamps. The usual."

"Do you need any help? Backup?"

"I have a feeling your mother would put a curse on me if I got you involved."

"She wouldn't have to find out," he says with a smile that I'm sure melts the hearts of all the women at the local bar. Too bad for him I've had my immunity built up by a master grinner.

"We don't really need a witch, I don't think," I say. "But thank you."

"What about a summoner?"

"A summoner?"

Joe closes those nice eyes and furrows his brow as he concentrates. He holds out his hand. At first there's nothing, but in the blink of an eye a sunflower appears in his fingers. He opens his eyes, smiling again.

"Wow," I say, really impressed.

He hands me the flower. "For you."

"Thank you," I chuckle. "Where did it come from?"

"No idea," he laughs.

"So you're the one responsible for all my missing left socks?"

"You've caught me," he says, holding up his hands. "What about you? I showed you mine."

I do the levitating coffee table trick again. "Ta da!"

"And I thought I was something."

"Oh, you are," I say, chuckling nervously. I meet his eyes but look away when my cheeks flare up. I'm blushing again, darn it. Me and my libido. Perhaps it's all the use I'm making of my "power," because I swear I did not used to be this slutty-minded.

Mercifully, the kitchen door swings open and Anna walks in holding three glass vials filled with a murky brown liquid. "Here you go," she says. I stand up after picking up my purse and smoothing my pants. Joe does the same. "Just have them drink it and whatever magical memory loss they have should reverse in a minute."

"Can I mix it in with a drink?"

"You better. It tastes like death otherwise."

"Okay. Thank you," I say taking the bottles.

Anna eyes the sunflower in my other hand then at her son. A small smile crosses her face but quickly disappears. "If you need anything else, don't hesitate to call. *Anything.*"

"I will."

"Joe, why don't you walk Beatrice to her car?"

"With pleasure," he says with a smile.

They both escort me to the door. Joe steps out first. I turn back to Anna. "Thanks again for all your help and ... everything."

"Just remember what I told you."

"I will."

"See you later," she says with a wink before closing the door.

Okay, that was weird.

Joe and I walk down the path toward my car side by side. "So, how long are you in town for?" Joe asks.

"I don't know, until we catch the bad guys, I guess. Why?"

"I don't know. I just thought you might not know where the best places in town to eat are. You can't leave Texas without trying our barbecue." He opens the gate and steps aside like the perfect gentleman to let me pass.

"Are you asking me out on a date?"

"I do believe I am," he responds with a smile. He's got a great smile. Sweet yet mischievous. I'm a sucker for that kind of smile.

Okay, if this happened three months ago, I'd be laughing nervously and trying to keep my knees from turning to Jell-O. A hot, former football player with a killer smile even *talking* to me would get this response. I was kind of easy to overlook. But it's not three months ago. I have one too many crushes, and I sure as heck don't need another, even if he has an awesome mom. And I'm working. Vamps killing people = no time for flirting with cute summoners. Wait, who am I kidding?

I raise an eyebrow. "And why would you do that? Are you asking me out just so I'll put in a good word with George?" I ask.

"Would I do such a thing?"

"I don't know. Would you?"

"Maybe," he responds with a sly smile.

"Huh. Then *maybe* I'll have dinner with you," I say flirtatiously.

"Then *maybe* I should get your telephone number."

"Maybe it's 810-555-7823."

"Maybe?"

I shrug. "Maybe." I open the car door and sit down. He rests his arm on the top of the door looking down at me with that sly grin before shutting the door for me. Beaming, I shake my head and start the engine. He stands there, cell in hand, watching as I drive away.

Maybe we'll meet again. Heck, maybe I'll be stuck here for two weeks and will take him up on the offer. It's just dinner; I'm not marrying the guy or anything.

Well, maybe.

EIGHT

BETTER LEFT FORGOTTEN

EVEN AT MID-DAY, WHEN everyone should be in the prison that is work, the roads to Arlington are clogged. Must be an accident. Stop, go. Stop, go. I like to think of myself as a patient person. I used to stand by with a grin as one of my students carefully put together a collage of their ideal vacation, picture by picture. But my patience is not limitless. I lost the bulk of it outside Dallas city limits. Not even Carrie Underwood or Reba McEntire improved my mood.

Two hours for a drive that should have taken one. I had to call Rochelle, victim number three's girlfriend, to push back our appointment. She gave me attitude but relented. We're meeting at a Starbucks near her work. I picked a coffee shop so I can easily slip the potion in. I doubt these people would be willing to take it voluntarily, even if I am an FBI agent.

In between the laments about pickup trucks and whiskey, my mind wanders. First to today. I made it all the way to Dallas without screaming at the cars in front of me thanks to thoughts of Anna and Joe. Stupid stuff like, I hope I look as good as her when I'm her age. And how she managed to survive all those years in the vamp world. If her experience was anything like mine last night, she'd have to walk around in a suit of armor. And how did she and this Asher live? Did she make him blood pudding while he slept in his coffin down in the basement? I just can't wrap my head around the logistics.

Then my mind wandered to Joe and—strangely—high school. His type never gave me the time of day. I was invisible, purposely so guys like him and the girls he hung out with would leave me alone. It's strange that men like that take notice now. He's cute, though. And I'll bet he's fun. If I get starved for human companionship, I'll take him up on his offer. I can just imagine what Oliver would think. He'll either come up with some cockamamie excuse at the last moment to keep me away, or he'll stalk me on the date. Or he wouldn't care at all. He'd pretend to care but take the opportunity for some alone time with Marianna. This train of thought just winds me up tighter than a rattlesnake about to strike, so I push the jerk out of my head.

After I get out of Dallas—alive, to my great credit—my thoughts wander to Will as they usually do several times a day. I wonder what he's doing right now. Right at this moment. Is he running through the woods chasing deer? Is he sitting down to a big lunch of ham, bacon, and other meats with all the other werewolves? Is he wandering around moping that I'm not there with him? Okay, what I'm really thinking is: is he thinking about me? Is he flirting with the female werewolves there? Lord, there's that high school thing again, analyzing every look and every pause in the conversation. And I do.

April's spent hours listening and theorizing about a man she's never met. I'm so pathetic. Once, during a particularly boring meeting, I found myself drawing hearts with our initials in my notebook. Irie almost caught me, but I scribbled them out in time.

Fudge, I am getting sick of this. Why don't I just ask him out? Oh, right. The same dozen reasons as the last time I considered this option. Such as, I'm not sure he likes me back. Sometimes I think yes, like when we're sitting in the library and I see him glancing at me over his newspaper. Or when we're in the field and he tries to give me the least dangerous task. I've reamed him a new one for that last one, but inside I light up that he puts my safety above everyone else's, I can't help it. But then there are other times when he refuses to go places with me alone. Like when I invited him to the roller rink in town, and he just grunted. Grunted! He's grumpy around me too. If I challenge his strategy in the field, he won't look at me all day. The mixed signals are doing my head in. And we live and work together, so if I try and he rejects me, it'll be awkward city.

He's also still in love with his dead wife. I think he blames himself for not protecting her during the werewolf attack that killed her and turned him. He was some hotshot detective in D.C. and couldn't save her. He never talks about her, but I've seen a picture. She was the anti-me. Tall, rail thin, olive skin, dark brown hair. And sometimes he plays with his finger as if the ring is still there, no doubt thinking about her. I can barely compete against live women, let alone the pristine memory of a dead one.

And then there's Oliver. He's definitely down on the list of the reasons I chicken out, but he's still on there. I admit I'm attracted to him. Mega attracted, as last night proves. But heck, any woman with eyes would be. And yes, I've entertained the thought of getting to know him in the biblical sense more times than I care to admit. But I'm not that kind of woman. I've only slept with two men. One I thought I was in love with; the other I'd been seeing for two months, and it seemed like the thing to do. For almost two years. Not his fault. We really didn't have that much chemistry, and there *was* my issue, which also contributes to the Will problem.

I can't have an orgasm. I mean, I can *have* one, I'm physically able, but I can't when there's another person there. I might kill him. The few times I've … double clicked the mouse—and I've done it more in the last two months than in the previous two years—my bed levitates or furniture breaks. I could easily give my partner a brain aneurysm. Poor Steven thought there was something wrong with his technique, which was very vanilla but somewhat enjoyable. I even came close a few times, but I have the feeling that having sex with Will or Oliver would be like rich chocolate and leave me covered in their brain matter. That sounded grosser than I meant it to.

Okay, for the sake of boredom and traffic, let's say I did try it with Oliver and there were no problems, then what? Once or twice and he'd get bored with me, and then there'd be awkwardness. And any and all chance with Will would fly out the window. They don't get along. Oliver blatantly flirts with me, like, more than usual when Will's around. And then Will's grump factor raises seventeen points. But I like things with Oliver the way they are. Despite him annoying me to no end, he's been there when I needed him. We have good conversations. He likes going to movies with me. I trust him. He's a good friend. So I'll never sleep with him.

My GPS tells me for the fifteenth time to turn right. Did I really think she was polite? She's bossier than a spoiled six year old. I complete the turn right after the dirty SUV I've been behind for twenty miles makes it first. I've returned to strip mall land again with a TJ Maxx and Taco Bell on every corner. I drive another mile behind the SUV when the GPS tells me I've reached my destination on the right. The Starbucks is nestled between a nail salon and a boutique that only sells turquoise outfits with fringe. Yuck.

Taking my now-empty McDonald's bag, which I procured just outside Garland, and tossing it in the trash, I walk into the coffee house. Wasn't I just in this place two days ago? They're all the same with small tables, dark wood booths, strange murals on the walls, and a line out the door. I'd like to get in line but instead snag the last booth in the back. The middle-aged man next to me smiles but returns to typing away on his laptop.

I'm about ten minutes early, so I pull out my cell phone and dial my best friend April's number. If I don't call at least once a week, she threatens to jump on the first flight. I don't know how much longer I can put off having her or Nana visit. They want to see my "apartment" and meet my co-workers who I keep gushing about, especially Will and Oliver. I've changed a few details for them, of course. I don't live in a mansion, but a one-bedroom apartment in Wichita. George is my boss, CEO of a nationwide security company. Oliver, Will, and the rest of us fly around the country setting up daycare centers at each company branch. So yeah, I've pretty much lied through my teeth. Hopefully something good came out of Brian's visit, like I can put them off for a year or so. The line rings.

"Reynaldo's Salon," Lynn, the receptionist at April's work answers.

"Hi, Lynnie, it's Bea," I say.

"Hi! How are you?"

"Surviving," I say with a smile.

"Aren't we all? I'll get April for you. She just finished a perm." I hear the phone get set on the desk, then a few seconds later the clattering of someone picking it up.

"Hey, girl," April says.

I can picture her now, standing at the counter, one hip out as it always is. She's gorgeous with light brown skin, full bee-stung lips, almond-shaped eyes the color of dark chocolate, curves in the right places, and thick black hair. I always felt like the Elephant Man next to her. Even after three kids, she has a better figure than me. I'd hate her, except she's always accepted me. She was the first one outside of my family I told about the psychokinesis, not that I had a choice. I spent the night once and levitated her stuffed panda by accident. She thought it was the coolest thing. We've been closer than sisters ever since.

"Hey, you got time to talk?"

"For you, I'd keep Madonna waiting. How are you? Where are you? I tried you at home last night. Hot date I hope."

"I wish. I'm stuck in Dallas working for the next few days."

"Dallas? Never been," she says.

"Lucky you. It's crowded and a thousand degrees outside."

"You know you should just quit and move back. I miss you."

"Aw. I miss you too!"

"Well, are the hot twosome there sweating with you at least?" April asks with a snigger.

"Only Oliver. Will's still on vacation."

"So you're all alone with tall, dark, and flirtatious? Is he laying on the charm?"

"I'm almost drowning in it," I say.

"Tempted?"

"Only to attack him with my curling iron."

April chuckles. So does the laptop man. How rude. Sure, everyone listens to others conversations, but we pretend not to. It's called manners.

"I am so not flying to Dallas to bail your butt out of jail," April says.

"I can handle him without violence."

"I have no doubt."

"And guess what else? A cute boy asked me out today," I say in a sing-song voice.

"Another one?"

"I know, right?"

"Did you change your perfume or something? Well, what's bachelor number three like?"

"Do you remember Troy O'Donnell, the football player I tutored in English? He's a lot like him, only cuter and with a cute little Southern accent," I say.

"Did you say yes?"

"I said maybe. I'm only in town for a few days, and there are … other people to consider."

"Look, until either of the cuties throws you to the ground, sticks his tongue down your throat, and makes you scream in ecstasy, you're fair game."

"How very graphic, April."

"What? You know it's true. If the guy calls, say yes. Promise me you'll say yes. Promise!"

I cross my fingers but say, "I promise."

A woman walks into the shop who I have no doubt is Rochelle, Antoine Baker's girl on the side. Barely out of her teens, low rider jeans, tight black tank with red bra showing, black hair in cornrows. She even walks with attitude, hips moving more than a normal woman's should. Just by looking at her I can tell she'd have no qualms about taking up with a married man. This will not be a fun interview.

"April, my appointment just arrived. I'll call you later. Bye." I flip my phone closed and stand up as the girl looks around. "Rochelle?"

Rochelle looks me up and down, not impressed judging from the sneer. "You the FBI?" she asks with a thick Texas accent.

"I'm Special Agent Beatrice Alexander," I say flashing my badge.

"Uh huh," she says, taking off her bag and sitting across from me.

Laptop man has finished gathering the things he started collecting the second he saw my badge and walks away, glancing nervously at me. The badge has that effect on some people.

"I'm sorry I was late. Traffic was a nightmare," I say as I sit down.

"Whatever," the girl says, glaring at me.

"Can I make it up to you? Buy you a drink?"

"Mocha frap with extra whip."

"Exactly what I'm having," I say standing up, this time taking my purse with me. I get in line, occasionally glancing back at Rochelle, who is busy texting. She seems unfazed meeting with the FBI. Most people are either scared or excited; she's texting.

Lord, I wish Will was here. Okay, I have to stop thinking that. It just makes things worse. But I do wish he was here. I've never done an interview alone before. He was always there to get me back on track. Usually the bad cop to my good one. In theory this should be relatively easy once the potion takes effect, but still. This student is nowhere near as good as her master.

I order the drinks and wait with the other impatient people, feeling like an addict in line at the methadone clinic. Almost ten bucks for two drinks. I bet heroin is cheaper. When I get our cups, making sure nobody is watching, I dump the vial into Rochelle's drink, swishing it around. Hopefully the coffee will mask the taste. She's still texting when I sit down.

"I—" I say, but she holds up a finger to stop me and continues texting. How charming.

She keeps typing away on the phone for about five seconds, then sets it down. Without a word, she grabs the coffee, taking a sip. My body tenses for a millisecond, ready for lots of double talk about the taste, but she takes another.

"Is it good?" I ask, sipping mine.

"Not enough chocolate," she says with a sneer.

"Sorry."

"Whatever. So you wanted to see me? I don't know why. I told the cops everything I know about twenty times."

"Occasionally, with time,"—and a magic potion—"people remember more. Little details. Just walk me through the night. What time did Antoine pick you up?"

"He didn't," she says after another sip. "My roommate Tamika drove me. 'Toine met us about an hour later after his shift."

"What time was that?"

"I don't know. Around ten?"

"And the woman Antoine was flirting with, was she there before you got there?"

Rochelle takes another sip. "I told the cops I didn't know nothing about her."

"Just close your eyes and picture the bar that night. Please."

She closes her eyes, but not before rolling them. "Okay." She's silent for a second. "The woman was there before us. She was in the back booth with a group. I'd never seen them before."

I fish around my bag for the composite sketches. Rochelle opens her eyes as I lay the pictures out. "Do you recognize any of these people?"

She studies the pictures. "Yeah, I recognize them. Especially that bitch." She flicks the paper. "She zeroed in on 'Toine the second he walked in the door."

"What can you tell me about the others in the group? How many were there?"

"Um, seven I guess."

"Did you have any contact with them?"

"No, just the ho," she says, sipping her drink.

I do the same. "What can you tell me about them?"

"Not much," she says with attitude. "There wasn't a brother in the bunch, I know that. There was this Asian chick and dude. They were making out pretty hard the whole time."

"How many men?"

"Four. Asian dude, the two pasty white dudes, and the hulk. That guy was like six-four, Terminator muscles, looked Hispanic. Long black hair, eagle tattoo on his left shoulder. He looked pissed off all night."

I jot all this down in my notepad. "And the other woman?"

"I don't know. Young, like still in her teens even. Short, thin, long blonde hair, short skirt. She spent the whole time dancing by the jukebox."

"Did you catch any of their names?" I ask, still writing.

"The ho said her name was Serena, like Serena Williams. I didn't hear the other names." She sips the drink again. "You're good at this."

"What do you mean?" I ask as I put the pen down.

"I've been asked these questions like fifteen times. I never remembered all this stuff before."

"I'm very good at my job," I say with a smile. "Okay, so you and Antoine were at the bar drinking when this Serena came up to you. What happened after that?"

Rochelle sucks on her drink. "She asked if she could buy him a drink, totally ignoring me. 'Toine smiles, bitch smiles, I politely tell her to step off. She ignores me! Then she just starts talking about how she and her friends are just in from Santa Fe, how they rented a house in Venus and are throwing a party that night—"

"Wait, did you say Venus?" I ask, still writing.

"Yeah, you know, the town, like, twenty miles from here? Anyway, I tapped her on the shoulder and the bitch twirls around and looks me in the eye. She ... I don't know. It was weird. She told me to go home, forget all about her and her friends. But I don't think her lips moved. Tamika came out of the bathroom, and we left. That bitch must have slipped me something, I don't know."

"Sounds like she did. Now, can you remember anything else about them?"

She shakes her head. "No. Sorry."

"And you're sure she said Venus?"

"I am now. Do you really think she killed 'Toine?"

"It's looking more and more like it," I say as sensitively as is possible.

"That sucks. I mean, we weren't in love or anything, but he was decent to me. Great in bed too." She takes a deep breath and sighs. "Are we done here?"

I pull out my business card and pass it to her. "If you remember anything else, no matter how unimportant you think it is, call me."

She slips the card into her bag. "Sure." With that, she puts on her sunglasses and walks out of the shop. I'm sure deep down, buried under ten feet of bricks and dirt and cheap-girl armor, she's crying inside.

———

The heat practically knocks me down when I step outside. I'm at the car in fifteen seconds, but the sweat still drips down my breasts. The air starts when I turn on the engine. A little better. I punch in the address in my GPS to the YMCA in Grapevine, where the file said Amanda and Petra, the second victim's friends, volunteer over the summer. Seatbelt on and I'm off.

When I safely reach the freeway, I pull out my cell phone and call Kansas. George picks up on the fifth ring. "Dr. George Black," he says gruffly.

"Um, it's Beatrice."

"Oh. Hello," he says, tone not changing.

"Are you okay? You sound stressed."

He sighs on the other end. I've never heard him do that before. Did the mansion burn down or something? "I've just been dealing with a particularly stubborn problem. It has used up all my good will and patience today."

"Anything I can do?"

"I'm afraid not. And it's nothing for you to worry about. I've taken care of it as best I can. So, I assume you have an update?"

I walk him through the whole day, starting with Anna then detailing my interview with Rochelle. He "uh huh" and "okays" through the whole thing. "Whatever you paid her, you should double it," I say. "Stuff worked like a charm—which I guess it kind of was."

"Anna always was a master potion maker."

"I really liked her."

"And I am more than sure the feeling was mutual."

Before I can stop myself I say, "And her son really wants to join the team. He's a summoner."

"Yes. Joe. I am well aware of his desire. But I promised his parents I'd never recruit him."

"Too bad. He seemed nice." And so very cute. I switch lanes so I'm now behind three semis instead of four. "Okay, so I'm thinking we check for all the homes rented in Venus within the last year.

Preferably ones with basements. I'll try to narrow it down when I talk to the girls."

"Very good. Call me when you're done."

"Roger, roger."

"And keep yourself safe. For both our sakes," he mutters.

I raise an eyebrow. "Um, oookay. Call you later." I flip the phone closed. That was weird. Something or someone must have done a real number on him. Bureaucrats are worse than vamps, I swear. At least vamps only take your blood, not your spirit.

The roads are halfway decent all the way to Grapevine. It's a nice little community with the standard strip malls and fast food places common everywhere now. The YMCA sits next to a lush green park where not even the heat keeps mothers and children from getting out of the house so they don't drive each other nuts. I pull into the small parking lot and shut off the car.

The building is a beige one-story with YMCA in black and red letters on the side. When I walk in, my heels clap on the beige and black linoleum, almost drowning out the sound of children's laughter and basketballs in the back of the building. A harried mother dressed in a business suit practically drags a crying four-year-old past me. Someone was naughty. I turn into the main office where a teenager waits behind the counter.

"Hi. I'm here to meet Petra Bowers and Amanda Chenoweth," I say with a smile.

"You're the FBI lady?" the girl asks.

"That's me."

The girl reaches for the microphone. "Petra, Amanda, please report to the front office," she says over the intercom. "Have a seat."

The girls arrive a minute later. I recognize them from the police photos. Both are a little on the tall side, almost six feet with lanky limbs they already seem to be growing into. Petra's blue eyes look me up and down, defiance already in them. She's the prettier of the two with Angelina Jolie lips and dark brown hair off-setting her pale skin. Amanda is more girl-next-door pretty, with dirty blonde hair hanging loose around her round face. She's very tan with a few freckles, but they look good on her. They're both in matching shorts and golf shirts.

They look a lot better now than in the police photos. There must have been about two dozen photos of each girl in the file; every bruise—and there were quite a few—had to be documented. The heaviest bruising was around the neck and thigh area. Petra had some nasty ones on her arm too, with the imprint of fingers clearly visible. They wanted to do a rape kit, but both girls, along with their parents, refused. Not that they would have found any evidence. Male vamps can't produce sperm. That organ system shut down like their digestive system. How they get an erection, or how a female vamp lubricates, is through sheer willpower and concentration. I so wish I didn't know any of this.

"Hello, I'm Special Agent Beatrice Alexander," I say. Neither smile. I am seriously not looking forward to this. "Is there some-place private we can talk?"

"The staff break room's open," Petra says.

"Okay, lead the way."

I follow the girls just across the hall to a small, cramped room. Counters with microwaves and coffee machines line the back wall. Two huge vending machines sit next to the counter filled with healthy items like bottled water, Gatorade, and granola bars. Probably so the kids can't sneak in and OD on sugar. As a former elementary school teacher, I can appreciate that. A small round table fills the rest of the room with four plastic chairs around it. The girls sit next to each other with their backs to the vending machines. I shut the door behind myself and walk to the machines. Neither watches me.

"I'm going to get something to drink. Do either of you want something? My treat," I say, plucking out my wallet.

"No, thanks," both say.

Crud. I feed the machine three dollars and get three waters anyway. If my limited experience at bars tells me anything, it's that if there is something free in front of you, say pretzels, given enough time, you'll sample them. That's usually how I spent my time in bars anyway.

"Do you girls like working here?" I ask as I pull out the last two vials of potion, making sure to put my body between their line of sight and my hands.

"It's okay," Amanda says.

I twist off two caps and dump the brown liquid into the small hole. The moment it hits the water, the brown turns clear, as promised. Anna's a genius, a full bloody genius. I dump the other vial into a second water. "Did Kate work here too?"

"No. She worked at Forever 21," Petra answers.

Holding the three bottles, I walk to the table, setting the two open bottles in front of the girls. They look at me curiously. "We're going to be doing a lot of talking," I say with a smile. "I don't want the flow interrupted."

Petra eyes the open bottle. "Can I see your ID?"

Once again I pull out my credentials. Petra takes it from my hand, studying the badge then the lanyard inside. She looks from the picture to my face. Satisfied I'm for real, she hands it back.

"Sorry," she says as if she's really not.

"It's actually a very smart thing to do," I say as I sit across from them. I open my water and take a sip. "Thank you for meeting with me today. I know it's the last thing either of you wants."

"It's okay," Amanda says in a small voice.

"Before we get started, Amanda you're seventeen and still a minor. You might want to have a parent or lawyer here. Do you want that?"

"No, it's okay."

"If you change your mind at any point, just tell me. It's not a problem." I take another sip of water. "So, tell me, how did you two meet Kate?" I take another sip.

"Middle school," Petra answers. "We all had math together."

I sip again. *Come on, girls. Join the fun.* Amanda lightly touches her bottle. "And you've been friends ever since?" I ask, taking yet another sip.

Amanda picks up the water and swigs. Psychology, got to love it.

"Yeah," Petra answers. "We were in track together too."

"What's her event?" I ask with another sip.

"High hurdles," Amanda answers. "She took second at the district meet last year."

Petra picks up her water and gulps. "Can we just get on with this? And you don't have to pretend she's still alive either, it's just patronizing."

I do a double take. "I don't mean to be. I know how difficult this must be for you."

"Really? *Your* best friend was probably raped and murdered while you were right there, and you can't remember a thing about it?"

Dear lord, the sadness coming from this girl is palpable. It makes my stomach lurch. Her face masks it with a deep hatred, but I can tell. This time I do need water to settle my stomach.

"Petra," Amanda says in a small voice, "she's just trying to help."

"We've seen a dozen police officers, psychiatrists, hypnotherapists, all for nothing. I am sick of this! We don't remember, okay? We can't help you! Why can't you just leave us alone?"

"Because," I say, not holding my temper. Her energy is just so strong it's contagious. "Because it is my job to find and capture the bastards who did this to you and your friends. To stop them from killing more people. So they don't hurt others the way they hurt you. To do the only thing we can do for your friend now: get justice. And I know it's tough and aggravating, but I need your help to do my job. So drink your damn water. Drink it!" Without protest both pick up their water bottles, and take a good chug. I should try the scary tactic more often. Petra's energy levels out a little. "So, tell me what you remember about that night. Start at the beginning. Who picked who up?"

"Kate did," Amanda says. "Around seven. We went to the new Zac Efron movie."

"What time did you get out?"

"Around ten?" Amanda asks Petra, who nods.

"Then where did you go?"

"My house," Petra says taking another drink of water. "We wanted to change clothes for the club."

"The Glass Cactus? How did you get in?"

The girls exchange looks. "Fake IDs," Petra answers.

"Do you go there often?"

"About once a month," Amanda says, drinking more water.

"We remember getting there, and that's it," Petra says. "We woke up the next morning at my house without Kate."

From my purse I pull out my pad and pen. "Okay, this is going to sound corny, but I want you to close your eyes and imagine walking into that club with Kate. You're all wearing the same clothes you were that night. It *is* that night, okay? The sounds, the smells, the horrible music they were playing. Picture it all."

"The therapists made us do this," Petra says. "It got us nowhere."

"Humor me."

The girls close their eyes. "Okay," Amanda says.

"Is Kate there with you?" I ask. "Do you see the club?"

"Yes," Petra says.

"What did you do first?"

"Went to the fire bar," Petra says.

"Did anyone hassle you?"

"No. Some asshole with a popped collar hit on me," Petra says. "We didn't stick around too long."

"Where'd you go next?"

"Found a couch," Amanda says. "Kate and I went to dance, and Petra kept our seats. We danced with a couple of guys."

"That's when she came," Petra says, faced scrunched up like she's just bitten into a lemon.

"Who?"

Petra opens her eyes. "Julie. She said her name was Julie. I remember her."

"Describe her."

"Our age. About five feet tall, I guess. Blonde hair with bangs. Pale. She had really blue eyes."

"Had you seen her before?" I ask.

"No. Never. She just came out of nowhere and sat down. Started talking about the lack of cute guys. I thought it was weird. She didn't talk like she was from here. I think she was Canadian. She kept saying 'aboot.'"

I jot that down. "Then what happened?"

"Kate and I came back," Amanda says. "We all talked to her. She asked about school. Said she and her family just came to town, and she was about to start a new one. Stupid stuff."

"And when you were talking, did you notice anyone watching you?"

"No," Petra says. "But then Julie waved to some guy and he came over. Said he was her brother."

"Describe him."

"Pale like her. Brown gelled-up hair, tall, early twenties. Said his name was Rick."

"Kate liked him," Amanda interjects. "She started flirting right away."

"Did they mention anything about themselves?"

"No," Petra says. "It was weird. Whenever we asked a question, they'd just ask us one back."

"So you talked awhile. Then what happened?"

"Julie asked if we wanted to go back to their place," Amanda says. "She said their parents were out of town."

"I said no," Petra says. "No way. But Rick looked into Kate's eyes and whispered something. Then she just stands up and says,

'I'm going with Rick.' I'm like, what the hell? She's our ride, and it's so not like her to do something like that."

"That's all she said," Amanda adds. "She followed him out like a puppy. It was so weird."

"What did you guys do?" I ask.

"We weren't going to leave her with those people," Petra says. "We followed them to the parking lot, and when we got there, Kate was already in the back of the car. I grabbed her arm, but it was like she wasn't in there. Like her brain wasn't there."

"Describe the car."

"New dark blue Mercedes," Amanda says. "Tan leather interior. Dirty, like covered in dust. And there was a black bat hanging from the rearview mirror. I didn't see the license plate number."

I jot all that down. "Then what happened?"

Petra says, "I started yelling at Kate, but Rick grabbed my arm real hard." Petra lightly touches her arm where the bruises in the picture were. "He looked me in the eyes and … I don't know. It was like … have you ever woken up in the middle of the night and you can't move? You can breathe and stuff, and you're telling your legs to move, but they just won't? That's how I felt for the rest of the night."

Amanda picks up the story. "He told you to get into the car and not to move or say anything until he said so," she says in a low voice. She wipes a tear away. "And you did. I couldn't believe it. That's when Julie did the same thing to me. It was like I had no control over my body, but it moved and got into the car too. The whole ride I didn't move, didn't say anything. None of us did. But I was, like, calm. Like this was no big deal."

"I didn't feel that way," Petra says. "I tried everything I could to move. I just couldn't. I was screaming and screaming, but no words would come out. They must have drugged us."

"On the car ride, did they say anything?" I ask.

"They kept fighting over the radio station," Amanda says. "It got so bad he slapped her. She just sat back and pouted."

"Then he apologized and kissed her," Petra adds with a scoff. "Like full on make out. But he kept looking back at us in the mirror."

"Anything else?"

"They talked about us like we weren't even there," Petra says. "Saying how 'Yummy' we look. How their friend Geraldo's gonna love me. I felt like throwing up, but I couldn't."

"I just felt numb," Amanda says.

"Where did they take you? Describe it."

"A farmhouse in the middle of nowhere," Amanda says. "I don't know what town. We took back roads without signs."

"It was two stories with a dirt road driveway," Petra says. "Beige, I think. Real run down, paint chipping a lot. The windows were blacked out, like, literally black, as if someone sprayed them with black paint. No porch. And the front was all dirt, but the backyard had dying corn."

"Were there any other cars?"

"Yeah. A huge black van with the windows blacked out."

"Wasn't there an old pickup all rusted out?" Amanda asks.

"I think so. It was the same color as the house."

"Then what happened?" I ask delicately. Both girls are visibly tense, backs ramrod straight and hands clenched. Amanda stares down at the table as if she can see through it. Petra's jaw is set in concrete.

"When we pulled up, a woman came outside," Amanda says. "She was black. Pretty. Rick and Julie got out, and the woman asked what took them so long. They didn't answer. They just opened our doors, and pulled us out. Julie said, 'Nice, right?' The woman huffed and walked back inside. Rick said, 'Get inside' and Petra started walking. He took Kate's hand and led her inside. Julie told me to move and I did."

"What did the inside look like?" I ask, writing it all down.

"I guess drab," Amanda answers. "Like my grandparents' house. Needlepoints on the walls. Old furniture from like the seventies. They did have a flatscreen TV."

"There was a girl passed out on the couch," Petra adds. "She had bruises all over her arms and neck. Like covered. I thought she was dead, but then Rick nudged her with his foot and she woke up. He told her he didn't need her that night. I think she went into the kitchen, I don't know. They told us to sit down. Then this really big guy with the same bruises came up out of the basement."

"He had a gun on his hip," Amanda says, all color draining from her face. "I saw that …" She shakes her head. "Do we have to keep going? I don't feel so good."

"We can take a break if you want," I say.

"Mandy, why don't you go outside and get some air," Petra suggests.

"Okay," Amanda says, standing up on shaky legs. The poor girl all but runs out of the room.

"You don't need a break?" I ask Petra.

"No. Let's keep going. I want this over with."

"Okay." I have the feeling that if this girl lost every one of her limbs she'd still try to run a marathon. Wish I was like that. "What happened next?"

"The guy with the gun told them he oiled their coffins and put more black paint on the windows. Rick thanked him, and the guy went upstairs. Then he asked the black woman where everyone was. She told him JR got hungry and was upstairs with Miles. I think she said Liang and Ken were out, and Gerry was in the basement."

"So there were ten people living there total?"

"I guess." She drinks more water, and then starts ripping off the label in small strips. "Rick sat down next to Kate and put his arm around her. That pissed Julie off. She fell into the chair next to us, just glaring at them. Then Rick yelled down to Gerry. He said, 'Dinner's here' just before he started kissing Kate. She didn't respond, but he kept doing it."

"Then what?"

"Then the black woman took Amanda's hand, and yanked her off the couch like a rag doll. She said, 'I'm fucking starving,' and they went upstairs. I have no idea what happened up there. And don't ask Amanda about it," Petra says harshly. "She can't handle it. I'll tell you whatever you want, just leave her alone or this interview's over."

I know I shouldn't, but I say, "Okay." I'm such a softie. "What happened next?"

"This guy came up from the basement. He was ... huge. Tall, like three hundred pounds of muscle. Um, he had an eagle tattoo if that helps. Hispanic, long black hair. He scared the fuck out of me.

147

"Julie was playing with her hair, just glaring at Rick and Kate and she said, 'Gerry, dinner's here' and pointed to me. The fucker smiled. That's when I saw them."

"What?"

A lone tear falls, but she wipes it away like an annoying bug. "His fangs. They were fucking vampires, weren't they?"

I could lie, but she deserves the truth. "Yes. They were."

"Right," she whispers, shaking her head. "Not just crazy assholes who like to pretend either, right? Fucking *Dracula* vampires?"

"I'm afraid so," I say quietly.

"Jesus Christ. I was afraid of them as a kid, you know? I grew out of it. Stupid, huh?"

"No."

"And you put something in this water, right? That's why I remember all this crap now," she says, relief replaced with anger. "The FBI drugs people now?"

"It was the only way to get you to remember. I'm sorry."

"So you stop vampires? That's your job?"

"Today it is." I meet her cold, hard eyes. "I'm sorry I tricked you. I really am. But I meant what I said; I need your help to stop them. To get Kate a little justice. But you need to keep going. I need as much information on these creeps as possible if I'm going to find them. You can be peeved off later. What happened next?"

After a few more seconds of icy glare, the scared teenager looks away. "Rick and Kate stood up. He said, 'I'll leave you two alone. Try not to make a mess.' Then 'Come on, Julie. We'll share.' She scowled but followed them upstairs. Gerry sat down and he...you know. You saw the bruises."

"Did he …" I can't finish.

"Rape me? No. I think he was going to, but then there was shouting upstairs. He went to check it out."

"Could you hear what they were saying?"

"'You stupid bitch! What the hell is your problem?' Stuff like that. Then another man said, 'Not again.' The two in the kitchen ran up to see what was going on. I still couldn't move. There was more shouting, then a loud thwack and someone fell down the stairs. It was Julie. She was naked. Covered in blood. Like, even her hair was red. Rick ran down the stairs after her, pissed off to hell. He was naked and bloody too. He got Julie up, punching her in the face. Gerry and some other guy I hadn't seen before had to pull him off. The black chick stood at the top of the stairs grinning."

"What did the third man look like?"

"Lanky, but with muscles. Black hair. He was in pajama bottoms. Anyway, they got Rick away from Julie. The thin guy kind of took control. Asked Rick what happened. He said Julie went bat shit and ripped her throat out." Petra tries to retain her composure but can't anymore. She starts crying softly. "He must have meant Kate. Fuck." She gasps a few times and shakes her hands to calm down. "I can get through this," she says to herself. "I have to get through this." The hands wiggle for a few more seconds in time with the gasps. She stops crying. "Shit."

"We can take a break if—"

"No. I need to finish." Petra takes in as much air as she can, slowly letting it out. "The thin guy got pissed off too. He said, 'What the hell is wrong with you guys? We have rules! Why can't you fuckers follow them? Do you have any idea how pissed he's going to be when he finds out?' The black woman said, 'Then don't tell him.'"

"Back up. Who is this 'he?'" I ask.

"No idea. The thin guy gave the woman a look, but she just smiled. Then he started barking orders. Told some guy named Bill to get the body, told Gerry to start digging a hole. Ordered Rick and Julie to get cleaned up. Then the bitch on the stairs asked, 'What about the other two?' Thin guy said, 'Drive them back to their car. Wipe their memories.' I guess he meant us. Then she said, 'We should just kill them.' Thin guy got pissed. Said, 'One dead teenager he'll accept, three and he'll have no choice but to kill us. Just do it.' And he went back upstairs. So did the black woman.

"A minute later, she led Amanda down the stairs. I was so happy to see her, I couldn't breathe. She looked so pale. But then the guy with the gun followed them. He had ... um, a bloody sheet wrapped around a body. Her hand was ... hanging out. I knew it was Kate from her blueberry nail polish. Rick drove us back to the club, told us to forget the whole night, and go home. He drove away. He'd given me the key to Kate's car, and I drove us home," she finishes quickly. "That's it. That's all. I'm done."

Petra stands up, not looking at me. "That's all I'm going to say." Then her eyes look into mine, chilling me to the bone. "Don't contact me again until you've killed them all." With that, she walks out of the room.

I close my notebook. I need a shower.

NINE

PURGATORY

I'M IN A CRAPPY mood the entire drive back to the hotel. It's not just the God-awful traffic that doubles my driving time, or the annoying commercials on the radio for mattresses, it's the fact that I feel like a degenerate who tortures teenage girls. Petra was so angry, so hurt, so scared. She's never going to forgive herself for what happened. I know she'll be going over that night again and again, looking for all the things she could have done to stop it. *What if they stayed home? What if she had screamed in the parking lot?* I do the same thing all the time.

The GPS finally tells me to turn off the interstate, and five minutes later I've completed the turn. Crud, I can't put it off any longer. I have to call the mansion and give my report. I should have called sooner, but I wanted to be by myself as long as possible. My mouth just seems to bring misery today. I dial, and someone picks up on the fourth ring.

"Hello?" Irie says on the other side.

"Hey, it's Bea," I say.

"Well, if it isn't our little troublemaker," she says. "How's Texas?"

"It's hot. Why am I a troublemaker all of a sudden?"

"Can't say. Sworn to secrecy. It might 'jeopardize the case,'" she says in a mock masculine voice. "You'll find out soon enough. Oh, here's George!"

"Irie, wait, what—"

"Hello, Beatrice," George says. "I was just about to call. How did it go?"

"Lousy. Why am I a troublemaker?"

"You aren't. You're doing excellent work," he says quickly. "Now, we did a search of the town you mentioned, and there have been no listed properties in over a year."

"I guess it's possible they found a house they liked and just … took it over. I have a description of it." I read off the characteristics of the house and cars. "I think we should instruct the local law enforcement officers to drive around looking for it. I can go out tomorrow and do the same. And they should be aware there are ten, not seven people in the house. I don't know the ratio of vamps to people, but at least one has a gun." I read off the descriptions too.

"Fantastic, just fantastic," George says. "I'll get them this information right away. What's your next step?"

"A bath. I'm wiped," I say with a yawn.

"You relax a bit. You've earned it."

"Thank you. I'll call if we develop anything else."

"I'll do the same. Truly impressive work, Beatrice. Stay safe."

"You bet. Bye." I flip the phone shut. Why is it whenever I call home, I end up more on edge than before? And why am I a troublemaker? Did they see the pay-per-view charges from last month?

Come on, there's only one video rental store within thirty miles, and they won't let me get a DVD subscription. I get bored. Know what? I don't even care right now. I'll deal with it later. Now, I just want to soak away the last few hours.

I make it back to the Dauphine without screaming at another driver, as I did half a dozen times in the previous hour or so. Locking the car behind me, I walk up to the house. The place is quiet until I'm halfway up the stairs.

"Good evening, Mrs. Smythe," Cole, the concierge, says behind me. "How was your day at the spa?"

Using my last reserve of energy, I turn around and smile down at him. "Wonderful, thank you."

"Excellent. Can I get you anything? Would you like to place your dinner order now?"

"I'll do it later." This time I run up the stairs before I have to field obnoxious questions. I make it to my room, locking up behind myself.

Oliver's still ... whatever, so I rip off my clothes, grab some sweats from the suitcase, and start the bath. I don't even wait for it to fill up. The lukewarm water envelops me, and the guilt and tension ease out of my pores. I breathe in and out until the knot in my left shoulder disappears. About an hour in here and the right one should clear too.

Whenever a thought, good or bad, starts creeping in, I push it away. I even ignore the knock on the bedroom door outside. Oliver's dinner. Some distant part of my brain tells me he'll be waking up soon, but I shut it up. I need oblivion for a while. Which is what I get when I fall asleep a minute later.

———

Knocking. Who's knocking?

I jerk awake on the third knock, sending water splashing everywhere. Crud, I fell asleep. I hate when that happens. I'll drown one of these nights, and then Will or Oliver will see my naked body floating in a tub of cold, no-longer-sudsy water. And water makes everything look bigger—I don't need any help in that department. The water's still warm, so I can't have been asleep that long. There's another knock.

"Did you fall asleep in there, my dear?" Oliver asks on the other side. "Do you need me to come in and check on you?"

I'm totally awake now. "Try it, and I'll pull your brain out through your nose."

"How vivid."

"Give me five minutes."

I shave, scrub, and rinse in record time. After toweling, I toss on my pink sweats that hide everything. Oliver's lounging on the bed watching the news in his boxers, sipping dinner out of a wine glass. Would it kill him to put on a shirt? I'm too exhausted to feel the usual lust, let alone engage in a verbal sparring match, so I keep my mouth shut. "Your cellular phone was ringing," he says not taking his eyes off the screen.

"Thanks," I say, toweling my hair. I get the phone out of my purse, and dial voicemail. "Hey, Beatrice. This is Joe West." A huge smile crosses my face. "I guess this is *definitely* your telephone number. No *maybe* about it. I hope you're still in town. I'll bet you are, and I'll bet you're hungry right about now. I know this great steakhouse, very *Urban Cowboy*. I thought we could have dinner there. Together. Tonight. So if you're not ankle deep in vamps, call me. 555-3427. Maybe I'll see you later. Bye." I flip the phone closed with a silly smile on my face.

"Was that the canary you killed on the phone?" Oliver asks.

"Close. A new friend."

"Of the male persuasion?"

"Well, if you must know, Mr. Nosey, that was Joe West. Anna West's son. She said hello by the way."

"You saw Anna West today?"

"Yeah. She gave me some potions. I made a lot of progress today. You should read my notes." I dig the notebook out, tossing it at him.

His eyes don't leave me even when he catches it. "And her son asked you out on a date?"

"Yeah. Do you know him?"

"We met briefly when he was a child."

"He's not one anymore," I say with another smile.

"Will you accept his invitation?"

"I don't know. I guess it depends on what we're doing tonight. Do I have time for dinner with a cute Texan?" I know I'm just blatantly antagonizing him now. Give me a break. After the day I've had, I can use a bit of fun. "It'd give you time for some more 'catching up' with Marianna."

Grin Number Two, partial fang. "Are you trying to make me jealous as punishment for last night, my dear?"

"You wish. It has nothing to do with you. I happen to like Joe. So can I call him back and make plans?"

"Far be it for me to create a roadblock between you and true love, but alas, we have plans tonight. Killers to catch and all that."

155

"Well, if you'd read my notes there, you'd see that I may have located them, or at least where they're staying."

He opens the notebook, scanning it while I peruse the room service menu. I know the chances of me actually going on a date with Joe are slim to none, and I'm hungry. I settle on a hamburger with red potatoes.

"Did you contact George with this information yet?" Oliver asks.

"Of course. They're looking into it right now. What do you think we should do? We could drive there and take a look around ourselves."

"At night? Two against ten? I think not. Let the local law enforcement do the busy work. No, we proceed as planned." Oliver jumps off the bed, then retrieves his suitcase. "We go to the club the Costarellos were last seen at, which means I'm afraid Mr. West will have to wait."

"How did I know you were going to say that?"

Oliver pulls out a pair of black jeans and black silk shirt. I love that outfit on him. The jeans leave nothing to the imagination, and the shirt brings out his eyes and almost red lips. He's doing this to torture me, I know it. He starts dressing right in front of me. I look away toward the menu again. "You should rest until it is time to depart. I do not want you to swoon on the dance floor."

"What will you do?"

He buttons the shirt up, darn it. "Marianna invited me to a reading at her bookstore. I believe I shall attend."

"Wait. You're allowed to go on a date and I'm not?"

"This is not a date."

"Right," I say in a huff. "I'm sorry, but aren't we supposed to be married? What kind of woman allows her husband to go out with another hot woman?"

"My dear, it is not a date. And people do not stand Marianna up."

"Beatrice Smythe's husband does," I say sweetly.

He looks at me, eyes wild with amusement. Grin Number One forms. "There will be consequences."

"That's nice."

"If you are adamant …" He starts unbuttoning his shirt, not taking his eyes off me.

"What are you doing?"

"Getting comfortable for a night in with my wife," he says with the final button.

"Cute." I stand up, rolling my eyes. "Put your clothes back on. We'll go to Venus, then the club. I don't want to spend another minute in this place."

"It will do no good."

"It can't hurt." I grab some slut clothes from my suitcase and go into the bathroom, slamming the door. Half an hour later, Beatrice and Oliver Smythe descend the staircase of the Dauphine dressed to kill. Oliver smolders in his black outfit and leather coat, hair slicked back into a ponytail. I've gone more sensible tonight with a knee-length black velvet skirt, matching hip-length jacket, knife bustier, two-inch Mary Janes, and spider-web black stockings. No fashion tips tonight.

I think we can make a clean getaway, as no nudists or incestuous vamps jump out while we're in the hallway—until we take that final step off the stairs.

"There you are," Marianna calls from the study. All my positive self-image feelings fade away as she walks toward us. Her long, supple limbs go for miles in tight black pants ending at ballet slippers. Underneath her satin jacket about ninety percent of her boobs hang out of her matching jeweled tank top. Even without a stitch of makeup, she's flawless. And boy is she not happy to see me. Her eyes give me the once over and her lips purse. "Oh, hello."

"I am sorry, Marianna," Oliver says. "I will not be able to escort you out tonight. Something has come up."

"What?" she asks sweet as pie, though her eyes narrow.

"My dear wife has managed to acquire a pair of Bruce Springsteen tickets and wishes us to attend. I am sorry but perhaps we can go another night. All three of us."

All pretense of niceness fades. "You disappoint me, Oliver."

"It was never my intention. Please do not be cross with me."

The sweet mask returns. Smiles ensue. "As if *anyone* could ever stay angry at you. Enjoy your night with your … wife." She all but chokes that last word out.

"We will," I say with a smile. I start walking again without a second glance. For once I welcome the blast-furnace air of the night. "How much trouble are we in now?" I ask as we walk toward the car.

"Do you remember Cleveland?"

"That bad, huh?"

"Worse."

———

We spend the next three hours driving aimlessly around Venus, Texas, and its neighboring towns. Well, I do the driving and Oliver does the looking. I can't see much past the dotted yellow line on the road, not that I think there's much to see. The few homes we've ventured toward haven't been that much to look at. Dirt, rundown farm homes, the occasional cow. Real exciting stuff. And Oliver hasn't exactly been Mr. Chatty Cathy. He's said the occasional, "Turn here," or "This is a good song." Finally, around nine o'clock, he demands I return him to civilization. I'm bored out of my skull, so I oblige.

We're half an hour outside Dallas when the twenty minutes of complete silence finally gets to me. "Me and my bright ideas," I mutter.

Oliver changes the radio station and Patsy Cline's "Walkin' After Midnight" begins. He doesn't say anything.

"Not going to agree with me?" I ask.

"No. I do not wish to anger you any further after a bad day."

"But you're thinking it." I pause. "Well, I'm sorry I ruined your date with Marianna."

"Now you are intentionally attempting to start a fight."

"I am not! But you have to admit it was a pretty lousy thing to do to your supposed wife. Going on a date with another woman."

"My dear, I know this may come as a shock, but as much as I love living in a basement in Kansas, constantly at war with a werewolf, I do sometimes miss the companionship of my own kind. Talking to them and—"

"Sleeping with them," I finish.

He looks at me, expressionless. "I did not bed her."

For some reason I feel like I've grown three pounds lighter. "You were gone all night. And you had plans tonight."

"We reminisced. We drank. We flirted. Not so much as a kiss was exchanged. She tried and I evaded."

"And why did you do that?" I ask nastily.

"I believe you know the reason." My head snaps to the right to see his expression. "It would ruin our cover." Oh. He looks out the window. "Just as you attending dinner with Joe West would."

I'm quiet for a moment, then sigh. "I wasn't really going to dinner with him."

"Why not? You are young. Unattached."

"It wouldn't work out. He lives here, I live in Kansas. Besides, I don't think I could handle a relationship right now. My life's difficult enough as it is, right?"

"I suppose. Though with all the agony and torment we deal with, there should be some joy to life, yes?"

"Not if it complicates things even more."

"But the complications make life interesting."

"Wow. Are we having a *real* conversation for once? People wouldn't recognize us."

"I could make another pass at you if we have stepped outside your comfort zone, if you wish."

"No, thank you," I chuckle. "I'm good. And I'm sorry I was such a jerk before. I'm just frustrated. If you had interviewed those girls today ... I don't know. I just want to find these guys and ... you know."

"I know. And we will find them, of that I am sure. We just have to let the local police do their jobs. There cannot be that many blue BMWs in this area. And tomorrow, if you feel you must, you may join them in their search. The best thing to do now is to continue asking questions. The motley crew you describe had to have been noticed. We will find them.

"And then you may chop their heads off."

———

Who knew there would be so many yuppies in Purgatory? I should have guessed though.

The dance club is split into four levels: Hell, Purgatory, Heaven, and Upper Heaven. We've cased all levels and decided that Hell has the scariest group. Purgatory with its peach, yellow, and blue lounging area clashed with my black velvet. Though, if I get bored, I can sit at the martini bar and watch boxing. Fun. That level was wall to wall twenty-somethings either wearing next to nothing or pastel polo shirts with popped collars. Pink on men is somehow disconcerting. No self-respecting vamp was found in Purgatory or the two heavens for that matter.

Oliver and I stood out in Heaven. It was all white. White chairs, white bars, white tables, white tile dance floor. Heck, even the waitresses were dressed as sexy angels, which is wrong any way you look at it. More popped collars and emaciated girls gyrating to horrible remixes of Madonna and Common. There were one or two vamps up there, younglings who can blend in, according to Oliver. We didn't, so we banished ourselves to Hell.

Hell is as uncomfortable as it should be, with concrete bar tops and dance floor. The seats my companion and I occupy are of the aluminum variety, and our drinks sit on a stainless-steel stool. The room is almost totally dark except for the orange and red swirls on the dance floor above, and the glow from the neon light under the bar. Hip hop (not my cup of tea) blasts from the DJ booth. Either they've turned down the music on this level, or I've gone deaf. Thank God either way.

Some vamp whose name I think is Colin chats with Oliver while I sit and watch the people and vamps dance. Judging from the lack of tans and seriously outdated clothes—Members Only jacket? Please—I'd put the vamp to human ratio at thirty to seventy and growing. Some dance, others attempt conversation with other vamps or their prey. I've delegated myself the task of keeping an eye out for the bad guys. Oliver has taken the role of talking to everyone but me. From the few words I've been able to hear, the conversations have nothing to do with the case, unless our cabal is on *Jersey Shore* or frequented Studio 54. I'll have to ask him about that last one. All in all, I was happier driving around. At least then I could hear myself think.

Oliver says something, and Colin laughs. This is the fifth vamp who has sat down in the last two hours, and each one has laughed. It's so unfair. I always get the boring job. I sigh and take a sip of my water. Ten bucks for a water, highway robbery. And now I have to pee. I tap Oliver on the shoulder and mouth "bathroom." He nods then returns to his conversation with his new best friend.

The bathroom is relatively empty, meaning I only have to wait in line for five minutes. After I'm done with Mother Nature's call, halfway back to my seat, I spot a young, petite blonde at the bar who wasn't there before. I can only see her in profile, but she matches the description. Right age, pale, talking to a girl about her same age. She's like half the girls in here, though a lot less tan. Instead of going back to the table, I cut across the dance floor. The girl vamp doesn't register my presence, she's too busy talking to a teenager in short shorts and pink halter. The girl vamp chuckles. She's dressed in a black and red bondage miniskirt with matching red sweater. Her dark blonde hair hangs down to her butt, with square bangs framing her elfin face. She reminds me of *Alice in Wonderland*, especially with a smattering of freckles across her button nose. Trying not to be obvious, I order a screwdriver. Over the music I can't hear what they're talking about. I sit and drink.

This continues for a few minutes where I glean nothing while being eyed by a few drunken frat boys. Okay, drastic measures. I "accidentally" sweep my arm, spilling screwdriver all over my quarry.

"What the fuck?" the possible Julie shouts, jumping off her stool.

"Oh, my God!" I say. She winces at that last word just as I hoped she would. Vamp. "I am so sorry!" The bartender hands me a towel, and I start dabbing her sweater. She looks at me with disgust, snatching the towel away. "Um, are you okay?"

"Fine," she spits back.

"Why don't we go to the bathroom and get you cleaned up. It might stain."

"Just leave me alone," she says. Okay, this is as far as my plan went. I have no idea what to say or do now.

Then, as if he can read my mind, Oliver saunters over, God bless him. The girl, sensing him, looks up. Her fear is immediate. I wonder how young she is.

"Is everything well here?" Oliver asks, touching the girl's arm lightly. Her body tenses.

"I spilled my drink on her," I say.

He smiles. "Your clumsiness will be the end of you someday, my darling."

"You two are together?" the girl asks.

"This is my consort, Beatrice." He takes this opportunity to slip his arm around my waist.

"I—I'm sorry, I didn't know."

Two men saunter up to us from the dance floor, and I force a poker face to hide my excitement. One is wiry but muscled in dark blue jeans with tight, dark green shirt. He has cheekbones that can cut rocks, full lips, and ink black hair. The other is tall and looks my age, with an average build, but with a gorgeous face and sandy brown gelled-up hair. It's them. No question. Oliver tightens his grip on my waist, no doubt afraid I'll attack them on sight. If I had my machete Bette, darn straight I would. For now, I'll play it cool.

"What's going on?" Rick asks.

"Nothing," the girl who I have no doubt in my mind is Julie says.

The two size us up. I smile nervously, but Oliver's face remains concrete. JR looks Oliver in the eyes but glances away a moment later.

"I spilled my drink on her," I say. I turn to Julie. "I really think we should wash that out before it stains."

Julie looks at me, then at her two companions. Geez, we're going to the bathroom, not Borneo. JR nods. Rick doesn't look away from Oliver. I pull away from him. "Be right back. Play nice."

I take Julie's cold hand, practically dragging her to the bathroom. We bypass the line, walking straight to the sinks. She waits as I grab some paper towels and wet them. I look down into the sink, then as I look up, she's pulling off her sweater. And she has no bra on. I see every rib through her translucent skin. Of course I can't take my eyes off her boobs. They're small like oranges with no areola and tiny nipples. Jesus Christ, she couldn't have been more than fourteen when she was turned. Sick.

"This is easier," she says, turning on the water and scrubbing the sweater. The women in line look at the naked girl, rolling their eyes. I just stand with my soggy paper towels.

"So, who are those two guys? I think I've seen them around before."

"That's JR and Rick. We live together."

"Where?"

"All over." She turns off the faucet and goes to the dryer.

"How long have you been in Dallas?" I shout over the dryer.

"About four months, I guess. JR knows some people here."

"Is he your boyfriend?"

The dryer stops. "Not really. We've had some threesomes together and stuff, but he mostly plays for the other team. Rick's the one who turned me."

"Oh, how long you two been together?"

She puts the shirt on. "Five years, I guess. What about you? Who's the old guy?"

"My husband."

"He's old. And powerful. I think he's more powerful than Lord Freddy even, but don't tell JR I said that. Your guy freaked me out when he came over."

"Don't worry about him. He's as harmless as a kitten."

"Cool. So how long you two in town for?"

"Not long. You know, I have seen you guys around though. Weren't you at the Church before?"

"Yeah, we go there a lot. Easy pickings."

"I thought so. Yeah, you were with that pretty African American woman."

"Serena? Yeah. She's a bitch. I don't know why JR keeps her around." She slips into her damp and clingy sweater and walks out of the bathroom as I follow. "So, where are you guys staying?"

"The Dauphine. What about you?"

"This stupid farmhouse in the middle of nowhere. I hate it."

"Is it near a town at least?"

"Venus. Which might as well be the planet. At least we go out every night, or I would have taken up sunbathing by now."

We both scan the dancing horde for our men, and Julie spots them in the back corner. They seem to have declared a truce as Oliver and JR seem deep in conversation. *Hey, hey, the gang's all here.* Two skinny Asians, a man and woman, sit at the edge of the couch making out hardcore, like rounding third base. Next to them is a bored Serena. The first thing I notice is that her lips take up a quarter of her face. Rick sits to her right watching the dance floor. Squished between Rick and JR is a vamp I presume to be Gerry. He takes up half the couch with all that muscle. The image of him writhing on Petra, his hands roving everywhere, flashes into my mind. I push it away. I have to play nice, at least until we get an address.

Rick holds out his hand to Julie, pulling her onto his lap. He plants one on her and she responds in kind. I feel like calling *To Catch a Predator.*

"I missed you," Rick says.

"Vomit," Serena says.

I second that.

Oliver takes my wrist, guiding me onto his lap as well. He slides his arm around my waist again, resting his hand on my thigh as if it was nothing. If I feel anything move, it will be the last time it does. "Beloved, may I introduce you to JR, Gerry, and Serena, and the affectionate two are Liang and Ken."

"Nice to meet you."

"We were discussing the nightlife. JR recommends the Lizard Lounge, is it? Quite a lot of willing donors."

"You don't feed from her?" Gerry asks.

"Only on special occasions," he says, patting my thigh.

"Do you share?" Serena asks.

"Never," Oliver answers in a predatory tone.

She actually shrinks back in fear. "Just asking."

Change of topic time. Don't want to alienate them just yet. "It must be nice for all of you to be together. Oliver was just complaining how he's dying for the company of other vamps. Julie said you all live in a farmhouse together?"

"Yeah," JR says.

"Oh, my G!" a girl cries near us. "It's you!"

The whole group, except the necking duo, gaze over at the oncoming girls. Oh, crud. The Stick and the Twig—Denise and Pam—scurry toward us. Serena rolls her eyes and JR plasters an obviously fake smile on his face. The others just watch.

"Pamela. Denise," Oliver says.

"We thought we might find you here," Denise says with a huge grin. "And you found your friend."

"Yes, we found a friend," I say quickly. "A lot of them actually."

"Hello, girls," JR says. "Not at Freddy's tonight?"

"We actually just came from there," Denise answers.

"Shut up!" Pam says. Her eyes jut to JR. "We have a phone call to make."

"What? Why?" Denise asks. Pam scowls at her. "Oh! Right! Will you excuse us? Urgent business and all. We'll stop by later." The girls totter back the way they came.

"What fucking morons," Serena says with a sigh. "And now I'm officially bored. You guys enjoy your time with Ma and Pa Kettle over here. I'm going hunting."

"No trouble tonight!" JR calls.

She rolls her eyes and scoffs. "I'll see you back at the farm," she shouts before sauntering off into the sea of bodies on the dance floor.

"I think we will follow suit," Oliver says, standing up, which means I do as well. "I have the strongest desire to dance with my beautiful wife. Will you all please excuse us?"

Oliver takes my hand, leading me to the center of the floor. We're surrounded by the sweaty and horny. The song is fast and pumping but Oliver grabs my waist, pulling me into his body. "What?" I ask.

"Act as if you are in love with me. We are being watched. Head on my shoulder."

I rest my head in the crook of his neck, inhaling the Gucci cologne. I wrap my arms around his torso, as he does with mine. Some of the other dancers give us sideways glances. Whatever. This is how people should dance.

"I can't believe we found them," I say as quietly as I can, which still means I'm kind of shouting.

"The fates are on our side."

"Do we have a plan? I only have the knives and Mace."

"No, striking now would be ill advised."

"So we do what?"

"I suppose we must try to finagle an invitation to their domicile. That way we may return on the morrow with the proper reinforcements."

JR, who has been watching us, looks away toward his pocket. He pulls out his cell phone and listens for a few seconds, talking a moment later. He glances at us, then speaks again.

"Can you hear what he's saying?" I ask.

"No."

A huge smile crosses JR's face as he looks away. He continues talking, not looking at us again until he hangs up. He turns to Rick, saying something, and Rick smiles. Gerry leans in to listen to the conversation. I'm getting paranoid. "So what's the plan? Schmooze now, search and destroy tomorrow? What if they … you know … want to do things with us when we get there?"

Oliver doesn't answer. The song ends, and he releases me. Guess it's time to rejoin the serial killers on the couch. Oh, goody. When we do, JR scoots over to let us sit.

"You two look really cute together," Julie says.

"Thank you. It's all him," I say.

"I hate to cut this love-fest short," JR says, "but I'm bored of this place."

"Me too," Rick says.

JR stands. "Just got a line on a party. We're going. You guys want to come?"

"Do you, my darling?" Oliver asks.

"I was ready to leave an hour ago."

"Fantastic."

We all stand and walk upstairs out of the club. Oliver keeps his hand on my shoulder the whole time. Rick leads Julie, and the make-out duo keep their hands in each other's pockets. When we reach the parking lot, JR stops.

"Gerry, give Rick the keys to the van. You're going with me," JR says.

Gerry tosses Rick the keys, which he catches one handed. "Thanks buddy. Good luck," Rick says. He, the twosome, and the pixie all stroll away.

JR smiles at us. "So, you'll follow us. Where are you parked?"

"Two lanes over," I say.

"Us too. Easy to follow, then." JR leads with the rest of us behind. A few college kids pass us, giggling or talking. It isn't until Gerry glances back at me that the creeps roll down my spine. When JR does it as well, a red light flashes in my head. Exhaustion has dulled the logical section of my brain.

"What kind of car do you guys have?" I ask.

"Why?" Gerry asks gruffly.

"So we can follow you?"

"Red Firebird," JR answers.

Oliver's grip on my shoulder tightens. He read my notes. They don't have a Firebird, and there isn't one in the row. My stomach drops to my knees. We're in trouble. Crud. We keep walking as I glance to Oliver. Him and his darn poker face. When we reach our car, the vamps stop. How the hell do they know it's our car?

"Who phoned earlier?" Oliver asks.

"I think you know," JR replies.

What the Sam Hill is going on?

"I shall not go willingly," Oliver says.

"We didn't think you would."

I don't see the men move until they've reached their destinations. When vamps move, they move fast. Faster than the human eye can process. I feel the breeze of quick movement, but nothing else until the moment someone grabs me. I don't have the time to react. A preternaturally strong arm wraps around my chest. Oliver reappears a few feet from me, punching JR square in the jaw, the crack curling my toes. JR smashes to the ground. That's when it registers that someone's got me in a bear hug. If that's not bad enough, cold steel presses against my temple. Oh, I really hope that's not what I think it is.

"Hey!" Gerry says.

Before Oliver manages another punch, his eyes dart toward us. His cocked fist lowers. He snarls, pointed fangs in full view. "Lower your weapon."

Crud. It is what I think it is. I've only had a gun pointed at me once, and it wasn't a pleasant experience. It ended with me having to kill the man holding the gun. I had nightmares for weeks.

"Leave him alone, or I splatter your skank's brains out," Gerry says.

Oh, no. I think the last few days' events have finally caught up with me. My body begins shaking like a jonesing heroin addict, and my knees just about give out. A whimper escapes my mouth, then another.

Oliver's gaze moves from the giant holding me to my eyes. He looks damn near as scared as I am. "Trixie, darling, calm yourself. Everything will be alright, my dear. I promise. I *swear* it to you. I will never let them harm you. We can handle this. *You* can handle this. Do you trust me?"

I nod. And darned if the shaking doesn't stop. How does he do that to me?

"Release her, and I shall do whatever you ask."

JR picks himself up, setting his jaw back with another crack. I whimper. I hate that sound. "She comes with us," JR says. "To keep you in line. Gerry, if either of them makes a move, pull the trigger. Get her in the car. You, passenger side." Gerry all but carries me to the back of the car. I don't struggle. "Oh, and asshole..." JR says when Oliver reaches the front. JR cocks his fist back, and with all this strength, punches Oliver in the face, then again in the stomach. Oliver drops to his knees.

"Stop it!" I cry, trying to wiggle out of Gerry's arms.

Ignoring me, JR picks Oliver off the ground by the hair, tossing him into the car, and slams the door. Still holding the gun on me, Gerry climbs into the car, dragging me behind him. "Close the door," he orders.

I slam it with all my might, scowling at the meathead. JR takes the wheel in front of me. "Keys, please." Gerry roots around in my purse until he finds the keys. Sadly, he also finds the silver/garlic Mace and cell phone, both of which he tosses out the window.

My already pounding heart joins a percussion band when the car starts. I've been taught since I was a girl to never get into a car with a stranger, that it's better to be shot in the parking lot. And I know what these guys are capable of. I glance at Oliver, who has turned halfway toward me. A trickle of blood runs down his chin where JR split his lip. He wipes it off, and spits out more blood on the dashboard of the Dauphine's car. If we survive the night, Marianna's going to be even more peeved at us.

"Oliver?" I ask with a trembling voice.

He looks back at me. "Beatrice…" He never uses my real name. Oh, God. We're going to die. "I need you to listen to me. Everything will be all right. You trust me, correct?"

"I do."

"Just do not do *anything* until I instruct you to, do you understand me? *Do nothing.* Tell me you understand what I am saying."

Gerry and JR look at Oliver, then at me. "I understand," I say.

"Then I *promise* you, you will survive this night.

Yeah, we have no weapons, no backup, two pissed off vampires, one with a gun, and now I'm not allowed to use my power? The odds are not in our favor.

And why didn't he say *we*?

TEN

LORDS AND MASTERS

THE GOOD NEWS IS they don't kill us on the ride over. The bad news is that our destination turns out to be an S&M club called Poison Ivy. Clothing optional.

After JR parks in the lot behind the red brick building, we all get out. JR keeps hold of Oliver's shirt, dragging him toward the front of the building. Gerry pushes me after them with the barrel of the gun. The bouncer, a stocky Mediterranean vamp in a tailored designer suit, takes one look at JR and opens the door, revealing a neon green sign with POISON IVY against a black backdrop. To the right are stairs, which I stumble down in near darkness. Luckily Gerry grabs me by the coat, all but choking me to hold me up. The stairs end at a black curtain with the club name written on it. That's when a topless vamp in black vinyl chaps and nipple clamps saunters out.

Okay. That's all I can take. Breaking point. I lose it. A hysterical laugh escapes before I can stop myself. "Holy crap!"

All four vamps look at me, and only Oliver isn't offended. I don't care. I just can't stop laughing! My entire body rocks with each guffaw as tears well up in my eyes. Chaps rolls her eyes then walks up the stairs. Her bare butt wiggles with each step, and I laugh even harder. "I'm sorry! I'm so sorry!"

"Shut up." JR pushes Oliver through the curtain, and Gerry does the same to me.

That's when I really bust my gut. Horrible techno-pop only popular in Germany plays on the stereos above, but that's not what gets me. A porn where a woman in a black vinyl bustier bull whips a man with a nice heinie fills the entire far wall, but that's not it, either. No, it's the people—or, judging by their beautiful bodies (which I can see every inch of), I suppose they're vamps. Males, females, and everything in between move around wearing little or no clothing. A few are in robes, but the motif seems to be leather or vinyl, with a few harnesses thrown in for good measure. Some even have piercings in places no metal should go. I've never seen so many penises, breasts, or chains on display. On a leather couch three feet from me, a man and woman go at it like rabbits.

I've never seen anyone have sex in front of me before. Heck, I've barely done the deed myself. I'm not exactly queen of the sex bombs so this is … I just can't help myself. I have a gun pointed at me, I'm probably being led to my death, and what do I do? I stop walking, point, and laugh. I laugh until I'm about to pee my pants.

The sex must not be very good because the couple stops mid-thrust to gaze over at me in disgust. "The hell is your problem?" the woman asks with an Irish accent.

"I—I—" is all I can say through the cackles.

Someone grabs my upper arm, spinning me around. Oliver glares at me, mouth set in a straight line. He jerks me away from the peeved couple, this time taking the lead to the back of the club. My laughter dissipates a little from the hard squeezing. JR and Gerry flank us with the gun still trained on me. We move past three men chained to a wall with handcuffs wearing nothing but zipped leather hoods, as their partners either whip or cut them, or in one instance does something that is still illegal in some states. Oliver grips my arm to make sure I don't start freaking out again. I try not to look at their unmentionables, but how can I not? They're at full salute, red, and uncircumcised, which I find odd. I've seen only a handful, in either pornos or on my two boyfriends, but they've all been circumcised. Then it hits me. I'll bet Oliver isn't circumcised. My eyes fly to his crotch as if I can tell through his pants. He doesn't notice, thank goodness.

We move away from the main showroom and stop at the bar, where a bald man in leather pants and spiked dog collar cleans blood off some glasses. My laughs finally subside.

"What's she on?" the bartender asks JR.

"My wife has never been to such a club before," Oliver answers.

"And you're still with her?" the bartender asks.

"She is an apt pupil," Oliver responds.

I so don't care if they're talking about me. Visions of uncircumcised penises dance in my head.

"We're here to see Freddy," JR says impatiently.

The bartender picks up the phone under the bar. "Sir? JR's here with some people. Should I send them up?" He waits for a reply. "Yes, sir." He hangs up the phone. "You know the way."

JR walks past the bar to a black door marked PRIVATE. Beyond that door is another stairwell with low lighting and dark green carpet. Oliver keeps hold of my hand, and Gerry doesn't move the gun from my back as we walk up single file. Any giddiness or lustful thoughts fade from my mind. Oliver keeps that damn poker face, so I have no idea how afraid I should be. Have we been found out? I've only seen a few movies where undercover officers are discovered, and they're either shot or given concrete shoes. Neither option holds much appeal.

We reach the top, which dead ends at a door. JR knocks.

"Enter," a man commands with a British accent.

JR walks through the door, and we follow like good hostages. Okay, wasn't expecting this. If downstairs is Sodom and Gomorrah, upstairs is where tweedy scholars study Sodom and Gomorrah. It's downright tasteful, with polished wood walls spruced up with pretty paintings of ballet dancers, cityscapes, and the odd portrait of a staunch man or woman from the Romantic era. An entire wall consists of books, hard and soft cover, from pop art to murder mysteries. A fellow reader; maybe he won't be so bad. The hardwood floor is covered with a deep red Persian rug that matches the color of the huge desk. On the wall behind the desk are two long swords crisscrossing each other, both with elaborate gold handles.

Two men wait in the study. The closer one lounges on the burgundy leather sofa, arm draped around the back. He wears a severe business suit, dark blue pinstripe with crisp white shirt, matching vest, and light blue tie. *Très* CEO. His wavy blonde hair is moussed to perfection. His aqua blue eyes appraise us, but no emotion surfaces.

The other man sits behind the desk and from across the room it seems as if the desk overwhelms him. He's attractive, but not beautiful like his friend, with wild curly brown hair, dull brown eyes, a pinched nose too small for his face, and a pointed chin. Still, the features suit him, especially with the goatee. He folds his arms on the desk, fingers lacing. A huge grin brightens his face.

"So glad you could join us, old friend," Deskman says with that clipped British accent.

Friend? Great. "You just make friends everywhere, don't you?" I mutter to Oliver, but he ignores me.

"As if we were given a choice," Oliver says.

Gerry finally removes the gun, stepping toward JR as Deskman rises. I judge him to be a little taller than me, but not by much. "Not happy to see me, I gather."

"Having your pathetic henchmen abduct me and my companion at gunpoint does not endear you to me, *friend*."

"I did not think you would have come otherwise," Deskman, who must be Lord Freddy, says as he steps out from behind the desk. He wears a conservative white shirt and gray pants. He looks like an architect, not the owner of an S&M club.

"I would not," Oliver replies.

Another grin from Freddy. "JR, Geraldo, please escort Oliver's pretty companion downstairs and make sure she has a good time."

Oliver steps in front of JR before he even moves. "You touch her and I will rip off your testicles and eat them in front of you, do you understand me?" He says it with such utter conviction, *I* get chills.

JR's eyes narrow, but Freddy smiles. "Now, now. Play nice, Ollie," Freddy says.

"She remains with me, that is all I will request from you," Oliver says. "Please."

Freddy is taken aback. He chuckles. "My, my Ollie. Has a heart actually grown where there was once an empty hole?"

"No. I may simply require her to save my life at some point during this meeting. She cannot do that from downstairs."

Freddy and the other suit eye me. "You believe *she* can protect you from us?" Freddy asks.

"I know she can."

Freddy mulls this over, pursing his lips and folding his arms across his chest. "I am intrigued. She may remain. Gentlemen, please wait downstairs, but do keep yourselves handy. Apparently I may need assistance in subduing this angelic creature later on."

JR and Gerry nod, then walk past us, glaring at Oliver, who glares right back. When the door shuts, Freddy hops up on the desk like it's his daddy's, legs dangling. "The years have been kind to you, Ollie. Modernity suits you."

"You as well." He looks to the suit on the couch. "Hello, Anton."

"Oliver," Anton says with an Eastern European accent.

"Oh, I am sorry. How rude of me," Freddy says mock serious. "I have neglected my hosting duties. I have not introduced everyone to your fetching bodyguard. Where are my manners?" He jumps off the desk and walks over to me. "I am Lord Frederick St. Clair and this is Anton Evanesky, my right hand. And you are?"

"Beatrice."

"Beatrice. Beautiful name. Were your parents fans of the Bard or Dante?"

"Neither. I was named after my mother's favorite soap opera character."

Freddy grins again. "Honest. I do hope that virtue has infected my old friend here." He eyes Oliver up and down, a little mirth leaving his eyes. "You did not think you could come to *my* town without me finding out about it, did you?"

"We did not intend to remain long," Oliver says. "How *did* you find out, Freddy? Was it your two child whores?"

"If you are referring to Denise and Pamela, they merely put the thought into my head and called when they found you. No, I am afraid Marianna alerted me to your presence this evening. She knows of our ... history."

That b-word!

"Of course," Oliver says.

"What are you doing here, Ollie?" Freddy asks.

"Just passing through. We were leaving tomorrow, but if you desire, we can depart tonight. You need not do something you shall regret."

I can feel it in the air as the worm turns. Freddy's smile drops as he stalks toward Oliver, fangs bared. "You do not tell me what to do, Oliver. You are in *my* territory, governed by *my* laws. Off the top of my head I can list five you have broken, all punishable by death."

"I have broken no true laws, and you know it. You cannot scare me with idle threats, and you are no fool. Killing me without cause would endear you to no one. Remember who my friends are."

"*Friends* is not a word I would use to describe them," Freddy says. "They would not lift a pen to save you."

"Do you wish to take that chance?"

"More than you know."

"Frederick," Anton says reproachfully.

Freddy's head whips toward Anton. "I have heard all your objections, Anton. They grow tiresome."

"He is correct about the possible political ramifications. We do not need to give anyone more ammunition, especially after the trouble your friends downstairs have caused in the last few months." Anton glares at me, mouth set straight.

"That is another topic I grow tired of. We will not speak of it in mixed company."

"Have you become lax in your duties, Frederick?" Oliver asks with grin Number Three.

"Stop it," I mutter. That is one of the things I don't get about men, their need to antagonize. That and the whole Chuck Norris thing.

All three men look my way. Oliver glares, Anton sizes me up, and Freddy smiles. "Ollie, you should listen to your consort. I believe she is as wise as she is beautiful." His smile widens. "Would you care to sit down? You appear exhausted, fair Beatrice."

I glance at Oliver, who nods. I don't know what the heck is going on, what their deal is, but me sitting down won't hurt things. I rest next to Anton, who remains emotionless. Freddy takes the seat next to me, so I'm wedged between two hostile vamps. Freddy leans back in the couch, draping his arm over the back on my side. He crosses his legs and smiles again. Oliver takes a few steps, but Freddy's head whips back. "I did not give you permission to move, Oliver," Freddy hisses.

"It's okay," I say to Oliver.

"I just wish to get to know your pretty friend, Ollie. Surely you do not object to a civilized conversation?"

I shoot him the "keep your mouth shut" look. A scowl forms, but he says nothing.

"Good," Freddy continues. "How did the angel meet the devil?"

"In a library. He hit on me, and I told him to buzz off. He didn't, and he just grew on me. End of story."

"Yes. He is quite like flesh-eating bacteria, is he not? He causes nothing but pain, and leaves his victim scarred for life. And how long has he been growing on you?"

"Two months," Oliver answers. "And we are not lovers to answer your next question."

"And yet you have been introducing her as your wife, Ollie. She is registered as your consort. And it looks as if you have marked her otherwise pristine neck. That is your handiwork, no?"

Oliver's scowl deepens. I've never seen him look at someone with such utter contempt, not even Will. Freddy revels in it, his face lighting up. Whatever happened between these two was bad, and I have the distinct feeling I'm about to be drawn into the middle of it.

"It was an accident," I say.

Freddy's attention returns to me. "Was it? And you forgave him?"

"I think forgiving past wrongs is the only way for us to move on. Otherwise they cripple us," I say.

"Some wrongs can never be forgiven," Freddy counters, all joy ripped from his face. He looks back at Oliver. "And on occasion the only avenue to cope with said wrongs is to destroy the source of them."

"It was over two hundred years ago," Oliver says.

"And I have missed Jules every hour of that two hundred years," Freddy snarls.

Oh, I knew it. *I knew it!* This is about a woman! Stupid Oliver couldn't keep it in his pants, and now I'm going to die because of it. Why am I not surprised?

"Wonderful, just wonderful," I mutter, rolling my eyes.

"Did you say something, Beatrice?" Freddy asks.

"Nope. Not a thing."

"Does it surprise you to learn this about your lover?" Freddy asks.

"Nope. He'll sleep with anything. I've seen him hit on trees." Okay, there was a pixie in the tree, but still. "And he's not my lover."

"You share a hotel room. He calls you his wife."

"I take the bed, he's in his coffin. And the wife thing was my idea so the other vamps would leave me alone."

"She does not lie," Oliver says. "I took her on this trip in the hopes of remedying her reluctance, but her will is too strong. I actually grow tired of her frigidity." He looks down at me, meeting my eyes. His grow wide. "I was planning to leave her on the next leg of our trip." Grin Number Four surfaces.

Oh!

"What?" I snap. "You were *what*?"

"I am sorry, my darling, but it is true."

"You were just going to abandon me in San Diego?" I cry, doing an Oscar-worthy performance of the wronged woman. Joan Crawford would be proud. "What about what you said in Chicago? That you'd give me as much time as I needed, huh? Forget about that, you creep?"

"I lied. I thought it would be amusing to see how long it would take for you to spread your legs. But the farce has grown ... dull. Rather like you."

I jump off the couch, hands on my hips. "Well, excuse me for having some morals! There are some of us who wait to fall in love before letting a living dead man into their most sacred place! And to think I stayed with you after you went crazy and bit me!" I look at Freddy. "You can stake him now! I don't care! Do us all a favor!" I flop back on the couch, folding my arms with a huff.

Freddy's smile stretches so far he looks like the Joker from *Batman*. "My, my. You have not changed, have you Ollie? Leaving broken hearts wherever you go." The smile fades. "Such a shame I did not believe a word of it."

"I want nothing to do with him," I say. "Believe it or not, but it's the truth." *For the love of Christ, believe me.*

"Beatrice, angel," Freddy says with a quick smile, "it does not matter if I believe *you*. It matters that I believe *him*."

"I—"

I don't see him move. I blink and the snarling Freddy is on top of me, his whole weight pressed against me. One moment I'm sitting up, and the next I have my head in Anton's lap while Freddy straddles me, two long fingers on either side of my windpipe. Anton seems as surprised as I am, his arms raised as if a tarantula just jumped on his thigh.

"Do not move!" Freddy roars at Oliver, putting pressure on my neck.

My eyes dart to Oliver, who hovers above wide-eyed in fear and hatred. "Release her," he says sounding more than a little afraid.

"Oh, I knew you cared," Freddy says mock serious. His grin forms cheek to cheek.

"Her ex-lover is an officer of the law," Oliver says quickly. "He knows she is here. There would be a nationwide manhunt."

184

"Frederick," Anton says, still not moving

"Silence!" Freddy shouts. He squeezes tighter. I can barely breathe now. My eyes water. I think they're tears.

"Killing a human is punishable by death!" Oliver shouts. "The F.R.E.A.K.S. will not let this pass!"

"They have not caught me yet," Freddy says to me.

"This time they will," Oliver shouts. "They know we are here! I am working with them!"

"Lies!"

Oh, God. I see spots. I try to use my power to push him off, but it doesn't work. He doesn't budge. The world starts spinning.

"Frederick, release her!" Anton orders. He shoves the insane vamp by the shoulders, pushing him off me and the couch. Freddy tumbles over the side. I gasp for breath the moment I feel the fingers leave.

"How dare you touch me!" Freddy roars from the ground.

Oliver is beside me in a blink, wrapping his arms around me as I gasp and cough. He strokes my hair, rocking me as I clutch onto his shirt, wiping my tears on it.

"He is employed by the F.R.E.A.K.S.," Anton says. "Do you really want them upon our heads more than they apparently already are? Is your revenge worth that?"

"Yes," Freddy snarls. "He must pay!"

Oliver pulls me tighter into his chest. I think he'd pull me inside him if he could. The gasps lessen. My throat aches with each breath. "Do what you will to me," Oliver says, "but leave her be."

Freddy glances at Anton, then Oliver, then back to Anton. He rises, smoothing his pants. He regains his composure by wiping imaginary dirt off his pants. "Then challenge me to a duel."

"I beg your pardon?" Oliver asks.

"A duel. I have kept up with my swordplay, have you?"

"This is ridiculous," Anton protests.

"No, it is not. If he challenges me, then we are protected under vampiric law and the F.R.E.A.K.S. cannot touch us." Freddy grins. "And if I remember correctly, our Oliver here was never confident with a blade." He takes a step toward us, the grin falling. "Challenge me, or I will call my men in to hold you down while I vivisect and flay your lover in front of you. *Challenge me.*"

"This is madness," Anton says. "I do not—"

"I care not what you think! Challenge me!"

Oliver's poker face has returned, but I'm sure his mind is working on every possible scenario. He drops his arms, pushing me away. "If I agree, she will not be harmed?"

"I will not so much as touch a hair on her head. Challenge me."

Slowly, Oliver stands while not taking his eyes off Freddy. "Then I, Oliver Smythe Montrose of no land challenge you, Lord Frederick Sampson St. Clair of North Texas, to a duel."

"And I accept," Freddy says, bowing. "Anton, call JR and Geraldo as witnesses. And retrieve the swords." Anton nods, glancing at us as he stands. He walks over to the phone. "We need to move the sofa, Oliver. Please stand, Miss Beatrice."

What the heck is going on?

Oliver holds out his hand. Good thing, because the world somersaults as I stand up. Freddy pushes the couch toward the back wall. JR and Gerry enter and immediately start moving furniture off to the side. I lean against Oliver as he helps me back to the moved couch. With the others setting the stage, Freddy saunters over to Anton, who hands him one of the swords from the wall.

It's as big as I am. Oliver plops me down on the couch, and then joins me. Freddy swishes the sword to and fro, testing it.

"You don't have to do this, you know," I whisper. "Do you really think he'll let me go just like that?"

"If I am dead then he has no reason to harm you," Oliver whispers back.

My stomach drops at the word *dead*. "'If you're dead?' You're planning on dying?" I whisper.

"I shall try my best not to," he says with grin Number Four, the "I'm in trouble" one.

"This is insane! Why don't we just arrest him?"

"If we attempt to arrest him here, there is an entire cadre downstairs who will not allow us to leave this building alive, no matter who we are. Plus, we have no weapons or holding cell. This is the only way." He removes his jacket and unbuttons his sleeves for better movement. "If something should happen to me, do not go back to the hotel. Call the others. Finish the mission, but do *nothing* to help me, do you understand?"

"Why?"

"It will null the contract. *Do nothing.*"

"Oliver," Freddy says in sing-song. "Are you prepared?"

I meet Oliver's eyes, which are steely with resolve. He cups my cheeks in his hands, pulling my face to his lips. Softly, he kisses my forehead. "I am sorry for this." He releases my face and stands. "My sword please."

Anton brings him the sword. Oliver takes the golden lattice handle. "Silver?"

"Naturally," Freddy says. "The very same one I used to kill Ravi for this territory seventy years ago."

Oliver joins Freddy in the center of the square. They're boxed in by the couch, desk, and far wall, which Gerry and JR lean against. JR has a huge smile on his face, but Gerry looks bored. He probably planned on spending the night raping teenage girls, not watching a sword fight. Anton takes a ringside seat beside me, throwing his arm over the side of the couch like a date at a movie. I clutch onto Oliver's jacket like a security blanket. My foot jiggles. Oliver's old. I'm sure he's done this lots of times. Dozens. He'll be fine. He *has* to be fine.

The men face each other, raising their swords to their noses in unison, faces blank. They lower the silver swords to the ground so the pointed tips touch the ground.

"I will enjoy gutting you," Freddy says.

"Jules said you were terrible in bed. Unimaginative. Could not wait to—"

Freddy lunges at Oliver with a roar I'm sure they heard all the way in Kansas. Oliver raises his weapon to block the blow, the swords clanking on impact. Freddy raises his sword again, but Oliver blocks. Without hesitation, Freddy continues bringing the sword down as if he's chopping wood. Clack, clack, clack. Oliver grips his sword with two hands as he lowers to his knee to brace the impacts. Freddy howls louder with each swing. Oliver's sword lowers to his forehead, and in that instant he punches Freddy in the stomach. The enraged vampire doubles over for a moment, which is all Oliver needs. He stands and leaps away.

Freddy recovers far too quickly. Just as Oliver moves, Freddy is on him again, sword gliding to Oliver's left side. He parries it away, then twists to make a blow of his own. Freddy blocks it. They continue like this for a few seconds: block, blow, block, blow, blow, moving so fast I lose track of who is doing what. I feel like I'm watching a live version of an Errol Flynn movie. The real thing is far more frightening and loud.

Oliver bends to the side to avoid a strike and at the same time spins around so he's on my right. Freddy attempts another axe move, but Oliver sidesteps it. Freddy stops attacking, glaring at the stony Oliver who holds his sword and other hand out to the side. "You are rusty, my old friend," Freddy says.

"As are you," Oliver says back. "You used to be able to take someone out in three thrusts. At least that is what Jules told me."

They circle each other like rabid dogs. "I enjoy toying with you."

"Well, stop it," Oliver hisses. "I grow bored with you, as all do."

"You would deny me my revenge?" Freddy asks, still circling. "You stole and then killed my lover."

"Vampire hunters killed Jules, not I."

"If Jules had been with me, it would not have happened!"

"I am not responsible for what happened. You drove Jules away with your neediness and weakness. Death was preferable to an eternity with you."

Freddy's eyes turn shark black. He lunges at Oliver, who steps to the side. Freddy jumps on his desk, and at the same time, brings the sword down and over, drawing blood on Oliver's left bicep. The skin sizzles like bacon on impact and smells like what it is: burnt flesh. I gasp. Oliver hisses in pain, involuntarily switching the sword to his left hand, right one pressing on the wound. He steps back but not far enough. Freddy kicks Oliver in the face, knocking him on his back.

"No!" I shriek.

Freddy leaps off the desk beside Oliver. He brings the sword down, but Oliver crosses his blade across his body in protection. So Freddy stamps down hard on Oliver's stomach. He recoils in pain, turning over onto his side. Freddy slashes across Oliver's back with the look of a man possessed. Oliver howls in pain. Blood pours out like Niagara Falls, pooling on the floor. He drops the sword. He's defenseless. Freddy kneels down beside him, drawing the sword to Oliver's neck. He yanks on Oliver's hair. "Beg for mercy," Freddy says with a snarl.

Anton yanks on my arm, drawing my attention away from the scene. "If you are able to do something miraculous," Anton whispers quickly, "and I believe you can, I would so it now."

"Beg!"

"Never," Oliver says through the pain.

Anton yanks again. "Now!" he whispers.

Screw it, Oliver is not dying on my watch.

Freddy begins drawing the sword across Oliver's neck like a violin bow, triumph written all over his face. That is until the sword flies from his hand as if pulled by invisible strings. All eyes follow the floating weapon until it lands with a clang in the corner of the room. Everyone's face but mine contorts into a look of confusion. Anton and I stand up.

"What the hell?" Gerry says.

The two goons take a step toward Oliver, but I hold up my hand to focus my power. They both fall back against the wall unable to move. At the same time, I look at the sword Oliver lost, picking it up with my mind. It floats into my outstretched hand. Freddy's look of utter confusion turns to wonder then anger. The other two continue struggling, worming their bodies as if trying to get out of rope.

"Get away from him," I order, my voice matching my fury. I whip toward Anton. "You. Sit."

He does.

Holding the sword at the ready—not easy as it weighs at least ten pounds—I step toward the motionless Freddy. "Try anything and I squish your two henchmen like bugs on a windshield."

"You always do know the most interesting people, Ollie," Freddy says in amusement.

"Oliver, get up," I command.

With a groan worthy of a porn star, he stands, grimacing in pain. He's so pale, almost the color of a real corpse.

"We're leaving," I say, edging back toward the door. Freddy doesn't move.

"This is not over, Ollie," Freddy says.

"Don't you move," I say as we reach the door. Both JR and Gerry scowl and seethe next to me.

"I'm going to kill you, bitch," Gerry growls.

"Not if I kill you first, pal. And I will. That's a promise."

Gerry makes another attempt with the lunging, but I tighten the invisible plank so he can't even blink. Oliver staggers through the open door, and I back out too. Oliver's halfway down the stairs when I close the door with my mind. I have to release the men, focusing my entire mind on that door. The men pull and push and smash, but it doesn't budge. Even as I'm running down those stairs as fast as my feet allow, I don't let go.

A bleeding Oliver pushes his way through the copulating crowd toward the front door. Some libertines actually look concerned, especially when they see the sword still in my hand. A few even stop having sex. The bartender moves toward me as I pass, but I fly-squirrel him across the room. Vamps gasp but don't move. Smart of them.

We make it out the main door without another incident. Outside is a problem. The bouncer grabs Oliver by the shirt when he steps foot one out, slamming him against the wall. Oliver cries out in pain when his back hits brick. Before I even realize I'm doing it, I jab the sword through the guard's stomach with a roar. It slides in like butter. The howling bouncer releases Oliver, who falls to the sidewalk. The burning smell of the bouncer's flesh almost makes me gag. I release the sword, and the bouncer steps away, staring down at his stomach as if an alien had just popped out. I toss Oliver's good arm over my shoulder, hoisting him up. We both groan from the effort. A thin, warm layer of blood coats my hand. *Just get him to the car, Bea.*

He leans on me, and we walk as quickly as possible to the car, which isn't that fast. I've been working out, but not enough to lug a two-hundred-pound injured vampire around. By the time I get him to the car, my thighs, arms, and back are all burning. The BMW's not locked, thank God. I open the back door, tossing Oliver onto the seat. If possible he's grown even paler. Thin blue veins cascade around his sickly alabaster skin. He flops onto his stomach, hands balled into fists to combat the pain. Dear Lord. The two foot gash puckers and bleeds. It's so deep I swear I can see his spine. His shirt is thick with blood. I look away, slamming the door shut. He needs blood. And fast. What the hell am I going to do?

I climb into the driver's side and reach for the ignition but realize I don't have the keys. "Crap!" I shout, hitting the steering wheel with both hands.

"What?" Oliver asks as if he's in a dream state. He's seconds from passing out.

"No keys! What—"

JR and Gerry round the corner, charging at the car like the bulls in Pamplona. I lock the doors, not that it will do anything. But me whipping my head back and picking them up does. They soar into the street behind us. I just bought us all of a second.

"*Red and yellow wires*," Oliver winces. "Hotwire."

The panel under the wheel falls into my lap, expelling a load of wires. Reaching under my bustier I pull out a dagger to cut the wires as my hands tremble. I start rubbing them together like in the movies, but the engine just sputters. Glancing in the rearview mirror, I see Gerry and JR running toward us again. I keep rubbing. I look again, and they've disappeared.

Glass smashes beside me, a thousand tiny shards raining like diamonds. I scream and duck down, instinctively protecting my face. A hand grabs my hair, yanking me up. I gouge the dagger into the offending hand. It works. JR pulls his bleeding hand away. The blade went all the way through, so the silver tip pokes out of his palm, dripping blood. I rub the wires again. *Oh, please. Please…* The car springs to life. *Oh, thank you, God!* I put it in reverse and punch it. The tires skid, but we move. Oliver groans in pain as his back slams into the seat behind. I step on the brake, and we come to a sudden stop. He groans again. I put the car into drive, and we're out of the lot.

There are few cars on the road, but channeling Richard Petty from NASCAR, I maneuver and speed, even going through a red light. I'm not stopping for anything. There's no noise but my ragged breath and the passing air outside. No cars follow us that I can see.

"Oliver?" I ask through the breaths.

He doesn't answer.

Very quickly, I turn around. Blood has smeared the brown leather interior like something out of a crime scene photo. His eyes are closed, and he's not breathing. Is he dead? My stomach buckles so hard I gasp. Wait, he's a vampire; they don't breathe. The knot in my belly loosens a little. He's just passed out. I have no idea how much blood he can lose before he dies for real. I have no idea what to do about his cuts. I just have no idea what to do.

Don't panic. That's what you do—you don't panic. I take a few deep breaths to calm myself, though it works only up to a point. My arms shake from the adrenaline coursing through my every vein. Okay, first step is to stop driving like a maniac. The last thing I need is to be pulled over with a bleeding man in the backseat. I stop at the red light this time.

He needs blood, and I have no idea where to get it. I'd donate, but until we're safe, I need all my strength. They have blood at the hotel. Our weapons are there too. I really, *really* want my machete right now. But Marianna is there. As is Oliver's cell phone. Call for help. I run though my options and can't think of anything better right now. I punch the address into the GPS with my trembling finger. The light turns, and I head for the hotel.

———

Oliver doesn't regain consciousness in the fifteen minutes it takes to reach the Dauphine. I didn't think it possible, but in that time he turns a whiter shade of pale with his cheeks sinking in too. And doubts about this plan fade when I look at him. He needs blood and I'm getting it for him, even if it means facing a house full of vamps.

The remote for the Dauphine's gate still works. Good sign. If I'm lucky, everyone's out and they have no idea we're wanted fugitives. Yeah. Right. I pull the BMW to the front of the house, leaving the engine on. Might need a quick getaway. The lights are on inside, but nobody runs out of the house. *Please God, let everyone be out. Please.*

I leave the car idling and get out. My legs wobble a little, but I can walk. Better yet, I can run. Which is what I do. I run through the unlocked front door, past the library and den, and up the stairs. Nobody stops me. I'm panting when I reach the second floor but continue as fast as my legs allow to the second stairwell. My heels thump on the stairs, but I make it to our room without incident. Crap! No keys!

No choice. My mind pushes the door. It swings open the wrong way. The hinges from the wall hang off the door, but I shimmy through the opening. After turning on the light I race over to the bed, falling to my knees and reaching under. I feel the black duffel and yank it out. All the weapons are there. I run around the room grabbing the essentials—thermos of blood, case papers, cell phone—and throw them in the bag. I'm over by the window picking up Oliver's other leather jacket when the door smashes in. I shriek and drop the jacket. The door falls to the ground with a thud. The male German twin still has his leg raised from the kick.

His sister and Marianna stand behind him, all three glaring at me. My luck just ran out.

I don't so much as blink when the trio step in. Marianna walks between the twins, so they flank her on either side like blonde pillars. She stops a few feet from the bed, folding her arms across her chest. "Checking out?" she asks with a sly smile.

"I don't want any trouble. I was just leaving." I don't move though.

She eyes me up and down. My entire body is sticky with blood. I'm like a prostitute to a recovering sex addict: temptation. She licks her lips. "Did Freddy kill him?" she asks.

"What?" I ask.

"Freddy. Did he slay Oliver?"

All the pain, all the nervousness sizzles out of me, replaced by red hot rage. "Why did you do that to him?"

She shrugs. "I thought Freddy might find it interesting. And judging from your appearance, he did."

"Go to hell, you bitch. I will kill you, I swear to—"

"Save your idle threats, little girl. Klaus, Ingrid, enjoy your midnight snack."

I don't wait for them to move. Their blonde heads twist like bottle caps around to their backs. Bones and tendons crack and break. Both fall to the ground, their gurgled screams filling the room. Sadly they won't die, but I'm sure it hurts like hell. Marianna's already huge eyes double in size as she looks to either side. Guess she didn't see that coming.

"You—" is all she manages.

Planning is key in this job. I came up with a dozen scenarios of what was waiting for me in this house. The one I face is closest to scenario four. I know exactly what to do. I rip off the front of the bustier as she finally looks back to me. Her eyes dart to the daggers. I pull out two, and before my arms even reach the level, they float out of my hands. As fast as bullets, they fire right into her chest at the heart, exiting on the other side with blood in their wake. Bull's-eye.

She doesn't have time to react before I yank out two more, launching them to the same spot. Her body jerks violently a second time, blood splattering all over her shirt and out her mouth. Marianna collapses to the floor next to her henchmen.

I feel her eyes follow me as I walk over to the bed. The once-confident woman whimpers and presses on her wounds as blood pours between her fingers. I feel nothing—not rage, not sadness, just nothing—as I pull Bette out. Marianna whimpers louder as the long blade comes into view. I gaze down at her. How many people has she killed? Hundreds? Thousands? She tried to kill me and my partner just because he wouldn't go to a book reading with her. I meet her eyes. They plead.

"Please. Do not," she says.

I feel nothing. "I'll tell Oliver you said good-bye."

With all my strength, I bring the machete down onto her neck. With the silver coating, it slices through as if the flesh and bone isn't there. Blood sprays like I've just turned on a sprinkler. Her head separates from the rest of her, blood spreading like wildfire over the floor. Her brown eyes glaze over. I yank Bette out of the floor with a groan. Then I throw up all over the nice bedspread.

ELEVEN

PLAYING DOCTOR

I RUN OUT OF that house as fast as I can carrying a sixty-pound duffel bag full of weapons. I left everything else—our clothes and other personal items—behind. God knows who else is in that house, and I don't want to find out. The only piece of clothing I did take is Oliver's jacket. We need a new place to regroup, and I don't think visible bloodstains would help us go around undetected.

Oliver is still passed out in the back when I jump into the car. Practically before I close the door, I step on the gas and get the heck out of there. I want as much distance as I can get between us and anything with fangs before I stop.

Glancing in the mirror, I watch him. He looks worse. His skin is almost transparent now with a map of blue veins crisscrossing everywhere. I make it three miles down the road before the smart part of my brain takes over. I pull over. Oliver doesn't stir.

I grab the thermos from the bag beside me and climb into the backseat. It's a darn slaughterhouse back here, blood smeared and in pools on the interior. I lift Oliver's head into my lap. What I wouldn't give for one of his crude remarks right now, he's so still and cold. With one hand I open his mouth to a pucker, and with the other pour down the blood. At first it pools in the hole for a few seconds, then slowly drains down his throat. I pour again. And again. The thinner blue veins disappear after the third time. I don't know how much he's absorbing because the wound on his back continues bleeding all over me. I pour a few more times until the thermos is empty.

His eyes remain closed, and he's still a sickly shade of white, but the veins have disappeared and his cheeks are back to their full state. "Oliver?" I whisper. Nothing. Maybe this will work. "Oliver!" I shout as I slap his face as hard as I can.

His head jerks up along with the rest of his torso. He howls in pain. "Fuck!" His eyes jet around the car wildly, not sure where he is. They stop at me. "Where are we? What has happened?"

"We're safe," I say. "We got away after you passed out." He groans in torment again. It's so deep, it sinks into my bones almost causing me pain. "Your back's really bad. It won't stop bleeding."

"I am starving," he says in a low voice. "I am so hungry."

"I gave you the last of the blood. I don't know what else to do."

"I need blood. Medical attention. It was a silver sword, the wound will not close on its own. And we need a safe location to wait for the others." His eyes meet mine. Oh, crud. They're as black as onyx. He's vamping out. "Put me in the trunk. If I am seen …"

Don't need to tell me twice. I race to the front, hitting the button to open the trunk. He all but tumbles out like a drunk, but at least he can move on his own. I so don't want to, but I throw his arm around my shoulder to help him walk. His mouth is a mere foot from my neck. He's dead weight, barely able to put one foot in front of the other. Those eyes don't leave my neck. "Where do we get this blood and medical attention?" I ask.

He doesn't answer. There is nothing in his world but my neck right now. We make it the ten steps to the trunk. I all but push him into it. He rests on his belly, closing his eyes. I slam the trunk shut. Now what? *Think!*

I close my eyes, taking deep breaths. He's just going to keep losing blood unless I get that wound closed. He won't make it the few hours it will take for Dr. Neill to get here, and I don't know of any vamp doctors. I'll have to do it. I so hate my life.

I pull out my cell phone and dial information. Within seconds, I have the address for an all-night pharmacy and peel rubber down the street, pulling into the parking lot five minutes later. Thank you, GPS. The realization that I'm covered in blood hits me when I step inside the store, but I can't do anything about it now. The place is deserted except for the clerk, and he doesn't look up from his magazine.

After grabbing a basket, I start going up and down the aisles grabbing items. As a former teacher I've had to take first-aid classes, though I've never had to put it to use before. I get the essentials: first-aid kit, gauze, gloves, tape, and rubbing alcohol. What he needs is stitches, but of course they don't sell suture kits here. Instead I get a tube of superglue next to the air fresheners. I pick up a few more items like a packet of XL T-shirts, water, paper towels, and Windex before checking out. When the clerk finally peels himself from an article on Jessica Simpson, he visibly tenses. I do my best to pretend there's nothing wrong, even though the blood on my shirt drips onto the white tile floor. He glances at my items, then at the blood.

"Are you okay, Miss?" he asks.

"Fine. Hit a deer. In a hurry." He shakes his head but starts ringing me up. I keep a sweet smile plastered in my face. "Do you by any chance, know a good hotel close by?"

"Um, the Embassy Suites're nice."

"And where is that?"

Reluctantly, he gives me directions. I thank him and almost run out of the store without paying. I toss all but the Windex and paper towels into the front of the car. In the back, I proceed to wipe up as much of the blood as I can, scrubbing with all my might. The clerk watches me from the window inside. If I was him, I'd be on the phone to the police the moment a bleeding lady set a foot into his store, but he hasn't picked up a phone as far as I can see. Maybe the deer story is more plausible than I thought. I just do a quick clean, sweat dripping off my nose, before driving off. It's still noticeable, but not as severe as before. I can pull into the hotel without someone thinking I've had a dying man in the back.

Next step. I root around my bag for the cell phone. Kansas is pre-set one. It rings five times before someone picks up. "Hello?" George asks, still groggy from sleep.

"George, its Bea. Oliver's been injured. It's really bad."

"What happened?" he asks, now awake.

I tell him. "I'm on my way to the Embassy Suites with him, but we have no blood and no coffin. He's bleeding like crazy."

"Okay, you need to calm down," he says as if he should take his own advice. "I'll rouse the team. They'll be there in an hour or two. Were you hurt?"

"Not really."

"Good," he says, relieved.

"George, I really have no idea what to do here."

"Just help Oliver anyway you can. We'll bring everything he needs."

"Bring some clothes. And weapons. The gang of vamps is definitely in Venus. We should find them soon."

"Okay. Call when you get to the hotel."

"I will." I hang up. One hour, maybe two before we're rescued. Just need to keep him alive until then.

I pull into the Embassy Suites' parking lot. It's a big place, eight stories of brick with a parking lot off to the side. The bored valets stand under the awning and watch as I park my own car. When I turn the engine off, I realize that my bloodstained hands quake. How long have they been doing that? I entwine the sticky fingers to stop them. It seems to work. The shallow breaths help too.

Crap, I'm really caked in blood. Smears run up and down my arms, neck, and cheeks. Marianna's blood all but geysered over me, so it's probably in my hair too. Bile rises into my throat again, and I almost can't stop it from coming out. She … I can't think about it now. I reach into the plastic shopping bag to retrieve the bottle of water. I pour it on my arms, my face, even my legs wiping as much off with the paper towels as I can. A lot sloughs off, enough not to arouse suspicion. Thank God I wore black tonight. The blood on my clothes is barely noticeable. I pull my coat back on, buttoning it up all the way before I run into the hotel.

The huge lobby is near empty with only the front desk attendant, bellboy, and a chatting couple on the sofa off to the side. The concierge smiles as I power walk over to her. "Good evening," she says.

"Hello. I don't have a reservation," I start. I worked this story out between the pharmacy and here. "Is it possible to get a room for the night? I think my husband has food poisoning, and we won't be able to make it all the way home tonight."

"Does he need a doctor?" she asks.

"No. Can we get a room?"

The woman checks the computer. "Of course."

After paying with the emergency credit card, I sprint back to the car to get the bags. I unzip the duffel, pulling out one of the guns and vamp pepper spray, stuffing them in my purse. I grab Oliver's jacket and pop the trunk.

His eyes have returned to normal, but some of the veins have resurfaced. "You drive like a madwoman," he says groggily.

"You have to get up," I say.

He lifts his right arm up a few inches without help, but I do the rest. I fling his arm over my shoulder again, wrapping my other arm around his back. He groans in pain. My thigh and back muscles feel as if they're on fire as I hoist him up. We both groan this time. He pushes, and I pull him out of the trunk. "I do not know how much more of this I can take," he says through the pain.

"Shut up," I say, out of breath. I prop him up on the bumper. "We're almost there. Here, put this on." I reach down and gather my purse, the bags, and his coat. He manages to stand, and I help him on with the coat. But if he doesn't stop wincing, I'll cut off his lips.

We stumble like a pair of drunks through the parking lot with me close to carrying him along with the bags. All of his two hundred muscled pounds lies against me like a Roman column. My poor shoulders will be beyond sore tomorrow.

"Is he okay?" one of the valets asks as we pass.

"Food poisoning," I manage to say.

The bellboy rushes toward us, mouth agape. "Do you need help, ma'am?" he asks. The jerk stops right in front of me. I cease walking. "Should I call a doctor?"

"No. All he needs is a toilet and some sleep," I say, sidestepping him.

"Sir?" the bellman asks.

"I will be fine. Never eat raw oysters, my son," Oliver says with a small smile.

This is good enough for him. The bellman gets on the opposite side and puts Oliver's free arm over his shoulder too. Oliver bites his lower lip to stop the whimpers. The weight is literally lifted off my shoulders by half. We both carry him through the lobby past the stunned people and into the elevator.

"Perfect end to a perfect night, right my love?" Oliver says when the elevator doors close.

I smile at the bellman. "We've had worse, pookie."

The doors open onto the fourth floor, and we haul him down the hallway to room 408. "Are you sure you don't need a doctor, sir?" the bellman asks as I find the room key.

"If I have not improved in an hour, I am sure my wife will phone one," Oliver says.

Handing Oliver off to the man, I open the door. First I turn on the light. "Let's get him face down on the bed," I say, resuming my supportive position. We toss Oliver on the red and gold comforter.

"Is there anything else I can do?" the bellman asks.

"No, I can take it from here," I say hustling him out of the room. I do put a twenty in his hand before shutting the door on his face. I lock every lock before spinning around to my patient.

"Nice lad," Oliver says.

"We have to close that wound ASAP." I yank off my jacket and kick off my shoes before tossing the contents of the bags onto the bed next to him.

Oliver flips his head to watch me. I open the gauze, superglue, kit, and gloves. "Done this before, have you?" he asks with a weak grin Number Four.

Ignoring him, I move to the other side of the bed with the scissors from the kit in my hand. "I have to cut your shirt off. It may hurt." He bites his lip when I lift up his arms to remove the coat. The shirt underneath is so drenched in blood it sticks like tape to his torso. Making sure not to touch the wound still weeping blood, I cut the shirt vertically and lay it open, getting the full extent of the damage. Wow. Freddy sliced at least two feet from shoulder to hip. The flesh creases like swollen lips with a gaping gash an inch deep. Every centimeter is bloody.

"This is not how I envisioned the circumstances of you tearing my clothes off."

I ignore him again. "I need to clean you up or I won't be able to see what I'm doing," I say more to myself than him.

I gather the white towels from the bathroom, soaking them in water before returning to my patient. He smiles weakly as I reach him. "Ripping my clothes off and now a sponge bath. It is as if you have been reading my mind."

"Will you please shut up?" I bark.

He doesn't utter a word as I delicately wipe over hard muscles and broad shoulders that comprise his back. This is intimate, I know it, but I feel nothing. This must be how doctors do it, shutting off everything but the logical side of their brain. No wonder they're such jerks. His hands clench when I pat around the wound. When I'm done, the towel resembles a maxi-pad. I toss it to the floor. Now comes the part I'm dreading. I open the superglue and slap on the surgical gloves.

"Superglue?" Oliver asks.

"It was used in Vietnam in combat situations when suturing would take too long or was unavailable." Thank you, History Channel.

"Fascinating."

I stare at the wound. Okay. Here goes.

I position my body above his, hands and instruments ready. But I can't move. I can't. Shoot. Blood continues to run down his alabaster flesh, slowly draining his life force out, but I still can't move. My hands tremble again. I am not going to glue pieces of my friend's flesh together in a room at the Embassy Suites. It's too surreal. I close my eyes and shake my head. I can't do this.

"What is the matter?" Oliver asks.

I close my hands into fists then open them again. *Just do it*. He could die if I don't. I have no choice. I open my eyes. "Nothing. This will hurt." Here goes. My hands move this time. I push together the loose edges of his skin and squeeze the glue between them. Oliver winces again, and my gag reflex spikes. I swallow the bile back down. "I think I'm going to be sick. You need to distract me. Talk to me."

"About what?" he asks through the pain as I move up the next inch.

"I don't know. Anything. What's the story with you and the lord of the swords? Who was this Jules chick I was almost killed over?"

"I met them in France close to two hundred fifty years ago. They were residing with my sire, Alain, when I came to visit."

I move up the wound. "Your sire? The guy who turned you?"

"Yes. He was Frederick's sire as well."

I move up again. The cut gets deeper. "So Freddy's like your brother? And you stole his girlfriend? Classy."

"It was not that simple. They were together for over a century, and Frederick was … smothering. Where Jules went, who Jules fed upon, Frederick insisted he be involved."

"And then you came along, offering to take her away from it all."

"Jules seduced me," Oliver says as if I've offended him.

"Sorry." I manage another inch, but cannot get an angle to continue. "I'm going to have to straddle your legs," I say, meeting his bloodshot eyes. "If you make one inappropriate comment, I will glue your eyelids shut when you're sleeping, got me?"

"I shall do my utmost to control myself," he says with a faint smile.

With a sigh, I throw my leg over his body, resting my lower half on his legs. I continue gluing. "So you and this chick ran off. How'd she die?"

"We were ill suited together. I was simply a means to an end to escape Freddy. I believe we lasted all of a week before parting ways."

"Then she died?"

"Vampire hunters. Jules was careless one too many times. Captured, and then left outside to burn in the sun. A horrible way to die."

"And Freddy's carried a grudge this whole time? He must have really loved her."

"Or as close as he is capable of."

I'm halfway done, thank God. I wipe the sweat off my forehead. "Why didn't you tell me about any of this?"

"I had hoped it would remain irrelevant. We would arrive, dispatch the gang, and leave without issue."

"I guess Marianna ruined that," I mutter.

"Yes, I suppose she did. We will no doubt make her regret it."

"I already did," I say to myself.

Oliver's torso moves as he pushes himself onto his elbows a few inches, twisting to look at me. "You went back to the Dauphine?" he groans.

"What the heck are you doing? Don't move like that! The glue hasn't dried."

"Why did you return?"

"Lie back down or finish the job yourself. Lie down!" He does as I say. Shaking my head, I move up the cut. "I went back because you needed blood, and I didn't know where else to go."

"That was the second most idiotic thing you did tonight."

"And what? Me saving your life was number one?"

"Yes."

Before I can stop myself, I smack the back of his head. "How can you say that?"

"You nulled the contract. By law he is now able to do whatever he desires to us."

"Well, excuse me for not wanting to see that hobbit decapitate you. Ungrateful much?" I pinch the next inch of skin as hard as I can and glue. "Besides, everyone is on their way. We should be gone by tomorrow."

"If Marianna and Frederick do not have their spies out in full force."

I pinch more gently this time. "We don't have to worry about Marianna." I finish the last bit over his shoulder and sit beside him. The glue holds, but blood weeps from one or two gaps. I blot them with the washcloth and pull off the gloves. "Keep still while the glue dries."

Everything after that is gravy. I put gauze over the red line and tape it up. The wound on his arm isn't that deep, so I just put butterfly band-aids on it and gauze it up too. "Excellent job, Nurse Alexander," Oliver says.

"Will it heal?" I ask, putting on the last piece of tape.

"It depends on my blood consumption, but it should."

"Good." I stand up, taking the packet of shirts with me. Oliver watches as I put them in the bathroom. Next I go to my purse and take out the cell phone. I hand it and the TV remote to him. "I need to take a shower. Don't move until I get out. And call George. Tell him the address and room number," I say, pointing to a small pad of stationery bearing the hotel's logo and information on the nightstand.

"Yes, ma'am," he says as he takes the gadgets.

Once again I find myself literally peeling off my clothes. I wish it was only sweat this time. From now on, I will associate Dallas with bodily fluids. I can't wait to get back to Kansas. I step into the warm shower and start scrubbing myself like a person with OCD who just stuck their hand into a vat of toxic waste. The water at my feet is as red as the soap in my hand. For five minutes straight, I scour and wipe until the water turns pink. I wash and conditioner my hair until the bottles are empty. I know I'm clean, but I feel the stickiness still on me like a phantom limb. I want to stay in this shower forever, but know I can't. He's not out of the woods yet. Despite his ribald front, Oliver still needs blood and fast. It must be sheer will and determination that's keeping him from lunging at my neck to chow down. I've gone this far, gotta finish the trip. I shut off the water and step out.

The white shirt I bought barely goes past my hips, revealing my not so long legs and cellulite. Having no choice, which is the story of my life, I rinse out and put back on my slightly bloodstained panties. Within seconds, my nipples stick out like erasers. At this moment, I regret both not taking my clothes from the Dauphine and ever setting foot inside a McDonald's.

Oliver says nothing as I return. His eyes are closed again.

"Oliver?" I ask, rushing over to him.

His eyes open. "What?"

I sigh. "Nothing. How do you feel?"

"My back itches. It is healing."

I look. The gauze is soaked in blood in places. "You're still bleeding."

"I know. It is fine. Can you help me move? This is not a comfortable position."

"Fine." I grab his feet, spinning them so they're dangling over the side. He does his best to sit up on his own but fails. He's still weak. I carefully throw his arm over my already sore shoulders and lift. We make it three steps before his legs give out. It's been a rough couple of days and my energy level is at negative three. I can't handle the dead weight. We both buckle to the ground, him on top of me.

"Shoot," I mutter.

"I apologize," he says. I wriggle out from under his body and he lands on his stomach. "Perhaps I should remain here. I do not wish to move farther."

"Are you going to be able to last two hours without blood? Honestly?"

He can't even lift his head to look at me. "I do not know."

That's a no. Crap. I don't want to do this, but I know I have to. It *is* sort of the theme of my life. "You need to feed from me."

"No."

"We're safe now. There's no reason I can't donate."

He uses his last bit of energy to turn on his side, move his eyes to mine, and set his jaw. "No."

"Why are you being so—"

"I said never again. I meant it."

"Last time was by force, and I'm volunteering now. You'll take just enough to heal, okay?"

"I will not do this. I can wait. No." He closes his eyes again.

A wave of rage swells within me. "Listen to me, you jerk!" His eyes open. "I'm exhausted. I have been kidnapped, strangled, attacked, I've seen you cut open with a sword, killed a few vamps, carried your sorry butt a mile, and done a frightening medical procedure. All of this because of you! And you're worried about drinking a little of my blood? Get over it!" I shove my wrist to his lips. "Now, bite me, you jackass!"

His eyes soften and study mine. His face falls. "It will hurt."

"I remember, and I don't care. Do it."

I expect more protests, but instead he opens his mouth, fangs exposed. I tense. It really does hurt. I look away as the teeth lower, but gasp in pain when the two huge fangs punch through skin. The blood flows into Oliver's suckling mouth. If it wasn't for the pain, it might feel as if he was kissing my wrist with the moving lips and roving tongue. Some find this erotic. I find it painful and disgusting. I whimper.

It takes thirty long, long suckling seconds for me to become lightheaded. The world tilts a little, and I instinctively pull my wrist away. His fingernails dig into my flesh. Everything full tilt boogies. Spots float all around. From experience, I know I have about ten seconds before I pass out. I do the only thing I can think of to get him to stop: I kick him in the crotch.

You fantasize about doing it a dozen times, but the reality is such a letdown. Still, it does do the job. He releases me, and I instantly scoot away, pressing against the two holes with my other hand. Blood spills between my fingers. I grab a towel and wrap it around the wrist. Oliver remains doubled over on his side, my blood dribbling down his chin. He rocks back and forth. My heavy breathing is the only noise.

"I apologize," he says a few seconds later. Still doubled over, he lifts his head. His eyes are the normal shade, no snake black at all. His color is better with a hint of pink resurfacing. The world does another one eighty. He meets my eyes. "I may have nicked your artery. I need to close the wounds."

"No. Just give me the glue. I can do it."

"Trixie, this is not up for debate. Trust me."

I can always kick him in the nuts again if I need to. And … spinning and spots are bad. I don't shrink away as he crawls toward me, still in pain as he grimaces every time he moves. He sits next to me. "Me and my bright ideas," I mutter.

A little smile forms as he takes my arm. "You trust me?"

"You know I do."

He unwraps the towel. Blood pours from the two holes onto the carpet. Blood. I can't escape it. Once again my wrist moves to his mouth, but no fangs press in. It's worse. His tongue licks over the wounds like a cat giving itself a bath. Vamp saliva has a clotting enzyme, so I'll be healed by tomorrow morning. After three licks, the blood slows. His eyes peer over my wrist to my own for a moment, but I look away. This is just too weird. He licks a few more times before releasing me. I fight the urge to wipe the cooties off. The wounds are still raw, and now itchy, but they've stopped bleeding.

"Thank you," I say quietly.

We sit side by side for a minute without speaking. I'm so tired now I don't think I can get my mouth to move anymore. He is so still, so quiet, if we were outside birds would perch on him. "Did I hurt you?" he asks finally.

"Not too bad," I find myself saying.

"I apologize for losing control. It was—"

"I know. And I'm sorry for kicking you in the crotch."

He smiles a genuine smile. "No, you are not."

213

"No, I'm not," I say, trying to stop the oncoming laughs.

He doesn't have my restraint. He chuckles, which becomes a full on laugh. It's contagious. I laugh harder than him, shaking my head at the ridiculousness of it all. "Geez, what a night."

"Oh, yes."

The laughs die down a moment later, leaving nothing but awkwardness and exhaustion. I sigh. "I think I need to lie down now," I chuckle for the last time.

I put my hand on his bare shoulder in an attempt to rise. I make it halfway before my knees buckle, and I fall into Oliver's awaiting arms. Oops. He gazes down at me, and I look up at him, our eyes locking. With his arms around my back, the tips of his fingers touching the edge of my breast, and the other supporting my bare legs, I suddenly feel like I am—wet, half naked, with adrenaline coursing through me. Because I am. Goosebumps erupt like Pompeii all over. The butterflies I normally get have multiplied and spread to every inch of my body. His ruby red lips hover mere inches from mine. Neither of us moves, not even our eyes as this glorious thing passes between us.

I know this is the days' events at work, I know it. I know we've been through a lot, faced our share of death in a short period of time, and what I'm feeling is just a product of that. Everyone gets this way. Irie and Wolfe hooked up right after she fought off a rogue witch. If I do anything, I'll hate myself tomorrow. But ...

Not tearing my eyes from his, I reach up to his lower lip, slowly wiping the blood with my finger. His grip tightens on my body. It feels so good, our skin touching. The more touching, the more every part of me turns deliciously warm like hot fudge. He's so handsome, the most beautiful man I've ever laid eyes on. Like a dark angel. Those lips, those eyes—God, everything about him does something to me. I could look at him for eternity, and the lust would never wane. He risked his life to save mine tonight. Damn it, I want him. More than I've wanted a man before. To hell with it. "We're always finding ourselves in hotel rooms alone to-gether," I say quietly, "with me half naked. And I always end up in your arms. Always."

His eyes jut from side to side as if trying to read my mind like a book. I don't think he likes the material. His eyes become almost sad for a moment before they leave mine. "And you always fall asleep. You are exhausted, my dear. As am I."

Wait. Am I getting the brush off from a priapismic dead guy?

He stands up with me still in his arms. He flinches in pain, but manages to get us both back to the bed, laying me on top before pulling the covers out. "Get under the covers, my dear," he says. When I do, I'm surprised he doesn't pat my head like a good girl. "I am going to clean myself up a bit. Try to sleep."

Without another word, he switches off the lights and retreats into the bathroom, leaving me alone in the dark. Water from the sink runs in the next room. Any warm feelings evaporate. I scoff. Um, what the heck just happened? I practically throw myself at him, and he does nothing. Okay, so he's still weak, but *nothing*? I don't get it. I want him, he wants me ... grr! You've got to be kidding me. Well, that's it. He missed his chance. I'm not giving him another one. Not ever.

He's in the bathroom about ten minutes and as each one passes, I grow angrier and angrier. How can he not want me? He flirts with me all the time. Nonstop. And he knows it annoys me. If he doesn't want to sleep with me, then why do it at all? I'm not crazy. I know I have limited experience with men, but any fool could tell he's into me. I *feel* it. And yes, I know, it would be a mistake. But *what* a mistake. He's had hundreds of years of experience. Is it my thighs? He saw my thighs and was grossed out. I know I'm not gorgeous like Marianna, but I'm not a psycho either. That should earn me some points. Who am I kidding? He's a man. Good and evil doesn't matter, just dress size. I was just sport for him. What—

The bathroom door opens and I close my eyes tight, pretending to sleep. I hear him check the curtains and turn off the bathroom light. I squeeze them tighter when he sits on the bed. The top cover rustles as he lies down next to me. What a gentleman, leaving a piece of hard cotton between our bodies. I turn on my side with my back to him.

"I know you are awake," he says. "Your breathing is not yet shallow."

Crud. "I was just about to fall asleep, thank you very much. You woke me. But since you're up, why don't you call downstairs and get yourself a cot. The bed's mine."

"You would throw an injured man out of a comfortable bed?"

I flip over to face him. It's dark, so I can only make out the outline of his face and bare chest. He lies on his stomach, so once again our faces just mere inches apart. My skin lights up again, damn it. "If he was you? Yes. Now get out of my bed."

"Do you not trust me enough to know I will not molest you in your sleep? Or is it the opposite?"

"You're a pig." I flip over again. "Just shut up and go to sleep, okay? Don't think about me and don't touch me, or I swear I'll throw open the curtains at sunrise." Damn it! I feel the tears on their way, and I almost draw blood when I bite my lip to stop them. I'm being wishy-washy and I know it, but I can't seem to stop myself.

We're silent again for a minute, with only my angered breathing filling void.

"Do you not think I long to kiss you?" he asks quietly.

"What?"

I feel him turn on his side with great effort. "Oh, my beautiful Trixie," he says in a breathy whisper. "Do you not think that it requires every inch of my resolve not to press my mouth against yours? To taste you? To touch you? To be inside you and watch as I bring you to ecstasy?"

I don't move. I don't blink. For some reason, I just want to disappear, vanish, so I don't have to have this conversation while I'm in just a flimsy T-shirt and panties.

"But when it occurs—and I have no doubt it *will* occur—it will be because *you* want *me*. Not because you want to block out the world."

If I wasn't already lying down, I'm pretty sure I'd swoon. But instead I say, "Well, don't hold your breath, buddy. I had a moment of weakness. It won't happen again."

"Oh, yes it will. And I have nothing but time, my beloved."

I smile despite myself but quickly drop it. "Whatever."

"You should try to sleep now. I will keep watch until rescue arrives."

"Do you think Freddy will find us?"

"No. Not tonight."

We don't speak for another minute.

"I killed Marianna."

He's silent for a moment and then says, "I know."

"I didn't have to. But I did." I flip over again to see his reaction. Nothing but sadness, for who I don't know. "She hurt us. She hurt *you*. I just … I did it. Are you mad at me?"

He pushes back a piece of my hair. "Never."

Tears well up in my eyes. "I—"

"Shush, my darling," he says, lifting his free arm to welcome me in. How does he do that? Knowing exactly what I need when I need it? I scoot the few inches between us as he drapes his arm over my shoulders. I scoot closer to him, hugging his arm with mine and resting my forehead against his. My safe haven. He traces circles on my neck, humming a lullaby until I fall asleep a minute later. Better than sex.

———

What the …?

Light streaming in from the hallway wakes me. My eyes are so blurry even rubbing them barely helps. I look toward the person standing in the light. The person's fury hits my head like a baseball bat. I sit up, dislodging my body from Oliver's. Then I make out the figure. Oh, shit. Yes, I think that. It bears repeating. *Oh, shit.*

I fell asleep on Oliver's shoulder with my body curled around his while he held me. He's shirtless, and I may as well be, the one I wear is so thin. This is how he finds us. At this moment, I so wish Freddy had killed me.

"Hi, Will."

TWELVE

EXTERMINATION

HE CUT HIS VACATION short. His first vacation in years, and he cuts it short. Why? Nancy and her big, stupid, *stupid* mouth. She just had to pick up the damn phone on George's desk. He was calling to check in, and she answered. It took her all of a minute to blab the whole story. He was on the next flight back.

Nancy and the entire team (minus Carl, since our psychometric never does say much, and Andrew, who stayed home since there are no ghosts around) have taken turns regaling me on what happened next, acting as if it was all my fault. Will arrived home, and before he even set down his bags, he tore into George. What was he thinking? How could he let me go without backup? On and on. It took half an hour to calm him down, and another half hour to convince him not to steal the jet and fly to Dallas. At least now I know why everyone was so stressed and cryptic.

It was horrible. The most gut-wrenching humiliating moment of my life, and that's saying something; I've had some doozies.

They arrived at the hotel, flashed badges, got the master key, and rushed upstairs. I'm told Will knocked, but I was so deep in sleep I didn't hear it. Of course he got the wrong idea. Anyone would, what with us half naked and clinging to one another. Without a word, he walked out. I dislodged myself from the barely awake Oliver and tried to follow. I was so lightheaded all I managed to do was fall back into bed. Irie and Chandler came in next. Now, the whole team knows. Such is my life: I do nothing wrong and I'm still punished.

Right now I'm at mobile command, a huge RV/trailer we fly in for missions. It has everything: medical equipment, a lab, temporary holding cell, and the conference room in which I now sit. We were quickly and quietly ushered out of the hotel in the dark of night and into SUVs. We drove to Love Field, where command waited in an abandoned hanger. Mobile command is kept with our jet and flown in behind us on an old military carrier. Will was in the other car on the way here. He didn't get out until I was already inside command. The rest of the team came out of the conference room to meet us. Nancy threw her arms around me, and I squeezed tight. Then Dr. Lynette Neill, our physician, examined both Oliver and me.

His wound was already healing, but she stitched up the few places I missed and his arm. Oliver didn't say a word to me on the ride, or while I watched him get patched up. He joked with Nancy and Andrew but barely glanced at me. Neill gave him a huge thermos of blood and sent him to bed in the holding cell where they set up a spare coffin. I haven't seen him since.

I was appraised, given pain relievers, a blood transfusion, my own clothes, and then I passed out on the couch in the conference room. I woke about ten hours later. Everyone but Agent Rushmore—a severe FBI agent who is never without a blue pinstripe suit and crew cut, much like the other three agents assigned to us—was gone. No doubt at the hotel doing what we normally do: waiting until something happens. I could have asked Agent Rushmore to take me there, but I still feel like crap and can't handle the looks and questions, so I start typing up my report.

I gave the CliffsNotes version on the ride to command about what the vamps were driving, where they lived, etc. I can only hope we find the creeps today, take them out, and get the heck out of this state. Then I am never setting foot in Texas ever again.

The front door of the trailer opens and closes as I finish the paragraph, followed by giggling. A moment later Irie and Agent Wolfe, whose first name has never been told to me but I think is Andy, stumble into the conference room, still laughing. They have that "We just had tremendous sex, tee hee" look about them. She's dressed in simple jeans and black tank top, long dark hair pulled into a ponytail. Agent Wolfe is in, surprise surprise, a dark blue suit. His brown hair sticks to his forehead, but it's endearing on him. Irie smiles and holds up what looks like my suitcase.

"I come bearing gifts from the Dauphine," she says.

"Have any trouble?" I ask as I shut the laptop.

Irie sits beside me. "Not really. There was this pipsqueak who started yelling, but we shut him up quick. Apparently everyone left in a hurry last night. You sure made a mess. Haven't seen that much blood in a long time."

"Yeah," I say quietly.

"Got all your stuff. Oliver's coffin too. They're taking it back to the other hotel now." She pauses. "You look like hell."

"Thanks. I feel just peachy; especially now that you're here to tell me how fabulous I look. You're a real friend."

Irie looks at Agent Wolfe. "Told you she didn't sleep with him."

My mouth drops open. "What?"

"If you had, you'd be in a much better mood."

"Of course I didn't sleep with him! We didn't even kiss! Everyone thinks we did?"

"Pretty much," Agent Wolfe says.

"Come on, it did look kind of bad. Lying together, limbs entwined, clothing thrown everywhere? As if you wouldn't think the same thing."

She's right. I cover my face with my hands. "I'm so embarrassed."

"About what?"

My hands, my stomach, and my intelligence all drop when I hear his voice. He stands in the doorway, handsome face neutral. Normally, when I lay eyes on him, I'm told my face lights up like a firefly, but I doubt it's doing it now.

Will is a little over six feet tall with a muscular build. I saw him without a shirt once, and I can attest there isn't an ounce of fat anywhere. That delicious body is now encased in black boots, black jeans, and loose azure T-shirt. His chocolate brown hair hangs loose across his forehead just begging for fingers to run through it. A Roman, slightly asymmetrical nose and strong jaw complete the package. He's not alabaster-statue perfection like Oliver, but I think he's perfect in his own way. I just wish those green eyes I love would look my way now.

"Nothing," Irie says. "She's just embarrassed she had to call us in so soon."

Will walks in, purposely not looking at me. How I wish I could turn invisible right about now.

"Well, she should have done it the second there was a *hint* of trouble," he says, hard as granite. "I doubt she'll be making the same mistake in the future."

Great. He's pretending I'm not even in the room. Classic. A moment later Nancy, Agent Chandler, Carl, and Agent Rushmore filter in as well. All make it a point not to look at me, especially Nancy. She has a huge crush on Oliver, so I guess I'm the enemy right now. She sits in the back, scowl affixed to her face. The rest take their seats around the table, all eyes on Will, who stands at the white board. I guess something finally happened.

"Did we miss something?" Irie asks Carl as he sits next to her.

"We got a call from the local police. They found a house matching Agent Alexander's approximate description. Even has a basement, which is rare in this part of Texas," Will says. "The cars Petra Bowers described were out front as well."

"Did the police raid it yet?" Agent Wolfe asks.

"No, we advised them not to. They're keeping surveillance until we arrive. Since Agent Alexander has not finished her report," Will says with a hard edge, "she will stand up and tell us what we're up against."

I will? *Okay*. I rise, smiling nervously. Nancy rolls her eyes. Will, still refusing to set eyes on me, stands like a sculpture with folded arms. Angry man in repose.

"There should be ten people in the house, three human and seven vamps. One of the humans has a pistol, the other two are unknown in regards to weapons. As for the vamps, there are four men and three women. They've killed one person for sure, possibly many more. Chances are they sleep in the basement in coffins."

"'Chances are?'" Will asks. "You need to do better than that, Agent Alexander."

"I'm just telling you what the witness told me, Agent Price," I say, glancing at him. "As I was saying, per the witness, the house is isolated with at least three stories and a cornfield in the back. That's all." I sit back down.

"Thank you, Agent Alexander," Will says. "We need to be safe about this people, by the book. Let's assume all the humans act as day guards and are armed. We enter in two groups, one taking the front and the other the back. We go in at the same time, neutralizing the humans before taking the basement. Irie, Alexander, and I will go down first, followed by Agents Rushmore and Chandler. Agent Wolfe will guard the top stairs and come down if needed. Carl, I want you there to assist Dr. Neill in the ambulance. We'll have the locals keep the perimeter."

"What should we expect in the basement?" Agent Wolfe asks.

"We're doing this in daylight, so they should be asleep. But keep in mind they are just that—asleep. It'll be just like the op in Tallahassee. Taking them out in tandem by cutting off their heads."

"And if they wake up?" Irie asks.

"We'll have shotguns and other weapons."

Nancy raises her hand. "And what should I do?"

"You stay here. Keep an eye on our friend in the freezer."

"Shouldn't his girlfriend do that?" Nancy asks.

The whole room except for Will and me chuckle. I turn bright red, I know it. Will all but snarls at the group. "That's enough!" he roars. The laughs cease. "We are about to embark on a highly dangerous mission. Keep your minds on that, not on the sex lives of your fellow teammates. Daylight is wasting, and that is a luxury we don't have. Suit up, people! We leave in twenty! Dismissed!"

All the cowed people around the table stand, looking at one another shamed to heck. Good. They whisper to each other as they file out. My ears are burning. Will passes me, scowl still there. I stand up. "Will?" He ignores me and keeps moving toward the door. "Will, stop!" I slide the door shut with my mind before he goes through it.

"Open the door, Agent Alexander," he says, not turning around.

"No. Not until you let me explain."

He spins around. "Why?"

"Because you want me…" His eyes dart to mine, anger replaced with surprise and a tinge of embarrassment. An electric current of I don't know what shoots down my spine, "…to explain."

His eyes return to their neutral state before looking away from me again. "You don't owe me an explanation. What you do after hours is none of my business."

I take a step toward him. "But nothing happened. Nothing! I swear on my mother's ashes. I patched him up. I fed him. We fell asleep. *That's it.* I would never…" I don't even say it. "I didn't even want to come here."

He doesn't respond for a moment, just staring at the carpet. "Why didn't you call me? Tell me what was going on? I could have…"

"We both know there was nothing you could do. You were on vacation, I didn't want you to cut it short or ruin it by worrying about me. I'm sorry, but… it's my job. I go where people need me, and do what I have to, to protect them. This was no different."

He finally looks at me. "I know," he says with a trace of sadness. It vanishes a moment later. I take a step toward him, but he flinches. "Um, thank you for clearing that up, Agent Alexander. Fraternizing with, um, other team members is strongly frowned upon. People end up making mistakes in the field. I would hate for that to happen to you. Now, go get ready."

He opens the now-released door and walks out. I don't follow.

Okay, I wasn't expecting him to take me in his arms or confess his undying love and threaten to cut off the hand of any man who touches me, but something more than company rhetoric would have been nice. Did he believe me? Does he even care anymore? I can't get a handle on him. I sigh.

And men think women are confusing.

———

The hour drive to Venus is almost unbearable. Every person in the SUVs almost vibrates with fear and anticipation. It's like this before every big op. We're like the soldiers in the boats as they approach Omaha Beach. There's no real way to know what to expect. Best case, we kill them all without a struggle and the rest remain asleep while we decapitate their friends. I know better.

Will, Agent Chandler, Dr. Neill, and Carl all ride in the first car with Agent Rushmore, Irie, Agent Wolfe, and me in the second. Irie and Wolfe sit in the back, holding hands while watching the arid wasteland of Texas pass by. Brown plots of dirt followed by either herds of cows or tall corn with rotting farmhouses nearby. Lovely. Oliver and I drove this exact route last night in the dark. I couldn't see anything then. Wish that was the case now.

We're decked out for battle. I even have my camouflage T-shirt and black army boots on over black jeans. This plus the bullet-proof vest, shotgun, 9mm, silver combat knife, and Bette all make me feel a little better about fighting seven peeved vamps in a cramped space. Will's SUV turns right down a dirt road, peppering us with so much dust Agent Rushmore starts the wipers.

"Rush, the roadblock is about a mile away," Will says over the walkie-talkie.

"10-4," Agent Rushmore responds.

"Guess we're almost there," I say with a sigh.

"You nervous, Bea?" Irie asks.

"Heck yeah," I answer.

"Don't be," she responds. "I'll protect you. This isn't my first cabal. Just trust your instincts. If you think it's beside you, don't hesitate. Shoot to kill. Aim for the head. Just don't hit one of us in the process."

"I'll do my best."

The SUV in front stops. As the dust clears, I see two police cars with flashing lights parked in front of a barricade. The bored, sweating cops holding shotguns wave us through.

"Get ready people," Agent Rushmore says as he drives through. I pull out the gold badge wrapped around my neck. It's just in case the bad or good guys can't tell who we are, even though the vests have "FBI" embossed on them in yellow letters. I yank my ponytail tighter as Irie and Agent Wolfe share one last deep kiss before the car stops.

I'll bet that every law enforcement officer within fifty miles has assembled in the field we've pulled into a mile from the house. There are easily a dozen police cars and thirty peace officers milling around in the hot sun. Some wait in their cars, others stand by the fire truck; two ambulances are also on standby. The largest subgroup assembles under a makeshift tent with fold-out table. As we pile out, the man at the center of the table breaks from the group on his way to us. He's in a sweat-stained white dress shirt, khaki pants, black cowboy boots, and matching hat. The sunglasses hide half his face, but I'd put his age at around forty. He's lean and his light brown skin glistens in the sun. There's little humidity today, thank God, but it's still in the mid-nineties. The people at the tent follow him, but the rest just watch, still talking to their neighbors.

"Which of you is Special Agent Price?" Cowboy hat asks.

"I am," Will says, extending his hand.

They shake. "I'm Chief Mitchell Montoya. We spoke on the phone."

"Nice to meet you." Another man sidles up to Montoya, about ten years older than him. He's sweating buckets in a khaki polyester uniform with silver sheriff's badge. "I'm Deputy Sheriff of Johnson County, Clyde Page." He shakes Will's hand too. "The sheriff's in Austin, otherwise he'd be here."

"Thank you both for being here, and for all your efforts in finding our suspects," Will says as he starts leading us all back to the tent.

"They're wanted in connection to kidnapped teens?" Montoya asks.

"Yes. We know for sure they've killed one girl and kidnapped two others. And there is evidence they've killed at least five others. We've contacted our Dallas field office, and they're standing by to collect evidence after we clear the house. We're fairly sure there are bodies in the field in the back."

The police officers rally around us as we reach the table. Blueprints of a house sit on it. I'm enveloped by the smell of BO and bad cologne. I have no idea what I'm looking at but put on my studious face to match everyone else's. "Once we spotted the cars from the BOLO, we pulled the blueprints from town hall," Montoya explains. "Basement was a good catch. Definitely the Martingales' house."

"Who are they?" I ask.

"Lou and Roz Martingale. Lived here all their lives. Old timers. I haven't seen either of them in months, only the granddaughter Kylie. They've always kept to themselves, though."

"The granddaughter. Is she very pale? Sickly looking of late?" I ask.

"Yeah," Montoya says. "She said they were all sick."

I glance at Will. "This has got to be the place."

"You didn't make your presence known, did you?" Will asks Montoya.

"Clifford?"

A man my age, face and body chubby in his uniform, steps forward. "I was making my rounds when I spotted the BMW in the distance. I called it in, and then the sheriff's department sent an undercover car by to make sure. The house, the cars—they all matched the eyewitness reports. We called the house, but there was no answer."

"Tell me what you know about the layout," Will says.

"Three levels," Montoya says, pointing to the blueprints. "Basement covers the entire base of the house. Only one way in or out. First level, two ways in and seven windows. Kitchen door in the back, front door visible from the driveway. One closet, living room, bathroom, and kitchen. Second floor has four bedrooms, two baths, one closet not counting the ones in the bedrooms."

"Okay," Will says. "I want Irie, Rush, and Chandler to enter through the kitchen door. Wolfe, Alexander, and I will go through the front. The noise should bring the three guardians downstairs, where we take them down. Then we go down to the basement."

"What do you want us to do?" Deputy Page asks.

"I need one man with necessary training to go in with us."

"I'll do it," Montoya says. "I was a Ranger. I can handle it."

"All I need for you to do is guard the people we bring out. Nothing more."

"I can do that."

"Everyone else, move the perimeter to fifty yards from the house the moment we move in. Keep it, and don't move in unless we tell you to."

"We have a SWAT unit standing by," Page says.

"I understand your desire to go in with us," Will says, "but we've dealt with these people before. They are the baddest of the bad. It would be irresponsible and downright dangerous for all of us if you went in. This is our raid. If we need you, we'll call you in, okay? Carl?"

Carl Petrovsky, all five-foot-six of him, steps toward Will. If the others notice the surgical gloves he wears, they don't let on. When he touches someone or something, he gets their whole history, emotions, the works. He's always wearing those darn gloves, even when it's a hundred degrees. Will and Carl step away from the group but I follow, nosy person that I am.

"Carl, I want you and the Doc to be in an ambulance when we go in, but the moment we do, I want you outside with a shotgun in case someone gets out. You're our last line of defense. Can you handle that?"

"Of course." Carl nods before running off toward Dr. Neill and the two paramedics.

"As for you," Will says to me, "are you okay to do this?"

"I'm fine. The blood transfusion last night—"

"I didn't mean that. I mean, will you be okay to do this?"

Why does he always ask me this before an op? I'm not three. I straighten my back. "These monsters killed six people. They terrorized two teenage girls. They kidnapped me. I'm ready."

"Okay, then. You stay close to me at all times. You are my shadow in there. I move, you move. If I tell you to do something, no matter what, you do it. Do we understand each other?"

"Yes."

I follow him back to the group. Irie is setting Montoya up with one of the hands-free com units we all have. I put my ear bud in and adjust the microphone. Montoya tightens his Kevlar vest. When they're done, he grabs the nearest shotgun and unclips his 9mm. "Montoya," Will says, "you ride with us. And you're driving."

"Coms check," Irie says over the earpiece. "Sound off."

Everyone says their last name.

"Deputy Page, are you on this frequency?" Will asks.

"Yes. We hear you."

"Okay then. Let's go to work," Will says.

Irie and Agent Wolfe share another deep, lingering kiss before starting to their separate cars. Carl climbs into the back of the ambulance, looking like a child holding a toy gun bigger than he is. All the police officers rush to their squad cars, kicking up as much dust as their vehicles. Agent Wolfe and I pile into the back, Montoya and

Will in the front. The butts of our shotguns rest on the floor with the barrels up toward the ceiling. This thing makes me nervous. I prefer my machete.

We pull out first, followed by the second SUV and ambulance. Agent Wolfe makes the sign of the cross. I just feel like puking. I can almost smell the tension and fear. Will stares out the window, deep in thought. I just keep my eyes on the shotgun. I can do this. I *can* do this.

"Stop the car," Will says. Montoya and the rest of the caravan do as he says. Without another word, Will jumps out of the car. Everyone else seems to know what's going on, so I follow. We gather around the back of the cars. "We run the rest of the way. Can't risk them seeing the dust. Weapons check, everyone."

Shotguns, knives, Mace are all examined. I pull Bette out of the back, fastening her black holster to my belt. Montoya's brow furrows when he sees Bette. "Those aren't standard."

"Neither are our bad guys," Irie replies with a smirk.

"Montoya, I need you to keep watch on the house as we approach. When we go in, bring the car to the front but do not enter the house. No matter what you hear. *No* matter what you hear, *do not* go in unless I call you in. No questions. Do you understand me, Ranger?"

"I do," he answers without hesitation.

"Good." Will hands him some binoculars. "Be our eyes. The rest of you, let's go."

Irie nods and starts running toward the house with Agents Chandler and Rushmore close behind. The rest of us tail Will at a nice trot. I hate running, especially in heavy Kevlar when it's a hundred degrees out. The farmhouse quickly comes into view over the horizon. It's just as Petra described it. Beige brown with cracking paint and blacked-out windows. I recognize the van and BMW from last night. I found you, you bastards.

"I don't see anyone in the upstairs windows," Montoya reports over the walkie. "Downstairs windows are blacked out. You're all clear."

Irie's group veers to the left, but we continue straight toward the door at a crouch until we take cover behind the van. Irie and the men disappear around the house. We all take this time to catch our breath, or at least I do. Will peeks over the hood of the van to check for movement.

"Irie, tell me when you're in position," Will whispers into his microphone.

The shotgun starts shaking in my hands. Too much adrenaline, not enough food. I can't believe I'm here. I can't believe I'm doing this. If someone told me a year ago I'd ever storm a house full of vampires with a machete and shotgun instead of teaching fractions, I'd have called a psychiatrist for them.

"We're at the back door," Irie says over the earpiece. "Movement in the kitchen."

Still crouching, Will starts toward the door again with me a foot behind him. As quietly as we can, we run up the steps to the front door. Will puts his ear to it. "One in the living room with the TV on," he whispers. Gotta love werewolf hearing. "Get ready."

I square my shoulders, grip the shotgun tight, and try not to throw up.

Here we go.

Will steps back. "On my mark. Three, two … one!" He kicks the door so hard it falls with the hinges still on. He's through the door first, shouting, "FBI! Hands above your head!"

I'm next through the door, with Agent Wolfe a split-second behind. I swing the shotgun at the only moving thing in the living room. A girl resembling a living skeleton, who I assume is the granddaughter Kylie, lies on the couch, all eighty pounds of her. There are very few places on her arms that aren't covered in bruises. She can barely lift them. Will is already pulling out the riot cuffs, a piece of adjustable plastic used to bind hands. As he yanks her off the sofa and cuffs her, the kitchen door swings open. I swerve my gun toward it on reflex, as does Agent Wolfe. A man in his late teens with spiky black hair, cargo pants, and T-shirt with a rainbow flag stumbles out. His hands are bound in the back. Irie pushes him out with the barrel of her shotgun.

"Kitchen clear," Irie says. She forces the man down on the brown and red striped couch next to Kylie. Both captives seem too out of it to know what's going on. Low blood volume does that—I speak from experience.

Out of nowhere, Will jerks his weapon toward the stairs, pulling the trigger at the same time. I hear the first shots before the shotgun blast overshadows them. An obese man in jeans and a white wife beater showing off every one of his tattoos runs down the stairs, revolver pointed at us. All gun barrels glide toward the man. His two shots hit Agent Wolfe square in the chest before Will's round takes out a huge chunk of wall inches from the man. He stops moving. Agent Wolfe's body jerks with each impact before he falls to the ground. "Do not move! Do not fucking move!" Will barks at the man. "Drop your weapon! Now! Now!"

The man does.

Irie slumps to the ground beside the groaning Agent Wolfe. They both fumble with his flak jacket. The two gold slugs lay on the outside, squished like two pennies. "Are you okay? Baby, are you okay?" Irie asks breathlessly.

Will runs to the man, cuffs ready. The man puts up no fight with three shotguns on him. The creep even chuckles. "That was stupid. *Really* stupid," Will mutters as he tightens the cuffs. The man scoffs as Will pushes him down the stairs toward the couch. "You okay, Wolfe?"

Agent Wolfe nods as Irie fawns over him, kissing his cheeks. "Thank God, thank God," Irie says, still kissing.

"He's fine," I answer.

"Everything okay in there?" Montoya asks over the walkie.

Will forces Fatty onto the couch next to the others. "Fine. We're coming out with three."

Irie pulls Wolfe off the floor. He winces and groans but stands without support.

"Agents Chandler, Rush, take them out to Montoya, and then rejoin us in the basement. Wolfe, get yourself checked out with the Doc. Everyone else, on me."

Chandler pulls Fatty off the couch, and the two others are escorted out of the house as the rest of us walk to the basement door. Will tries the handle, but it doesn't budge. With one swift kick it falls away, making enough noise to wake the dead as it tumbles down the stairs. I can't see anything down there. We're going in blind.

"Stay close," Will says to me before stepping into the abyss with me one stair behind him. He leads with the shotgun, almost gliding down the steps. Werewolves have great night vision. Me, I almost fumble on the third step. My heart thumps triple time when I reach the bottom. None of us moves for a moment. It's quiet. Nothing jumps out at us. *Thank you, Lord, they're asleep.*

A light flicks on, one of those that hangs from the ceiling. Will lowers his hand and grips the shotgun again. With the light on, I notice the tiny windows near the ceiling are boarded up. We do a cursory check of the room but find nothing except six coffins lying on the concrete floor side-by-side. Two are onyx black, one is wood, and the rest are silver colored.

"There's only six," I whisper.

"Maybe two sleep together," Irie whispers back.

Shotgun trained on the nearest casket, Will reaches down and attempts to lift the lid. It doesn't budge. "Locked," Will whispers. "Irie?"

Irie steps over to the coffin, putting her shotgun down. After rubbing her hands together, she places them on one of the hinges. The metal lights up poker red, then melts into nothing. She's a pyrokinetic, so she can create fire at will. After picking up the shotgun again, she stands. "I'll start on the rest." She walks to the farthest coffin and does the same to it.

Will quietly lifts the top lid off the coffin while I keep my shotgun pointed on it. Serena, now nothing but waxy skin and bones, lies inside. She doesn't move or breathe. "Do you recognize her?" Will asks.

"Yeah. She was there last night. Serena."

"Get out your blade," he orders.

I lean the shotgun against the wall to pull out Bette. Someone cleaned her up from last night. This is what killed Marianna, and now it's doing the same to Serena. I don't know how I feel about that. I kind of want to throw up. Will meets my eyes, and his turn soft. "I'll do it. You cover me, okay?"

I nod. We exchange his shotgun for Bette. Our skin briefly touches and my hand goes hot, as does my face. Great, the perfect place for a hormone attack. His expression doesn't change.

Will positions himself above Serena. Without a moment's hesitation, he brings Bette down on her neck. When the machete makes contact, her eyes jerk open and her mouth forms into a scream, though no sound comes out. Blood pools in the coffin. Serena's black eyes and mouth close. That's it. She's dead. May God have mercy on her soul.

A scream fills the quiet room. Agent Chandler runs down the stairs with Agent Rushmore staying up top, gun aimed at us. Everyone freezes. The lids of all five coffins fly open, barely giving us enough time to jump away. Oh, crap.

As fast as lightning, so they're nothing but blurs, all five vamps leap out of their coffins. I blink and they're lying down, and the next thing I know a naked Rick has me by the neck, flinging me across the room. I'm airborne, weightless, until I land against the wall, knocking all the marrow from my bones. I'm dazed. Every inch of me aches. The gunshots and shouting echoing through the room seem distant. Things are blurry until I blink a few times.

Agent Chandler pulls the trigger on his shotgun, face contorted in fury. A huge hole of blood and gristle blooms from Ken's chest. He crumbles to the floor. Two down. The smell of gunpowder is overwhelming.

At the same moment, Irie aims her gun at Liang, to no avail. She bops around the room so fast Irie can't get a chance to pull the trigger. Will swings at Gerry with Bette but keeps missing. Julie grabs onto Agent Chandler as he re-cocks the shotgun. Agent Rushmore tries to pull her off, wrapping the barrel of the shotgun across her throat. I have no idea where JR is.

Rick appears before me, snarling. The clouds in my brain part. Instinct makes me reach for the shotgun, but I lost it on the trip into the wall; it's too far away. Rick yanks me off the floor by my vest, teeth bared. I kick him square in his exposed hairy nuts. Works every time. He releases me as he doubles over. Not missing a beat, I use my power to drag the shotgun into my hands. Aim and fire. His head explodes into a thousand tiny pieces all over me. Something cuts my cheek. I think it's part of his skull. I wipe the blood and brain covering my face with my forearm. "That's for Kate."

"No!" someone screams at the top of their lungs. "You bitch!"

With vamp speed, Julie charges toward me. There isn't enough time to expel the empty cartridge before she's on top of me. Her weight throws me off balance, and we collapse to the ground. She claws and squirms on top of me, lunging at my neck with those sharp fangs. One quick bite to the carotid artery, and I'm done for. "You bitch! You bitch!" she repeats between bites. She mauls again, but I head butt her nose with my forehead. She falls off me, but I'm phased too. My head thumps with its own pulse, and the blurs return.

Julie recovers before me, standing up and pouncing again as blood dribbles out of her nostrils. I can't think fast enough to do anything. I can't even sit up. She makes it one step but can't take another. Her body moves, but not her head. Will stands behind her clutching onto her blonde hair. With one fell swoop he slices across her neck with Bette. Her tiny body crumbles to the floor, but her head remains in Will's fist. Blood drips out of the stump onto his boots. He tosses her head down with disgust. I just stare at it.

Will helps me up, and I take the hand that just held a severed head. Eww. He yanks me up, eyes quickly giving me the once over. "Are you okay?" he asks as his eyes stop at my cut cheek. He cups my chin as his thumb wipes off the blood from the cut. I shiver with lust. *My hero.* If it wasn't for the howl of pain on the other side of the room, I'd kiss him right beside the severed head.

We look as Liang sinks her teeth into Agent Rushmore's forearm, ripping a huge piece of meat off as he bellows. Will passes Bette to me while simultaneously pulling out his Glock and aiming. He squeezes the trigger, hitting her in the chest. She releases him. Agent Rushmore falls to the ground clutching his bloody arm. Will pulls the trigger again, but Liang vanishes from the spot. The bullet ricochets on the wall. "Chandler, get him out of here!" Will shouts. Agent Chandler grabs Rushmore, and they run up the stairs. Wish I could. Liang reappears near Irie. Irie doesn't notice. She's too busy training her gun on Gerry. Good thing I'm here.

The moment Liang materializes, I grip her body with my mind. She struggles as I lift and toss her through the boarded-up window with all my strength. The wood snaps and glass breaks as she floats like a brick outside. Sun streams into the basement, blinding us all. Gerry hisses and jumps to the other side of the room. Outside Liang shrieks in agony from her impromptu sunbathing session. The odor of burnt flesh wafts in. The screams stop a second later. All eyes and guns point at Gerry. We win.

"What are you waiting for?" he asks.

"How many people have you killed here?" Will asks.

"I'm not telling you shit," he spits back.

Will pulls the trigger, hitting Gerry in the leg. The vamp howls in pain. "Easy or hard. Your choice."

Gerry clutches his leg, groaning either from the bullet or the utter contempt showing all over his face. "Eight. Nine. I don't remember. They're out in the field."

"And where's JR?" I ask.

The air shifts from quick movement.

No more grimace. Smile instead. Crap. "Here."

Before he utters that word, a creaking emanates from beneath the stairs. Will checked there—I saw him. On instinct, we turn our heads as a blur of solid matter races toward us at the same moment Gerry does. There's only time for Will to knock me into the sunshine before the blur reaches me. Bette clatters beside me. JR grabs Will's gun arm as my butt hits concrete. With a crack, Will's arm twists at a ninety degree angle. The veins in his neck and forehead pop, but he doesn't cry out. With his good arm, he cold cocks the vamp. JR releases him. That's when Irie screams.

Gerry is lying on top of her. It takes me a moment to realize he's not kissing her neck but biting. "No!" I shout. Gerry raises his blood-caked face and smiles, blood dripping from pointed fangs. Irie's body convulses under him. The already stifling room becomes ten degrees hotter. JR roundhouse kicks Will in the face, and he falls into Irie's pooling blood. JR uses this opportunity to grab the nearby shotgun, cocking it.

He doesn't keep it for long. The gun soars out of his hands into my lap. With one swift movement, I swing the gun and fire. JR's head vaporizes. I cock it again. Gerry, impervious to everything but the blood he laps up, doesn't notice when his friend dies. He doesn't even notice as I aim at the window near him, shooting it out. The moment the light hits his face, his skin boils and blisters.

Yowling, he jumps off Irie. I shoot again, severing his leg at the knee. The hulk collapses near me. Will rushes to Irie's side as I cock again. No more bullets. I pick up my girl Bette and pull myself off the floor. Gerry cries blood tears. Half his face is nothing but burns and soot. I raise Bette and put him out of his misery. "Told you I'd get you."

"Bea! Help me!" Will says.

I whip my head toward him. Will kneels beside Irie, his good hand pressed against her wound. I rush over. "Oh, God," I say, falling to my knees on her other side.

"Put pressure on it," Will groans.

We switch places. Damn, it's really hot in here. Easily over a hundred just around her. He slips his fingers out of the gaps in her neck, and I put mine in—without gagging, to my credit. Blood runs like a creek out of the holes. Irie blinks rapidly and writhes in pain. She tries to say something, but just sputters out blood. I swear it's getting hotter in here by the second.

Will stands, pressing on his earpiece. "We need a medic! Now!"

Irie violently shakes her head, and I almost lose my grip. She attempts speech again, but I only understand the word *out*. Sweat drips off me everywhere.

"Will!" I shout. "She's trying to say something!"

He bends down. "What?"

"Can't," Irie sputters. She takes a deep breath. "Hold ... on."

"No!" I cry. Tears join the sweat on my face.

"Go!" she manages, grimacing in pain. "Hurry!"

"Okay," Will says quietly.

"No!"

Irie convulses, and a huge gust of hot air blasts me onto my butt. What the …? Will hooks his fingers in the armpits of my vest and yanks me up from the floor. "Run!"

Taking my hand in his, our sticky fingers entwining, he yanks me toward the stairs. We step over bodies and make it halfway up before another burst of hot air explodes in the room. I almost fall against Will when it hits. He pushes me in front of him and I run up, taking the stairs two at a time. Another blast, this time hotter than boiling water, erupts from the basement. The stairs ignite, fire crackling behind me. It chases us out of the house.

"Run!" Will shouts as we race out the front door.

Montoya and Agent Chandler take a few steps toward us, confusion all over their faces. Then they stop, as they must also feel all the air being sucked into the house. Will and I keep sprinting away from the crappy farmhouse until a loud boom pounds my brain out on my forehead. Everyone is flattened to the ground as the house explodes. Scalding hot air and flames envelop everything. I can't even scream. The world burns.

A huge weight covers my entire body, forcing my face into the dirt. I close my eyes and don't breathe. The onslaught is over as soon as it started. The heat, the ear-shattering noise—it all evaporates. There's peace for a few moments. Then there isn't. I hear the sound of large objects falling to the ground now. Metal, wood, glass all rain from the sky. I twist my head to the side but see nothing but flesh. Wait. The weight breathes. And it smells like sweat and blood. Oh.

I lie facedown under Will, barely able to inhale or exhale for a few more seconds, until the torrent of house debris stops. After a few moments of calm, his body lifts off mine, moving beside me instead. I flip onto my back, panting in the still roasting air. All that remains of the house is burning wood and foundation. There's nothing but scorched earth as far as the eye can see. Pieces of furniture and plaster smolder on the ground. Will lies on his stomach panting as quickly as I am. His back is nothing but blisters and burnt skin. I meet his tear-filled eyes with mine. We say nothing. I just take his hand in mine before closing my dry eyes.

———

Agents Rushmore, Wolfe, and I were rushed to the hospital before the fires burned out. Nobody said anything the whole ride. Wolfe just stared off into space, lost in his disbelieving grief. I felt every inch of his pain, thanks to my abilities. It's a miracle I didn't start crying. Shock, I guess.

After I was checked out by a doctor, they let me take a shower. The police took my clothes as evidence, but there was a woman officer about my size who gave me a spare pair of sweats. I got off lucky. No stitches for the cut on my cheek, nothing broken, only first-degree burns on my legs and arms. It stung when I showered, but I dealt. It was almost nice to feel the physical pain instead of the numbness inside my gut.

Now, I sit on a gurney off to the side, watching the doctors' and nurses' feet go by. Some of the policemen from the scene meandered around, occasionally glancing at me, no doubt itching to ask me the details. A house blew up. People are dead. More are buried in the backyard. It's only natural they're curious, but I couldn't handle their gazes. I closed the curtain. I'm just waiting for the doctor to pop by with my discharge papers, then I'm so out of here.

I don't know where Will or anyone else is. I've been here about three hours and haven't seen a familiar face. Agents Wolfe and Rushmore were whisked away by medical personnel when we arrived, and none of my other teammates have stopped by. I guess I'll have to hitch a ride with the police back to mobile command. Not that I'm in a hurry. By now, Nancy's been told about Irie. Poor girl. I don't know how she's going to get through this. They were like sisters. Bickering, snooty at times, but close as all get out. She'll be inconsolable. Wolfe too. Me, I'm numb. It hasn't hit yet. No more trips to the nail salon to pamper ourselves. No more midnight margaritas. My chest tightens. Maybe I'm not that numb.

Footsteps stop in front of the curtain. The doctor's I hope. The person pulls the curtain back. Will stands there, now in a brown sheriff's department T-shirt and black slacks. His arm is wrapped in a cast, but otherwise he seems fine. Wish I had super healing.

He shuts the curtain, but before he closes it all the way, I jump off the gurney and rush into his chest. He winces but wraps his arms around me after only a moment's hesitation.

"Thank God you're okay," I whisper. "Thank God."

I don't want to let go. Never. Ever. He's so warm and ... solid. I needed this. I've wanted this since this whole fiasco began. This comfort. This closeness. With him. I've missed him so much.

He pulls me in tighter, putting his cheek on top of my head. "I'm okay. It's okay." I move my arm a little, and he winces again.

His back. I hurt him. Again. I let go, but he clings for a moment, clutching onto my shirt. "Are you okay?" I ask.

"I'm healing. I'll be fine." He releases me. "I'll be back to normal in a few days."

"You didn't have to do that for me," I say.

244

"Better me than you." His eyes dart to my cheek. "Have they released you yet?"

"I'm just waiting for the paperwork. Then I can go and ... has anyone told Nancy yet?"

"Oliver's with her now."

"That's good. He'll know what to say. We should get to her soon, though. She'll need us too."

Will gazes down at the floor. "You should go. I'll ... just make things worse, I think."

I don't need to be an empath to tell he's in turmoil. His beautiful eyes are clouded with pain. It physically hurts me. "Hey. What is it?" I ask.

He scowls. "Nothing."

"Hey," I say, touching his arm. "What? You can tell me anything, you know that." I take his hand again. "Talk to me. Please."

Those stunning eyes look into mine, and the mask falls. "This is my fault," he whispers desperately. "I got her killed. I should have checked under the stairs more carefully. I didn't secure the room. If—"

I lace my fingers with his. "Hey. No. Don't do this to yourself."

"Bea, I'm the leader. I'm responsible. The successes, the failures—they're all on me. I *failed* her."

"No." I take him into my arms again, but he doesn't hug back this time. "You listen to me, okay? The only person responsible for her death was the vamp who bit her, and he's paying for it. We got them. They won't hurt anyone else ever again. We did good. *You* did good." I squeeze harder. "And for what it's worth, you saved my life. I'd be dead twice over if it wasn't for you. No question. So, thank you. Thank you for my life, Will."

My words have the desired effect. He takes a deep breath and his body relaxes a little. Better yet, his arms encircle my back, hugging me, pulling me in as close as possible. We don't speak for a few seconds. He smells of smoke and musk, which I inhale greedily. He could smell like dung and still have an effect on me. No doubts, no darkness can touch me as long as I'm in his arms. If God struck me dead at this moment, I wouldn't even mind. I wish I could read his mind. I wish I could lead him to the gurney, shed our clothes, and really touch. No man has ever made me feel this way. Not even Oliver. This is different. When I'm near him all reason, all logic vanishes and I just want to do this.

I don't know what it is about this man. I've felt it the moment I first saw him. You hear about it. Electricity, sparking something inside you, changing you. That's what I feel every time I even think about him. Alive. But when he's touching me like this, it's as if a nuclear explosion moves through me. It's unnerving, petrifying, and the most exhilarating experience of my life. I'm addicted. I never want it to end.

I find excuses to be near him. I eat at the same time so we can chat. I volunteer for whatever he's doing in the field. I've read half a dozen books on the Navy, his favorite topic. I suffer through intense physical training just so I can touch him. But this is the first time that touch has been deliberately loving, and it is ... divine.

But cut short. The curtain flies open, darn near giving me a heart attack. Agent Chandler takes one look at us, and his mouth droops open with embarrassment. Will and I uncouple, each of us turning red enough for it to show through the burns. "Um, sorry," Agent Chandler says. "Um, they, just found another body in the field. There's some issue over where to take it."

"Yes. Okay. Thank you," Will says.

Agent Chandler nods, then closes the curtain. Neither Will nor I can look at each other. "Uh, you better get over there," I say.

"Yes. I should," he says, eyes jutting everywhere but toward me. He starts backing up to the edge of the curtain. "Carl's on his way to pick you guys up. Take you back to the hotel. I'll just—I'll call Oliver and tell him you'll be there soon."

"Okay."

With an awkward smile he opens the curtain. He takes one step, then suddenly spins around, face filled with bafflement. "Uh, um, thank you. For …" He can't say another word. He just smiles nervously, then shuts the curtain. I take a deep breath. *Okay butterflies, he's gone. Stop fluttering in my stomach.*

God, what kind of person am I? My friend just died, and I'm about three seconds from jumping Will's bones. Why do inappropriate moments bring out the slut in me? I sit back on the gurney, but leap off a second later. I've suddenly got a case of the wiggles. Staying is no longer an option. I toss open the curtain and walk over to the nurse's station. "Bathroom?" She points down the hall.

I'm stepping into the bathroom when a man behind me says, "Beatrice?"

I spin around. *Oh, crap.* The vamp bartender from Poison Ivy, dressed in blue scrubs, stands a foot away. Before I can do anything, he's got a rag over my face coated in a chemical, and his other hand presses me into it by the neck. A few seconds of confused panic fades into oblivion, just like everything else.

I really hate Texas.

THIRTEEN

WITH OR WITHOUT YOU

I EMERGE FROM THE darkness of unconsciousness to, well, darkness. I know I'm awake because I hear someone behind me shuffling papers around. I try to move my arms and legs, but something—rope, judging from the scratchiness—binds them in place. Great, I'm tied to a chair and have apparently gone blind. No; tape covers my eyes. I swear I must have been Stalin in a past life to deserve all this.

"Excellent. You are awake."

I'd know that British accent anywhere.

The paper shuffling ceases, and a chair moves. Footsteps come closer until I feel him next to me. I'm sure if I wasn't so tired I'd be afraid, but I can't muster it. Hurrah for exhaustion. "I will remove the tape, but only if you promise not to use your gift against me. You have my word that I will not harm you, unless you make me. Do I have yours?"

"Sure," I say reluctantly.

His cold fingers graze my face as he slowly pulls the tape off. I blink a few times before the spots and blurs disappear. Freddy grins, fangs in full view. He's in black slacks and a light gray dress shirt. All dolled up for my kidnapping. We're back in his study, and I am in fact tied to a chair facing the door. I glance around and the only thing that's changed in his office is the pulley and rope hanging from the ceiling. "If you attempt to escape, just know, I can snap your neck before the furniture lands."

"I know."

"And I do apologize for any discomfort. Given the choice, I would have had Judd capture your mind and force you to remain motionless on the couch. Chloroform is so barbaric."

"You know I'm immune?"

"I attempted to dull your pain last night when I was strangling you. It did not work."

"Oh. Thank you?"

He shrugs. "In all my years, I have only encountered a handful of humans with immunity. Did your mother ever mention waking one morning with an unexplainable bruise while she was pregnant with you?"

It would not surprise me if my mother tangled sheets with a vampire in her day, what with her being a "free spirit" and all. But I'm not sharing anything with this creep. "None of your business. What do you want, Freddy?"

"You seem a clever woman. I believe you already know the answer to that."

I do. "He's not that stupid. It's obviously a trap. He won't come."

"You do not think he cares enough for you to risk his life?"

I don't know. "He'll know what you have planned. He'll send someone else, most likely one of my fellow *federal agents*. If you let me go right now, maybe the men with guns *won't* storm this place and shoot you on sight."

"I am well aware of your affiliation with the F.R.E.A.K.S., Agent Alexander," he says with another smile. "However, if you recall your vampiric law, by assaulting me last night during a legally sanctioned duel, I can by all accounts shoot *you* on sight and your organization could not lay a finger on me. I have no desire to harm you, mind you, but I will if your lover does not show his cowardly hide here this evening. Once again, I ask: Do you think he will?"

The exhaustion isn't strong enough to mask the fear anymore. My heart rate doubles. "I really don't know."

He's satisfied with the answer, giving me a half smile. "He was always selfish. Never gave any thought to others, your lover."

"For the nine hundredth time, he isn't my lover," I say through gritted teeth. "We've never even really kissed, okay?"

Freddy pulls up a chair to sit beside me. He crosses his legs and folds his hands on his knee. "And yet he showed such devotion last night."

"We're friends. That's what friends do for each other. You should get some."

"I learned the heart-wrenching way what closeness with others brings," he says coldly. "Misery. Contempt. Even those we hold above all others, whom we never thought could harm us, are not above betrayal. I choose mine carefully now. And as this current situation shows, you should have as well."

"They really hurt you. Oliver and Jules."

"Oh, yes," he says, eyes haunted. "More than words can express."

"Oliver told me a little about it. They ran off together?"

"Yes. He swanned in and seduced the love of my life in less than a fortnight. I thought I could trust them, my blood brother and lover." He wrings his hands. "Jules paid for that betrayal at the hands of executioners, and now two hundred fifty years later, so will Oliver."

"It was forever ago," I say. "How can you still be—"

"If you knew the first thing about true love, you would not make such an asinine statement. I ache for Jules every day. Part of my soul died when Jules did," Freddy says, as if each word physically hurts.

"I'm sorry," I say, meaning it.

"Thank you," he says, patting my bound hand. "I would have understood if they were truly in love, but Oliver just used him as he does all. Poisoned him against me. He—"

Huh? What? Did he just... "Wait," I say, holding up my hands as high as they can go, being tied down and all. "Whoa. Did you just say *him*? Who is *him*?"

"Jules. Julian."

If this were a cartoon, my head would spin around with steam coming out of my ears. "Jules is a dude?" I ask, flabbergasted. "Oliver stole your *boyfriend*? A man? With a..." Holy heck.

"You seem surprised," Freddy says, puzzled.

"Um, yeah! He hits on anything with boobs! I've never see him even look at another man that way. Women, yeah, like... all the time. Nonstop. It's just... huh." Oliver's bisexual. Didn't see that one coming, and I'm from Southern California.

"He always favored women over men. That was why I thought nothing of a minor flirtation between them. The many times I have looked back on it, I suppose I should have suspected, especially after the night we were all in bed together. He and Jules—"

"Wait! Whoa. You two *slept* together? All three of you? At the same time? How does that even work? Where does everything go? Who—"

Freddy chuckles. "How innocent you are, Agent Alexander."

"Stop laughing! I just found out one of my good friends is bi and into threesomes! It's a lot to take in!"

Freddy continues chuckling. "You know, I finally do believe you and Oliver have not made love. Quite a shame. I will say one thing in his favor, he was quite a lover. Tender, yet rough all at once. I am sorry you will not have a chance to experience it before I gut him."

Freddy stops smiling, as do I. Vivisection is a terrific mood killer. We both look away from each other, staying silent for a few uncomfortable seconds. I don't know what to say, but my mouth takes over. "I am sorry about your boyfriend," I say quietly. "I'm sorry you're in so much pain. But killing Oliver won't bring him back. It might not even make you feel better."

"It certainly is worth a try." Freddy rises, peering down at me with another smile my way. He walks back to his desk and sits. I try to scoot the chair, but can't. "Two hundred fifty years of plotting and planning, and the night is finally here. I cannot tell you how many scenarios have crossed my mind. Staking him outside naked as the sun rises. Burning him alive. The rack. I . . . I am almost happy for the first time in centuries. The only thing that vexes me though, and perhaps you can shed the proverbial light on it, is why would he even dare to come here? Why risk venturing into my territory?"

"Because it's his job. You don't understand. He's a changed man. He doesn't hurt people anymore, he helps them. He has for thirty years."

"So it was JR's antics that brought the fly to the spider," Freddy says while I'm sure doing the diabolical hand gesture popular with James Bond villains. "If the boy was not dead, I would thank him."

"Did you know what he and his pals were doing?"

"Of course. JR and I have what you might call a past. I could not hurt him, and he would never stand by and let me punish any member of his little family. There was no real problem with it. They cleaned up after themselves, though not as well as they should, seeing as they are now dead. I suppose I should thank you for that as well, doing what I could not."

"Huh?"

"I could have warned them, I suppose. I almost did, but thought better of it. I had no idea where you and Oliver were hiding, but I knew if I waited long enough you would surface to do what you came here for. I am glad it was sooner rather than later."

"You used your old boyfriend as bait?"

"Two birds, one stone. And you took care of several thorns in my side and are now helping me fulfill my wildest dream. I am so very glad our paths crossed, Agent Alexander. I should like to do something for you after all this unpleasantness is over."

You can die, you psycho creep.

There's a knock on the door. Anton steps in. If he's surprised to see me tied to a chair, it doesn't show. Once again he's dressed in a dark blue suit, white shirt, and matching silk tie. "Cameron has just arrived with Susan and Jamal."

"Excellent. I do hope they wish to stay for the show." I hear the chair move as he stands. "I will go greet them." He walks up to Anton, putting his hands on the man's shoulders. "This is a good night, my friend. I am glad you are here to share it with me."

"As am I," Anton says with a nod.

"Watch her." He looks back at me. "Now, be a good girl. If you attempt to flee, Anton has my permission to harm you." He smiles at me before walking out. Thank God.

"Your friend is insane," I say.

Anton moves beside me. "I know."

I look at the vamp. "There's no chance you're going to help me, is there?"

"None. If you attempted an escape, you would not leave the building alive. And I would be punished, or worse. It would serve neither of our purposes. I do apologize for this. I did not think it would go this far when I phoned Oliver."

"I knew it!" I say. "I knew it! *You're* the tipster."

"Oliver did not tell you?"

"He doesn't tell me a lot of things, apparently." If we survive the night, he and I are going to have a long talk about sharing the important stuff. "Why did you call us? Why rat out your friend?"

"To take over, of course," he says matter-of-factly. "If he is removed from power due to negligence, I would immediately ascend as appointed successor."

"What?"

"He has grown weak over the years. More volatile. Our business ventures are suffering. It cannot stand."

"Then why not just duel?"

"He would defeat me. And by having a third party—a powerful third party—remove him, not only would my hands be clean, but I would retain the devotion of the F.R.E.A.K.S. for reporting the crime."

"In other words, all of Freddy's loyal subjects wouldn't blame you and then come after you for betraying him, *and* we'd cut you some slack in the future? Someone's been reading their Machiavelli."

"At least twice a year," Anton says without an ounce of humor. "But Freddy was not supposed to discover Oliver's presence."

"Well, he did. And now he's going to kill him. We have to do something."

"I have spent all my waking hours since last night attempting to arrive at a solution, but none has presented itself. Oliver will come. He will die. Your organization will return to kill Freddy for complacency in multiple murders, and I shall ascend."

"And you don't care he's going to torture and kill Oliver?"

"Not particularly."

Jesus Christ, this guy scares me more than Freddy.

"And if Oliver doesn't show up, then what? He's not an idiot, you know. He knows what's waiting here for him."

"I saw the way he looked at you last night. There is not a doubt in my mind he will come. Not one."

———

Around the time they put the tarp down to cover the rug, I got shaky. I haven't a clue how long I've been tied here, but every minute feels like an hour. My neck hurts from all the times I've twisted it to see what they've been up to. The pulley and rope were just the beginning. Men and women continue to arrive with the oddest things. Tool box, shackles, and then a silver cage they assembled with gloves on. They built the darn thing in front of me. Strangely, the woman in black leather everything, Greta, seemed to be the only one who knew how to use the tools. The cage she put together was almost flat with just enough space for a human—or in this instance a vamp—to lie down in. They hoisted it onto the rope and pulley. Then came the tarp. For the blood.

As Freddy's minions anchor the tarp with paperweights, Anton returns with a brown leather satchel, which he places on the end table next to the tarp. Freddy smiles, as he has done with the arrival of every piece of equipment, and opens the bag. He pulls out a huge knife, followed by a smaller one. Then he draws out an Indiana Jones–type whip. I look away, biting on my lower lip to stop the oncoming panic.

"Is this all of them?" Freddy asks.

"I brought one of each," Anton answers.

"Good. Let us just have hope that I have the opportunity to use them all before he expires." He pauses. "I do grow impatient. Where is he? No manners."

"Perhaps we should phone him," Anton says. "They might not know she is missing."

"We shall wait fifteen more minutes. Let him think I have already disposed of her." The whip cracks mere inches from me, loud as a firecracker. I scream and jerk in the chair. All the vamps in the room chuckle, but I don't care. I slow my breathing to stop the oncoming heart attack. "I am sorry, Agent Alexander," Freddy chuckles. "I did not mean to frighten you." He steps in front of me, whip still in hand. "You have been the most agreeable hostage. I do appreciate it. As a token of my esteem, I believe I will abandon my prior plan of slitting your throat in front of Ollie. You have won me over with your charm and obedience."

"Stop this, please just stop this," I whisper. "Just let me go. We'll leave tonight. You'll never see him again. *Please.*"

"Never."

He's enjoying this too much. He's going to kill my friend, and he's smiling about it. Fear fades, replaced with something a lot more powerful. Hatred. I absolutely hate this man. He has strangled, kidnapped, and threatened me. He wants to torture my friend. *No.* No way in hell.

I peer up at him, eyes as hard as my heart. "Then you had better kill me," I growl in a low voice. "Do you hear me, you pathetic piece of shit? Because I *swear* to you, the moment you lay one finger on him, your life is forfeit. I will rip your black heart out with my bare hands as you scream for mercy, and I'll be laughing the entire time. I *promise* it. Ask Gerry and JR if I keep my promises."

His mouth sets into a straight line. "You do not frighten me, little girl."

"Then you're even stupider than you look."

The ringing of the telephone on the desk breaks the ice cold eye contact. Anton picks it up, listens, then hangs up. "That was Judd. They have arrived."

"They?" Freddy asks.

"He brought a werewolf," Anton replies. "They were frisked. No weapons or communication devices."

"Who is the wolf, Agent Alexander?"

"Another member of the F.R.E.A.K.S."

"What are they to each other?"

"Rivals. Oliver wouldn't give a damn if you hurt Will, and vice versa. I'm sure he's just here to make sure I get out safe."

Freddy studies my face. "You are telling the truth. They may come up."

In an instant, Freddy disappears from in front of me only to reappear behind me. He holds one of the knives to my neck, yanking my head back by the hair at the same time. Ow. I wince in pain. The blade presses into my neck, about to draw blood. He pulls tighter on my hair when there's a knock on the door. "Enter."

The vamp from the hospital walks in first carrying a shotgun, followed by Oliver, Will, and two hulking vamps with more shotguns trained on my friends. They have their hands up, both expressionless. Me, I'm trying not to hyperventilate. Will's eyes dart to mine, and for a fleeting moment fear fills his face, but he recovers. Oliver keeps his gaze trained on Freddy. "So glad you could make it," Freddy says. "We were beginning to worry."

"Has he harmed you?" Oliver asks, not taking his eyes off my captor.

"No," I pant. The knife digs deeper into my neck but doesn't draw blood.

"Good. Then my associate here shall promise this goes no further than tonight. There will be no recriminations if he and Agent Alexander leave this establishment unharmed."

"Really?" Freddy asks.

"I swear it by the authority bestowed upon me by the President of the United States as a sworn Federal Agent," Will says. "If she and I leave without incident, there will be no charges filed. Nothing will happen to you. I have a written statement to that effect in my back pocket."

"And what about you, Oliver? Does this pact extend to you?"

"I would not be so foolish as to include that as part of the terms."

Freddy presses the knife deeper, this time cutting me. I wince. "Or I could just let my subjects blow away your wolf, then force you to bleed your friend before I turn her. Your last dying thought would be of all the despicable things I will force her to do."

"You need to shut up, *right now*," Will snarls. Will takes a step, body trembling with rage, but Oliver stops him.

"No," Oliver says through gritted teeth.

Freddy is silent for a few seconds. He yanks my head back so I can see his grinning face. "Oh! I believe I understand now," Freddy says. "You have not fallen prey to our Oliver's charms as your heart and body belong to another." Okay, he can slit my throat now. Better that than to die of embarrassment. Freddy looks back at Will. "Then I am doing you a favor tonight, friend. Our Oliver has a penchant for taking things that belong to others. You should thank me."

"Just let her go," Will says.

Freddy glances at Oliver, then down at me. He leans down, kissing my forehead. "Remember, fair Beatrice, I am a man of my word. Go to your Dante. Satan is releasing you from his clutches." He removes the knife from my neck to cut the ropes. I jump up, rubbing my raw wrists. I fight the urge to leap into Will's arms, instead walking calmly over to them. I raise my hands in surrender as I join them. Neither man looks at me, and they keep their faces blank. Okay, they have something planned. The rest of the team is downstairs waiting to raid this place. Will's already figured out a way to get the guns away. That has to be it.

But neither Will nor Oliver move.

"Get the written authorization," Anton says, all business per usual.

One of the vamps reaches into Will's back pocket. Freddy is all smiles again. "There now. All civilized. Shawn, Robert, please escort the agents to the holding cells downstairs. I will release you both alive as promised after I am finished with your comrade. Just insurance, I assure you. If Oliver here attempts to escape or fight back, I will have no choice but to harm you. I believe that is fair."

"I will not attempt escape," Oliver says.

"We shall see. Robert?"

The vamp with his hair in a ponytail points his gun at me, and the henchman behind Will pokes him to get us walking. "Wait!" I say.

I sidestep the men. They can shoot me for all I care. I need to do this. I wrap my arms around Oliver, squeezing as hard as I can. I close my eyes, breathing in his scent, savoring the moment. No smoke or musk, only rich cologne. Just as good, though. The tears I'd managed to suppress all this time trickle out of my closed eyes. He doesn't hesitate. He clutches onto me as tight as I do him. "You don't have to do this," I whisper.

"Yes, I do," he whispers back. He releases me first, but I can't let go. This is it. We'll never touch, we'll never laugh together again. I can't let him go. He held me when I cried. He made me feel beautiful. He accepted me for who I am. He's my friend. *He came for me.* "Trixie…" His hands wrap around my wrists pulling me out of the embrace. A small smile crosses his handsome face. The most stunningly perfect face I ever have or will ever see. With his thumb he wipes a tear off my cheek. "I shall be fine. Go rescue Will."

Shawn yanks my arm, pulling me away from Oliver. "I'm sorry," I cry out as the goon drags me out.

"Goodbye, beloved."

The door slams shut.

———

I push the cage, the cage pushes back. All the pressure I focus on the door with my mind boomerangs back, and once again I'm flung to the back wall with the force of a car crash. My butt lands first, no doubt adding to my bruise collection. No swimsuits for me anytime soon.

"Crap!" I cry out. "Crap, crap, crap!"

"Will you please stop doing that?" Will asks in the jail cell next to me. "It's protected by magic. You're just going to keep hurting yourself."

The goons forced us into the basement, which can only be described as dungeon chic. There's a heavy lead door, three old-school cells with huge key holes, and sliding doors. I think this place was built in the Wild West days, though I doubt Wyatt Earp ever chained people to the back wall with silver shackles. The bondage theme spread down here too. I guess I should be grateful they didn't chain us up. I've been bound enough today, thank you very much.

"Can't you try again?" I ask as I pick myself up a third time.

Will just holds up his burnt hands in reply.

Not only are the cells guarded by an anti-magic spell, but they're also made of silver. Poor Will found out the hard way. And the bars are super strong. He tried with his hands covered with his shirt material, and the cell door didn't budge.

"This sucks!" I scream. "There has to be something we can do!"

"We wait. It's all we can do."

I start pacing again. "I don't believe that."

"He'll let us go in the morning. He has to, otherwise we can legally kill him."

"And Oliver?" I ask, looking him square in the eyes.

"He knew what he was doing," Will says emotionless.

I scoff. "And you're just, what? Okay with what's going on upstairs?" I ask angrily.

"Of course not," Will says, matching my tone. "No one deserves that. But we had no choice!"

"So, this was your plan? Show up with a piece of paper, hand over your teammate to a psychopath, and just walk away? 'Cause, great plan! We're locked down here! And he's upstairs where ..." I can't think it, let alone say it. "*That* was your great plan?"

"Bea, it's not like we had a whole lot of time to pull together some great assault. You were missing! You vanished from the hospital. Carl couldn't find you; Oliver said you weren't at the hotel. We weren't exactly thinking clearly! Not after everything today. He knew, *we* knew, what had to be done—and we're doing it."

"Sitting on our butts while he's being tortured to death? Yeah, we're doing our jobs," I say, choking back tears. I plop down on the cold stone floor in a pile, cupping my face in my hands. I will not cry. I *won't*. He needs me strong to save him. Strong people don't cry. They keep their heads and figure out how to fix things. I breathe heavily to stop the waterworks. It helps, but not enough.

"Bea?" Will asks softly. I gaze up at him in the next cell, barely registering that he's calling me by my first name, which is rare. He leans down to my level, careful to avoid the silver bars. "I wish there was something I could say or do."

I look away and shake my head. There has to be something, *anything* I can do. Think logically. Magic and strength don't work. So what does that leave? What...

Occam's razor. I'm a genius. The easiest, simplest answer is usually the right one. So how do normal people break out of a locked room? "They pick the lock," I say to myself.

"What?" Will asks.

All hopelessness fades with those words. I jump up, the first genuine smile of the day crossing my face. "You can pick a lock, right? I saw you do it in Cleveland when Nancy wasn't there."

"Yeah, but I don't have any tools." He stands up, walking over to the lock on his cell. "I'd need metal, at least two pieces. I have nothing on—"

He stops talking after glancing at me.

I reach into my shirt after unclasping my bra. I take off the straps, pulling my bra out of the armhole. Guys are always amazed when they see women do this, and Will isn't immune. My white bra is speckled with brown spots of dried blood. I'd have thrown it out anyway. "The underwire should work, right?"

Even in life and death situations, men are still men. His eyes lock on my free breasts under the sweatshirt for a moment before he snaps out of it. "Um, yeah," he says, getting the bra from me. Breaking the underwire in half, he rips the metal out. I watch, transfixed, as he bends the first half lengthwise and gets to work on the lock, careful not to touch the silver bars with his skin. It takes a few minutes and multiple swear words until we hear that blessed "click." We both smile cheek to cheek as he kicks the door open and walks over to my cell. I bend down right with him as he fiddles with my lock. "You're a genius," he says, still smiling.

"I just watch a lot of movies," I say with a matching grin. I reach through the bars, touching his moving wrist. He stops. "I'm sorry I yelled at you. I do appreciate you coming to my rescue. You didn't have to."

"Of course I did," he says, meeting my eyes.

Not now, hormones, friend dying upstairs. I pull my hand away. "Then get on with it."

One minute later, I'm free. Next phase, get out through the metal door. Easy. Look ma, no hands. With all my power, I push the door. It tumbles down like a domino, landing with a huge clank. The two guards standing on either side of it are momentarily dumbfounded. Perfect. Will cold-cocks the one to the left, breaking his nose. He's down and out with one punch. At the same time, I twist the second's head around. He falls next to his buddy. "That was easy," I say as my victim twitches on the ground.

Will removes the vamp's gun from the holster, handing it to me. He takes the shotgun. "Come on."

We run up the stairs but wait at the top as Will listens for people on the other side. A moment later, he opens the door. The S&M club is empty and fully lit. With lights on, it's still as seedy as before. The space is empty. I guess everyone—

A blood curdling scream echoes above. The pain I feel with each moment of noise must be just a hint of the agony Oliver is experiencing. My God, what are they doing to him? Whatever it is, they sure as hell won't be doing it much longer. I step toward the stairs, but Will grabs my arm.

"What the hell are you doing?" I ask, jerking my arm back.

He doesn't let go. "No. We're leaving."

"What? No!" This time I get my arm back. "I am not—"

"Listen to me!" he hisses in a high whisper. "I counted ten vamps on my way in. We barely survived today when we were evenly matched. The only thing you going up there would do is get the both of you killed! I am not losing you too. Especially not today. Not ever."

If I wasn't so damn scared and angry, those words would put me on cloud nine. Oliver's wail of anguish snaps any joy out of me. "I. Am. Not. Leaving. Him." I take another step toward the stairs, but he seizes my arm again.

"No! Goddamn it, Bea! I promised I'd get you out of here safely, no matter what. It's what *he* wanted. He sacrificed himself for you. Don't let it be in vain. Please. You can't win this one."

For a moment, for a gut-wrenching moment, I want to run away. I really do. I want to turn around and just go. As fast as I can. I want to go with Will and have him drive me as far from this place as possible. I want to go home and forget the last few days. Forget Oliver and Irie, just let them fade from memory. Climb into bed and watch TV. Sleep. And I almost do. I almost can.

Until I see his face as clear as if he was right in front of me.

I see him as I did last night: pale, languid, bleeding. Dying. No more teasing. No more grins. No more flirting. No more hugs and chess games, and knowing in my soul that there will always be someone who will fight, steal, or kill for me. *No matter what.*

That scares me a hell of a lot more than anything up there.

This time I yank my arm away with enough force to almost dislocate it. The fury coursing through my cells locks my body, my eyes, my jaw into such a pose of hatred and resolve that I'd frighten any creature on this planet. I meet Will's eyes and for the first time they're filled with fear. Of me.

"Always underestimating me."

I run to the stairs, then up them as Oliver cries out again. I don't even bother with the door handle. With one look, the door explodes. I'm through it before the shards hit the floor. I count eleven vamps: some standing, others sitting all around the room, shielding their faces from the blast. Oliver hangs on his belly in the silver cage about six feet off the ground. His face is nothing but bloody pulp. The front of his hair is missing. Scalped. Blood spews out into buckets at his head, chest, and stomach. Freddy stands next to him near a machine that resembles a crank. It takes a moment for my brain to register that the rope wrapped around it and connected to Oliver's torso is his intestine. Shock takes over, pushing away all the horror I should feel. Wrath replaces it.

The vamps remain confused just long enough for me to shoot the nearest one right between the eyes as both my feet make it inside the study. She falls just as I swing my arm the opposite way, pulling the trigger and hitting the African American vamp to my right through the heart. Annie Oakley, eat your heart out.

The rest finally get their wits about them and start moving toward me. Anton, Freddy, and two others move to the back of the room to let the others fight. I open fire at anything that moves. One, two, three, four gunshots in quick succession. Another vamp goes down. I somersault to the right just as they're about to pounce. I fire twice more. Blood spurts out of the bartender's chest. He's down. And I'm out of ammo.

The woman in leather, Greta, lunges, but I hold up my leg so she lands on it. I grab her arms and roll her behind me into the wall, just like I practiced with Will a dozen times. One of the cowards in the corner leaps over Freddy's desk to join the fight as Greta touches the ground. Just as he lands, a loud now familiar boom vibrates though the room. The vamp's head disintegrates. Will stands in the door like an action hero, expelling the cartridge and taking aim again. Greta disappears from the floor then materializes in front of him. He fires just as she vanishes again. A huge chunk of desk blows off. He can handle her. I have my own problems.

Two vamps, both in leather pants and T-shirts, grab my arms and pull me off the floor just as Greta appears behind Will, biting down on his shoulder. He cries out, but butts her head with the gun. I'm on my own here. I kick the Latino one to my right in the knee, but it does nothing. One takes my bucking legs and the other my shoulders. I squirm and twist, but they don't let go. Will aims and fires at Greta, missing again. He cocks the gun, but it's empty. We're weaponless and outnumbered. This should scare me but doesn't. I wiggle my foot free and kick the vamp at my legs in the jaw. The force sends me and the vamp at my shoulders down to the ground. This moment of freedom is all I need.

My head whips to the right. The swords from last night glide from their stand, one to my awaiting hand and the other toward Will. He drops the shotgun as the sword reaches him. Mine lands in my hand just as Legs recovers. I smash my head back with all my force onto the nose of the vamp underneath me. His nose cracks, and he releases me. I swing my now free arm toward the other one, slicing down. His head separates at a diagonal, blood spurting like a fountain for an instant. I don't even spare a thought for how gross it is. The second vamp clutches me again, but I elbow him in the ribs hard. This frees me and I roll off him, stabbing him in the side for good measure.

Will's foe disappears just as he slices at her. She materializes to his right, kicking him in the stomach with her stiletto boot. He buckles, dropping the sword. The tip lands mere inches from the rest of the knives and other torture devices that have fallen to the floor. Perfect. Before she pops away again, I pick them all up. They lift off the floor by my will and zoom with the force of cannons into her back, all thirteen of them. One even pokes though her throat, blood spewing out of the small hole. Gurgling, she falls onto the tarp.

I stand. I'm the only one on the right side of the desk who does. The vamp that held my arms is smart enough to stay on the floor, clutching onto his bleeding nose and side. The remaining three in the corner can't take their eyes off me. The young one huddles on the floor behind a cool Anton, and Freddy is almost vibrating with fear. I meet his brown eyes. "I told you, you should have killed me."

"Yes," he says with a quaking voice. "I see that now. Well."

Will manages to get to his feet. His shirt and cast are caked with his blood, though the flow has ceased. He's a little pale, but I think he'll be alright. "Will? Get Oliver."

Will picks up the discarded sword, walking over to the hopefully unconscious Oliver. No one moves as Will lowers the cage to the ground. I can only watch out of the corner of my eye as Will lifts Oliver's nearly lifeless body out of the enclosure. His alabaster skin is cut in so many places it would take a mathematical formula to count them all. Will carries the body to the door. "Bea?"

I catch Freddy's fearful eyes again. "Right behind you. Go."

Will's either too tired or too weak to protest.

Freddy squares his shoulders. His jaw sets. "Go ahead. Kill me. But know … the man you just saved is not worth the effort. He is no friend of yours. He will betray you, leave you, and not look back. So do it."

"Oh, I'm not going to kill you." I look beside him. "Anton is."

Freddy's head swivels to his friend. "What?"

Sword pointed at him. I slowly walk toward the desk. "He called us here, you know. Tattled on you. He's wanted you dead for years. He was just waiting for the perfect opportunity. You didn't know that? Huh. He betrayed you, your best friend. Your *only* friend. Just like your lover." I smile at Freddy. "And you know why? Because you're stupid. And selfish. And nobody likes you. You're totally alone. Forever and always. And you get to die knowing it." I toss the sword to Anton who catches it one-handed. I didn't think it possible, but the vamp smiles. Freddy backs away from him. Anton glances at me. "You can say I did it."

"Thank you," he says with a nod.

"Just know …" I say, voice hard. "I will be watching you. Don't make me come back here. Ever."

"I understand."

With that I turn on my heels and walk out, stepping over the bodies in my wake. I don't look back, even when I hear the slices and screams.

Adios, Texas.

FOURTEEN

IN THE BEDROOM

I can do this.

It's easy.

Just lift up my hand and knock.

Now.

Crap.

I'm standing outside his door holding a warm mug of blood, and I can't move my hand. This is ridiculous. I *know* it's ridiculous, so why can't I move? Okay, I know the reason. I don't want to find out what's on the other side of the door. Will he be fully recovered, or did we get there too late? Will that once-dazzling body and face be ravaged with scars or camera-ready? And what the hell do I say to him? *Sorry you were tortured because I let my guard down?*

I should just go back upstairs and check on Nancy. From what I hear she's been crying almost nonstop since she got home. Andrew and George have done their best, and since I got home a few hours ago I've been up there, but it hasn't done much good. I don't know how she'll get through the memorial service tomorrow. I should have been here with them, not still in horrible Texas filling out paperwork and trying to answer questions that I just didn't have answers for.

Carl, Agent Chandler, and I were the only ones not in need of serious recovery time, so we had to clean up the mess at the farmhouse. The FBI, Sheriff's department, and Venus Police Department were all demanding answers as to why eight people died in an "explosion." I had to lie like a used car salesman. The only highlight was when Petra came in. Her smile when I told her we got them was almost worth the whole experience. We found ten bodies in the backyard.

Will came to save us from bureaucracy heck halfway through the second day, answering almost all their questions and squashing all egos. He passed out right next to Oliver on the drive to mobile command. I'm told he had to change to wolf form to heal. I wouldn't know, though. Carl and Agent Chandler had to drag me kicking and screaming out of medical as Dr. Neill fixed up both men. I didn't find out until the next day that Oliver survived. I'd managed to keep it together until that moment, but when Carl told me, I immediately burst into tears in front of about fifteen law enforcement officers. At least they stopped yelling at me after that.

The change did help Will. The bite, burns, and broken arm all disappeared, through the awkwardness has remained. We've barely said anything to each other that wasn't work related since that night. I alternate hourly between furious and grateful. If I hadn't been there, he would have left Oliver to die, of this I have no doubt. What does that say about him? Do I even want to be friends, let alone lovers, with a man who wouldn't raise a finger to help someone escape certain death just because he dislikes him? I know it was what Oliver asked him to do, but still. On the flip side, he did come to rescue me. When I needed him, he was there. He showed up. I would have died, and he almost did. He cares about me, but I'm too tired to sort this out now. I anticipate many sleepless nights pondering these questions.

Screw it. I lift my hand, gently knocking.

"Enter, Trixie," Oliver says on the other side. Here goes. After a deep breath, I open the door.

I've never been in his room before, but I like it. It's … tasteful. It's about as big as my room, so it's huge. There's an antique rosewood armoire, matching desk with computer, bookshelves off in the corner, and plasma TV hooked up to a DVD player. The only odd thing is that the TV is surrounded by maroon curtains in the red wall. The screen shows a starry night with a full moon so realistic I almost forget we're underground. I'll bet he has a sunrise on sometimes too. No porno music playing on a loop either.

The bed is the centerpiece, though. Like mine, it's a four poster with head board, but his lacks the canopy. The sheets he's under aren't satin or leopard print, as I would have guessed. They're gray and the comforter is black and white. No sex den; it's just a room.

Oliver sits propped up by pillows. He's still too pale and he wears a black scarf on his head to cover the scalped part. He's hooked up to a blood IV, but otherwise he's fine. He's okay. Alive.

There was a part of me that didn't believe it. Like it was just something they told me to stop me from going nuts, but seeing him with my own two eyes, all the fear and anger lift. That horrible rock in my stomach vanishes. I can breathe without forcing it.

"Is that for me?" he asks with a small smile.

For a moment I'm confused. What's he talking about? But then I remember the cup in my hands. I really need some sleep. "Yeah, but it looks like you've already got some."

"I can always use more," he says with grin Number Three.

I pull the chair from the desk over to the bed, handing him the mug before sitting on the edge of the chair, back straight. "You're looking well," I say with an awkward smile.

He sips. "The scars are almost gone. I shall be back to normal in another day or two."

"Good," I say.

Neither of us speaks for an uncomfortable minute. I mean, what do I say? My eyes dart around the room, and his remain on the cup. I have no idea what to say to this man. None. "Thank you" seems too little for someone who almost sacrificed their life for yours. I should have written down a speech or something. I can't do this. "Well," I say as I stand, "I'll let you rest. You must be—"

His cold hand catches my wrist. "Wait. Sit. Do not leave me." When I obey, he releases my wrist. "I was told what you did. It was foolish, reckless, and ... words cannot express the gratitude I feel."

"So you're not mad I killed your ex-girlfriend and ex-boyfriend?" I chuckle nervously. "Because if you have any more, I'd—"

"Stop it," he says. "I am being serious. I need to say this; please let your guard down and allow me to do so."

I'm about to let another smart remark pass though my lips, but his expression stops me. "Okay."

After a weary sigh, he says, "I am sorry. I am sorry for everything. I am sorry I put you in that situation. I am sorry I let that madman get so close to you. I am sorry ... for so many things.

What I let happen was unforgivable. And even after that, you ..." He looks away. "I am forever in your debt."

"Oliver ..." I move to the edge of the bed, taking his hand in mine just as he did for me two months ago in my room when I couldn't go on anymore. "*I* should be thanking *you*. You knew what he was planning. You knew what would happen if you showed up. But you did. And what he did to you ..." I shake the image of his ravaged body out of my mind. "You were willing to die a savage, vicious death to save me. You showed up. There aren't that many people who would do that. Not for me. Not for anyone."

His eyes catch mine again, this time they're as serious as a death sentence. "You listen to me, Beatrice Alexander. If I have to crawl through glass. If I have to walk a thousand miles. If I have to fight through a legion of demons to storm the gates of hell, come what may, I will *always* come for you. *Always. Never* doubt that."

And I don't. With every fiber of my being, I believe it.

I don't know what I feel. I don't know what to do. Everything I've felt for him—heck anything I've ever felt for anyone—nothing is quite like ... I don't know *what* I feel for this man. I've never felt it before, and I doubt I'll ever feel it again. The only way I can describe it is ... *beautiful*. Accepted. Safe. The way, I realize, he's always made me feel. My dark angel.

I lean in slowly, closing my eyes. I want to savor this. My lips touch his, warm on cool. He doesn't respond at first, but then kisses back, soft and slow. I release his hand to cup his jaw. I feel everything, his skin, his mouth, and all of me. From my toes to my hair, I *feel*. You know what? It's better than I ever imagined. I pull away a moment later, once again meeting his eyes. "And I will always come for you," I say.

I pull my hands away as I stand from the bed. He watches, face deceptively neutral, as I saunter back to the door.

I shut it quietly without another word.

We've said all that needs saying. For now.

THE END

ACKNOWLEDGEMENTS

First, to Sandy Lu at the Lori Perkins Literary Agency for pulling me out of the slush pile all those years ago. Ditto to Terri Bischoff at Midnight Ink. Also to Nicole Edman for the edits, and Courtney Colton for spreading the word. May we all make lots of money.

Last time I forgot to thank all the wonderful women who gave me blurbs, so I'm making up for it now. To Victoria Laurie, Kat Richardson, Karen Chance, Leanna Renee Hieber, Kelly Meding, Jeannie Holmes, and Carolyn Crane: I'm so honored you took time to read about (and actually liked) Bea and all her friends. I'm humbled to be in your company. And I still owe you all a drink.

Thanks to all the other Midnight Inkers, especially Alan Orloff, Beth Groundwater, and Lois Winston, for taking time to answer my questions and helping me navigate through publishing waters. You taught me a lot.

Thanks to my always wonderful beta readers Jill Kardell, Ginny Dowis, Theresa Friedrich, and Susan Dowis for your suggestions.

Thanks to Marti Gullatt of the Arlington Public Library for writing me about my Dallas mistakes. And for liking my books. Keep spreading the word!

Thanks to the Prince William, Fairfax, Huntington Beach, and Newport Beach public library systems for giving me a quiet place to write. And to stare at cute boys.

Thanks to those of you who hosted my blog tour and Roxanne Rhodes at Bewitching Book Tours for coordinating it. You all really are the wave of the future.

Thanks to my family for putting up with me full stop. I know sometimes it isn't easy.

And finally, thanks to my readers for posting nice reviews on websites, writing fan letters to me, following me on Facebook and Twitter, and just giving *Mind Over Monsters* a chance. I will do my damndest to never disappoint you.

"I don't mean to pry, but are y'all really married?"

Crud. I am going to stake that creep for not sharing our cover story with me. "Um, yes, in ... Vegas. About a year ago. I wouldn't let him, um, *bite* me otherwise."

"Oh."

"My parents love him." *Shut up, you idiot!* We reach the top of the stairs and enter another hallway. More paintings and gaslights. The bay window at the end is the only thing making it possible to see. "The house looks good for being so old. It's pre–Civil War, right?"

"Yes. Mistress Marianna kept almost everything the same as it was originally."

"Wait ... no electricity or indoor plumbing?"

"Oh, no. There was a massive renovation back in the fifties. Bathrooms, lights, air conditioning, even an elevator was added when the hotel opened." Cole stops in front of a door with a metal fence across it. A thick metal wire is the only thing visible down the dark hole. "I have to ask that you refrain from using the elevator, however. Safety issues."

"Not a problem."

The door creaking behind us startles me. Creepy old houses give me the chills, even in the best of circumstances. Both Cole and I turn, but only my mouth drops open. Walking out the door is the naked woman. Still naked. And she's not a natural blonde. I'm staring, I know I'm staring bug eyed and gawking, but she's just so ... naked! And walking toward us. Smiling. If I weren't trying so hard not to giggle, I'd hate this woman. Long, straight hay-colored hair. Full red lips. Unnatural, gravity-defying breasts to rival Pamela Anderson's. Long, lean legs without a hint of fat on them. Ugly stepsister, meet porno Cinderella.

"Hello," the woman says.

"Hi," I mumble, eyes finally moving down to the hardwood floor. I have a feeling I'm going to know the floors here quite well.

"Cole, has my Gucci come back from the tailor yet?" the nudist asks.

"It should be done tomorrow," Cole says. "There *was* extreme ripping."

"When Sal gets in the mood...," she giggles. Eww. I hate it when people share details of their sex lives. It happens at least once a month, more now that Irie's getting some. Positions, costumes, yuck. Thank goodness for soundproof rooms. "Are you just checking in?"

"Um, yeah," I say, not looking up.

"Gloria Van Buren," she says, holding out her hand at chest level.

It's like a train wreck. I have to look. Darn, if those are real then I'm the Queen of Sheba. "Beatrice Smythe," I say shaking her hand but staring at the watermelons.

"Wonderful, aren't they?" Gloria asks. "Present from Sal. He doesn't age, why should I? I can give you the name of my surgeon if you like."

My face heats up. "I'm good, thanks," I say.

"So, I guess we're going to be neighbors for the next few days. Maybe we can do some shopping or other ... things." She starts slowly running her finger over the top of my hand. Her suggestive smile turns up the furnace under my face. I pull my hand away.

"Sure. We can play Monopoly," I chuckle nervously.

Her smile widens. "You're funny. I like that in a woman."

The elevator begins whirring. Oh, thank you Jesus, Mary, and Joseph. "That'll be my husband," I chuckle. "I better take care of him."

"Of course," Gloria says. "The four of us should have drinks tonight."

"Maybe," I say. "I'll see what he says."

"And if you get bored or lonely, I'll be just next door."

Not in a hundred million years. "I'll keep that in mind."

"Cole," she says with a nod. Turning around, showing a perfect upside-down-heart-shaped heinie, she walks back to her room. Wonderful. There's a nymphomaniac next door. When Oliver stops being dead meat at sunset, he's dead meat.

The elevator stops, and Cole opens the gate. My "husband's" black, pod-like coffin waits on a folding stand with our suitcases right on top. A man in a white tank top, exposing steroid-sized muscles and bald head, pushes it out of the elevator. Cole leads the way to our room, pulling out two keys. He unlocks the door handle first, then the top dead bolt. Good, big on security. Cole opens the door and steps aside as the man pushes Oliver in like a room service tray. I step in next.

It's dark in here, more than it should be. I really don't think it's in the government budget if I break a hundred-thousand-dollar vase, so I stay by the door. Cole, with no problem seeing in the near pitch dark, picks up a black blob and a motor begins humming. Slowly, light filters in as two slats lift, revealing windows and trees outside. I'll say one good thing about Oliver; he has great taste in hotels. The room's as big as a normal house's living room with an antique armoire, small desk, plush white carpet, and periwinkle

43

French silk lounging chair that matches the walls. The huge man reaches under the king-size four-poster bed and pulls out a wooden stand long enough to fit the coffin.

While the men move the casket, I meander around the room. Good, only paintings of flowers and meadows. The bed has half a dozen pillows the same baby blue as the thousand thread count sheets. A white and blue comforter completes the bed set. It's … charming. Not at all what I expected. No mirrors on the ceiling or animal prints. I'll bet there isn't even a heart-shaped tub in the bathroom. Two vases full of sunflowers and blue irises sit on top of the dresser and between the huge windows. I walk over to the dresser and smell.

"Are the flowers to your liking?" Cole asks, looking up from the coffin.

"Yes. They're my favorites." And they are.

"I know. Your husband wanted to make sure the room was perfect."

I can't believe he remembered my favorite flowers. I told them to Nancy once in passing when she was doing one of those meme quizzes. Oliver was in the room reading. Huh. Well, it was nice of him. "It's very cozy," I say. I walk to the closed door on my right, opening it. Wow, nice bathtub. Claw footed and deep enough to fit all of Lake Arrowhead. I know where I'm spending my downtime. Hey, a robe. I pull it off the hanger. Soft as a rabbit. This place sure beats the Days Inn where we normally stay.

"Mrs. Smythe?" Cole calls.

"Yes?" I say stepping out of the bathroom.

"We've finished."

44